·A·WORLD·OF·
FAIRY TALES

Retold by Andrew Lang
Illustrated by Henry Justice Ford

Selected and introduced by Neil Philip

ALBION

An Albion Book

First published in 1994 by
The Albion Press Ltd,
Spring Hill,
Idbury,
Oxfordshire, OX7 6RU

Distributed by
Melia Publishing Services Ltd,
P.O. Box 1639, Maidenhead,
Berks SL6 6YZ

Designer: Emma Bradford
Project manager: Elizabeth Wilkes

ISBN 1 871927 04 8

Typesetting by York House Typographic, London
Colour origination by York House Graphics, London
Printed and bound in Hong Kong by Dai Nippon

Contents

Introduction

The world of the fairy tale is the first world of our imagination, in which the everyday hopes and troubles of mankind are acted out in poetic narratives which never lose their power. The need to tell stories, and to hear them, is central to what makes us human.

This book contains a selection of fairy tales from around the world, made from the series of twelve Fairy Books by Andrew Lang which started with *The Blue Fairy Book* in 1889 and closed with *The Lilac Fairy Book* in 1910. The stories have been chosen for their beauty, drama, and comedy, but also to show how similar — yet how different — the storytelling impulse is in different cultures. Andrew Lang writes of them, "They are our oldest legacy, they will be our last bequest, flitting from mouth to mouth when the printing press is in ruins and the alphabet has to be re-invented."

I have deliberately avoided well-known stories which can be found in countless other books of fairy tales. *The Blue Fairy Book* alone contained "Cinderella," "The Sleeping Beauty," "Little Red Riding Hood," "Puss in Boots," and "Beauty and the Beast" from Charles Perrault and "Rumpelstiltskin" from the Brothers Grimm, together with the famous stories of Dick Whittington and Jack the Giantkiller. In later volumes, Andrew Lang drew much more widely from the world's folk literature. The books were immensely popular, though Lang was criticized for taking liberties with his sources. He freely admitted, "The stories are not literal or word by word translations, but have been altered in many ways to make them suitable for children."

Andrew Lang, one of the most influential and productive men of letters of his day, wrote around a hundred and twenty books and edited over a hundred and fifty more, including twenty-five story collections for children, of which twelve were Fairy Books. While he superintended and advised, much of the actual work of retelling and translation was performed by helpers, chief of whom was his wife, Leonora. Lang himself provided the impetus and the knowledge which made the books so superior to anything that had come before, and to much that has come since. Soon his name was so closely associated with the fairy tale that he had to issue stern denials in every volume that he himself was the author of every fairy tale ever written: "*I do not write the stories out of my own head.*"

Two factors in particular ensured the success of the Fairy Books. The first was Lang's lifelong love of popular tales, which was more than a scholar's interest. He wrote that, "When I was a little boy I read every fairy tale I could lay my hands on." As a man, he continued to do so. The second was Lang's responsiveness to the real tastes of childhood. He carried on lively correspondences with child friends, and never underestimated them. He remembered that, "A boy of five is more at home in Fairyland than in his own country." His attitude to children's reading was refreshingly unprescriptive. He argued, "It is my wish that children should be allowed to choose their own books. Let their friends give them the money and turn them loose in the book shops."

I think that Lang was correct in assuming that some of those children, given complete freedom of choice, would still select a book of fairy tales. For in fairy tales the transforming power of the imagination — the basis of all childhood make-believe — is the most crucial element. Take, for instance, the first story in this book, "The Boys With the Golden Stars," from Romania. In it, two enchanted brothers, "with golden hair and stars on their foreheads," are persecuted by a wicked stepmother. They are murdered and buried, and from their graves spring two aspens. The trees are chopped down, to make two beds. The beds are burned, leaving only ashes. The ashes are scattered to the four winds, but the two brightest sparks fall into a river, where they become two little fishes with golden scales. The fishes are caught, and, when they have swum in the dew and been dried by the sun, turn once again into "two beautiful young princes, with hair as golden as the stars on their foreheads." Thus, in what Lang's friend Joseph Jacobs called "bright trains of images," fairy stories unfold their deep truths about human nature and human behaviour.

In the fairy tale world, it is true, the kindhearted and the humble always vanquish the wicked and the proud. It is not so in life. Yet the fairy tales contain suffering and cruelty as well as magical help and happy endings. We want them to end well, for the natural justice of the tales satisfies our sense of what is right; but the anguish the characters endure is real and painful to us. "Once upon a time" means *now*: and if we suffer with the heroes and heroines of fairy tales in their times of trial, we can allow ourselves to rejoice with them in their hours of triumph.

NEIL PHILIP

The Boys With the Golden Stars

ROMANIA

Once upon a time what happened did happen — and if it had not happened, you would never have heard this story.

Well, once upon a time there lived an emperor who had half a world all to himself to rule over, and in this world dwelt an old shepherd and his wife and their three daughters, Anna, Stana, and Laptitza.

Anna, the eldest, was so beautiful that when she took the sheep to pasture, they forgot to eat as long as she was walking with them. Stana, the second, was so beautiful that when she was driving the flock, the wolves protected the sheep. But Laptitza, the youngest, with a skin as white as the foam on the milk, and with hair as soft as the finest lamb's wool, was as beautiful as both her sisters put together — as beautiful as she alone could be.

One summer day when the rays of the sun were pouring down on the earth, the three sisters went to the wood on the outskirts of the mountain to pick strawberries. As they were looking for where the largest berries grew, they heard the tramp of horses approaching, so loud that you would have thought a whole army was riding by. But it was only the emperor going to hunt with his friends and attendants.

They were all fine handsome young men, who sat on their horses as if they were part of them, but the finest and handsomest of all was the young emperor himself.

As they drew near the three sisters, and marked their beauty, they checked their horses and rode slowly by.

"Listen, Sisters!" said Anna as they passed on. "If one of those young men should make me his wife, I would bake him a loaf of bread that should keep him young and brave forever."

"And if I," said Stana, "should be the one chosen, I would weave my husband a shirt that will keep him unscathed when he fights with dragons; when he goes through water, he will never even be wet; or if through fire, it will not scorch him."

"And I," said Laptitza, "will give the man who chooses me two boys, twins, each with a golden star on his forehead, as bright as those in the sky."

And though they spoke low, the young men heard and turned their horses' heads.

"I take you at your word, and mine shall you be, most lovely of empresses!" cried the emperor, and swung Laptitza and her strawberries on the horse before him.

"And I will have you," "And I you," exclaimed two of his friends, and they all rode back to the palace together.

The following morning the marriage ceremony took place, and for three days and three nights there was nothing but feasting over the whole kingdom. And when the rejoicings were over, the news was in everybody's mouth that Anna had sent for corn, and had made the loaf of which she had spoken at the strawberry beds. And then more days and nights passed, and this rumor was succeeded by another one — that Stana had procured some flax, and had dried it, and combed it, and spun it into linen, and sewed it herself into the shirt of which she had spoken over the strawberry beds.

Now the emperor had a stepmother, and she had a daughter by her first husband, who lived with her in the palace. The girl's mother had always believed that her daughter would be empress, and not the "Milkwhite Maiden," the child of a mere shepherd. So she hated the girl with all her heart, and only bided her time to do her ill.

But she could do nothing as long as the emperor remained with his wife night and day, and she began to wonder what she could do to get him away from her.

At last, when everything else had failed, she managed to make her brother, who was king of the neighboring country, declare war against

The Emperor meets the Three Sisters

the emperor, and besiege some of the frontier towns with a large army. This time her scheme was successful. The young emperor sprang up in wrath the moment he heard the news, and vowed that nothing, not even his wife, should hinder his giving them battle. And hastily assembling whatever soldiers happened to be at hand, he set off at once to meet the enemy. The other king had not reckoned on the swiftness of his movements, and was not ready to receive him. The emperor fell on him when he was off his guard, and routed his army completely. Then when victory was won, and the terms of peace hastily drawn up, he rode home as fast as his horse would carry him, and reached the palace on the third day.

But early that morning when the stars were growing pale in the sky, two little boys with golden hair and stars on their foreheads were born to Laptitza. And the stepmother, who was watching, took them away, and dug a hole in the corner of the palace, under the windows of the emperor, and put them in it, while in their stead she placed two little puppies.

The emperor came into the palace, and when they told him the news he went straight to Laptitza's room. No words were needed; he saw with his own eyes that Laptitza had not kept the promise she had made at the strawberry beds, and though it nearly broke his heart, he must punish her.

So he went out sadly and told his guards that the empress was to be buried in the earth up to her neck, so that everyone might know what would happen to those who dared to deceive the emperor.

Not many days after, the stepmother's wish was fulfilled. The emperor took her daughter to wife, and again the rejoicings lasted for three days and three nights.

Let us now see what happened to the two little boys.

The poor little babies had found no rest even in their graves. In the place where they had been buried, there sprang up two beautiful young aspens, and the stepmother, who hated the sight of the trees, which reminded her of her crime, gave orders that they should be uprooted. But the emperor heard of it, and forbade the trees to be touched, saying, "Let them alone; I like to see them there! They are the finest

The Stepmother digs a Grave for the Babies

aspens I have ever beheld, and bring me great joy!"

And the aspens grew as no aspens had ever grown before. In each day they added a year's growth, and each night they added a year's growth, and at dawn when the stars faded out of the sky, they grew three years' growth in the twinkling of an eye, and their boughs swept across the palace windows. And when the wind moved them softly, the emperor would sit and listen to them all the day long.

The stepmother knew what it all meant, and her mind never ceased from trying to invent some way of destroying the trees. It was not an easy thing, but a woman's will can press milk out of a stone, and her cunning conquer heroes. And so one morning the empress sat on the edge of her husband's bed, and began to coax him with all sorts of pretty ways. It was some time before the bait took, but at length — even emperors are only human!

"Well, well," he said at last, "have your way and cut down the trees; but out of one they shall make a bed for me, and out of the other, one for you!"

And with this the empress was forced to be content. The aspens were cut down next morning, and before night the new beds had been placed in the emperor's room.

Now when the emperor lay down in his bed, he seemed as if he had grown a hundred times heavier than usual, yet he felt a kind of calm that was quite new to him. But the empress felt as if she was lying on thorns and nettles, and could not close her eyes.

When the emperor was fast asleep, the beds began to crack loudly, and to the empress each crack had a meaning. She felt as if she were listening to a language that no one but herself could understand.

"Is it too heavy for you, little brother?" asked one of the beds.

"Oh, no, it is not heavy at all," answered the bed in which the emperor was sleeping. "I feel nothing but joy now that my beloved father rests over me."

"It is very heavy for me!" said the other bed, "for on me lies an evil soul."

And so they talked on till the morning, the empress listening all the while.

By daybreak the empress had determined how to get rid of the beds. She would have two others made exactly like them, and when the emperor had gone hunting they should be placed in his room. This was done, and the aspen beds were burnt in a large fire, till only a little heap of ashes was left.

Yet while they were burning, the empress seemed to hear the same words, which she alone could understand.

Then she stooped and gathered up the ashes, and scattered them to the four winds, so that they might blow over fresh lands and fresh seas, and nothing remain of them.

But she had not seen that where the fire burned brightest two sparks flew up, and after floating in the air for a few moments, fell down into the great river that flows through the heart of the country. Here the sparks had turned into two little fishes with golden scales, and one was so exactly like the other that everyone could tell at the first glance that they must be twins.

Early one morning the emperor's fishermen went down to the river to get some fish for their master's breakfast, and cast their nets into the stream. As the last star twinkled out of the sky, they drew them in, and among the multitude of fishes lay two with scales of gold, such as no man had ever looked on.

They all gathered around and wondered, and after some talk they decided that they would take the little fishes alive as they were, and give them as a present to the emperor.

"Do not take us there, for that is where we came from, and our destruction lies there," said one of the fishes.

"But what are we to do with you?" asked one fisherman.

"Go and collect all the dew that lies on the leaves, and let us swim in it. Then lay us in the sun, and do not come near us till the sun's rays have dried off the dew," answered the other fish.

The fisherman did as they told him — gathered the dew from the leaves and let them swim in it, then put them to lie in the sun till the dew was all dried up.

And when he came back, what do you think he saw? Why, two boys, two beautiful young princes, with hair as golden as the stars on their foreheads, and each so like the other, that at the first glance everyone would have known them for twins.

The boys grew fast. In every day they grew a year's growth, and in every night another year's growth, but at dawn, when the stars were fading, they grew three years' growth in the twinkling of an eye. And they grew in age, and wisdom and knowledge too. And when three days and three nights had passed, they were twelve years in age, twenty-four in strength, and thirty-six in wisdom.

"Now take us to our father," they said. So the fisherman gave them each a lambskin cap that half covered their faces, and completely hid their golden hair and the stars on their forehead, and led them to the court.

By the time they arrived there it was midday, and the fisherman and his charges went up to an official. "We wish to speak with the emperor," said one of the boys.

"You must wait until he has finished his dinner," replied the official.

"No, while he is eating it," said the second boy, stepping across the threshold.

The attendants all ran forward to thrust such impudent youngsters outside the palace, but the boys slipped through their fingers like quicksilver, and entered a large hall where the emperor was dining, surrounded by his whole court.

"We desire to enter," said one of the princes sharply to a servant who stood near the door.

"That is quite impossible," replied the servant.

"Is it? Let's see!" said the second prince, pushing the servants to the right and left.

But the servants were many, and the princes only two. The noise of a struggle reached the emperor's ears.

"What is the matter?" he asked angrily.

The princes stopped at the sound of their father's voice.

"Two boys who want to force their way in," replied one of the servants, approaching the emperor.

"To *force* their way in? Who dares to use force in my palace? What boys are they?" said the emperor all in one breath.

"We know not, O mighty emperor," answered the servant, "but they must surely be akin to you, for they have the strength of lions, and have scattered the guards at the gate. And they are as proud as they are strong, for they will not take their caps from their heads."

The emperor, as he listened, grew red with anger.

"Thrust them out," he cried. "Set the dogs after them."

"Leave us alone, and we will go quietly," said the princes, and stepped backward, weeping silently at the harsh words. They had almost reached the gates when a servant ran up to them.

"The emperor commands you to return," he panted. "The empress wishes to see you."

The princes thought a moment. Then they went back the way they had come, and walked straight up to the emperor, their caps still on their heads.

He sat at the top of a long table covered with flowers and filled with guests. And beside him sat the empress, supported by twelve cushions. When the princes entered, one of the cushions fell down, and there remained only eleven.

"Take off your caps," said one of the courtiers.

"A covered head is among men a sign of honor. We wish to seem what we are."

"Never mind," said the emperor, whose anger had dropped before the silvery tones of the boys' voices. "Stay as you are, but tell me *who* you are! Where do you come from, and what do you want?"

"We are twins, two shoots from one stem, which has been broken, and half lies in the ground and half sits at the head of this table. We

THE BOYS WITH THE GOLDEN STARS

have traveled a long way, we have spoken in the rustle of the wind, have whispered in the wood, we have sung in the waters, but now we wish to tell you a story that you know without knowing it, in the speech of men."

And a second cushion fell down.

"Let them take their silliness home," said the empress.

"Oh, no, let them go on," said the emperor. "You wished to see them, but I wish to hear them. Go on, boys, sing me the story."

The empress was silent, but the princes began to sing the story of their lives.

"There was once an emperor," they began, and the third cushion fell down.

When they reached the warlike expedition of the emperor, three of the cushions fell down at once.

And when the tale was finished there were no more cushions under the empress, but the moment that they lifted their caps, and showed their golden hair, and the golden stars, the eyes of the emperor and of all his guests were bent on them, and they could hardly bear the power of so many glances.

And there happened in the end what should have happened in the beginning. Laptitza took her rightful place next to her husband at the top of the table. The stepmother's daughter became the lowest kitchen maid in the palace, while the stepmother was tied to a wild horse, and everyone knew and has never forgotten that whoever has a mind turned to wickedness is sure to end badly.

The Punishment of the Stepmother

The Princess Bella-Flor

SPAIN

Once upon a time there lived a man who had two sons. When they grew up, the elder went to seek his fortune in a far country, and for many years no one heard anything about him. Meanwhile the younger son stayed at home with his father, who died at last in a good old age, leaving great riches behind him.

For some time the son who stayed at home spent his father's wealth freely, believing that he alone remained to enjoy it. But one day as he was coming downstairs, he was surprised to see a stranger enter the hall, looking about as if the house belonged to him.

"Have you forgotten me?" asked the man.

"I can't forget a person I have never known," was the rude answer.

"I am your brother," replied the stranger, "and I have returned home without the money I hoped to have made. And what is worse, they tell me in the village that my father is dead. I would have counted my lost gold as nothing if I could have seen him once more."

"He died six months ago," said the rich brother, "and he left you, as your portion, the old wooden chest that stands in the loft. You had better go there and look for it; I have no more time to waste." And he went his way.

So the wanderer turned his steps to the loft, which was at the top of the storehouse, and there he found the wooden chest, so old that it looked as if it were dropping to pieces.

"What use is this old thing to me?" he said to himself. "Oh, well, it will serve to light a fire at which I can warm myself; and the comforting flames shall be a reminder of my father's love."

Placing the chest on his back, the man, whose name was José, set out for his inn, and borrowing a hatchet, began to chop up the box. In doing so he discovered a secret drawer, and in it lay a paper. He opened the paper, not knowing what it might contain, and was astonished to find that it was the acknowledgment of a large debt that was owing to his father. Putting the precious writing in his pocket, he hastily inquired of the landlord where he could find the man whose name was written inside, and he ran out at once in search of him.

The debtor proved to be an old miser who lived at the other end of the village. He had hoped for many months that the paper he had written had been lost or destroyed, and, indeed, when he saw it, was very unwilling to pay what he owed. However, the stranger threatened to drag him before the king, and when the miser saw that there was no help for it, he counted out the coins one by one. The stranger picked them up and put them in his pocket, and went back to his inn feeling that he was now a rich man.

A few weeks after this he was walking through the streets of the nearest town, when he met a poor woman crying bitterly. He stopped and asked her what was the matter, and she answered between her sobs that her husband was dying, and to make matters worse, a creditor whom he could not pay was anxious to have him taken to prison.

"Comfort yourself," said the stranger kindly. "They shall neither send your husband to prison nor sell your goods. I will not only pay his debts, but if he dies, the cost of his burial also. And now go home, and nurse him as well as you can."

And so she did; but in spite of her care the husband died, and was buried by the stranger. But everything cost more than he had expected, and when all was paid, he found that only three gold pieces were left.

"What am I to do now?" he said to himself. "I think I had better go to court, and enter into the service of the king."

At first he was only a servant, who carried the king the water for his bath, and saw that his bed was made in a particular fashion. But he did his duties so well that his master soon took notice of him, and in a short time he rose to be a gentleman of the bedchamber.

Now when this happened, the younger brother had spent all the money he had inherited, and did not know how to make any for himself. He then thought of the king's favorite, and went whining to the palace to beg that his brother, whom he had so ill-used, would give him his protection and find him a position. The elder, who was always ready to help everyone, spoke to the king on his behalf, and the next day the young man took up his work at court.

Unfortunately, the newcomer was by nature spiteful and envious, and could not bear anyone to have better luck than himself. By spying through keyholes and listening at doors, he learned that the king, old and ugly though he was, had fallen in love with the Princess Bella-Flor, who would have nothing to say to him and had hidden herself in a mountain castle, no one knew where.

That will do nicely, thought the scoundrel, rubbing his hands. It will be quite easy to get the king to send my brother in search of her, and if he returns without finding her, his head will be the forfeit. Either way, he will be out of *my* path.

So he went at once to the Lord High Chamberlain and craved an audience of the king, to whom he declared he wished to tell some news of the highest importance. The king admitted him into the presence chamber without delay, and bade him state what he had to say, and to be quick about it.

"Oh, sire! The Princess Bella-Flor — " answered the man, and then stopped as if afraid.

"What of the Princess Bella-Flor?" asked the king impatiently.

"I have heard — it is whispered at court — that your majesty desires to know where she lies in hiding."

"I would give half my kingdom to the man who will bring her to me," cried the king eagerly. "Speak on, knave. Has a bird of the air revealed to you the secret?"

"It is not I, but my brother who knows," replied the traitor; "if your majesty would ask him — " But before the words were out of his mouth, the king had struck a blow with his scepter on a golden plate that hung on the wall.

"Order José to appear before me instantly," he shouted to the servant who ran to obey his orders, so great was the noise his majesty had made; and when José entered the hall, wondering what in the world could be the matter, the king was nearly dumb from rage and excitement.

"Bring me the Princess Bella-Flor this moment," he stammered, "for if you return without her, I will have you drowned!" And without another word he left the hall, leaving José staring with surprise and horror.

How can I find the Princess Bella-Flor when I have never even seen her? he thought. But it is no use staying here, for I shall only be put to death. And he walked slowly to the stables to choose himself a horse.

There were rows upon rows of fine beasts with their names written in gold above their stalls, and José was looking uncertainly from one to the other, wondering which he should choose, when an old white horse turned its head and signed to him to approach.

"Take me," it said in a gentle whisper, "and all will go well."

José still felt so bewildered with the mission that the king had given him that he forgot to be astonished at hearing a horse talk. Mechanically he laid his hand on the bridle, and led the white horse out of the stable. He was about to mount on his back, when the animal spoke again:

"Pick up those three loaves of bread that you see there, and put them in your pocket."

José did as he was told, and being in a great hurry to get away, asked no questions, but swung himself into the saddle.

They rode far without meeting any adventures, but at length they came to an anthill, and the horse stopped.

"Crumble those three loaves for the ants," he said. But José hesitated.

"Why, we may want them ourselves!" he answered.

"Never mind that; give them to the ants all the same. Do not lose a chance of helping others." And when the loaves lay in crumbs on the road, the horse galloped on.

By and by they entered a rocky pass between two mountains, and here they saw an eagle that had been caught in a hunter's net.

"Get down and cut the meshes of that net, and set the poor bird free," said the horse.

"But it will take so long," objected José, "and we may miss the princess."

"Never mind that; do not lose a chance of helping others," answered the horse. And when the meshes were cut, and the eagle was free, the horse galloped on.

They had ridden many miles, and at last they came to a river, where they beheld a little fish lying and gasping on the sand, and the horse said:

"Do you see that little fish? It will die if you do not put it back in the water."

"But, really, we shall never find the Princess Bella-Flor if we waste our time like this!" cried José.

"We never waste time when we are helping others," answered the horse. And soon the little fish was swimming happily away.

A little while after, they reached a castle that was built in the middle of a very thick wood, and right in front was the Princess Bella-Flor, feeding her hens.

"Now listen," said the horse. "I am going to give all sorts of little hops and skips, which will amuse the Princess Bella-Flor. Then she will tell you that she would like to ride a little way, and you must help her to mount. When she is seated, I shall begin to neigh and kick, and you must say that I have never carried a woman before, and that you had better get up behind so as to be able to manage me. Once on my back, we will go like the wind to the king's palace.

José did exactly as the horse told him, and everything fell out as the animal prophesied; so that it was not until they were galloping breathlessly toward the palace that the princess knew that she was taken captive. She said nothing, however, but quietly opened her apron that contained the bran for the chickens, and in a moment it lay scattered on the ground.

"Oh, I have let fall my bran!" she cried. "Please get down and pick it up for me." But José only answered:

"We shall find plenty of bran where we are going." And the horse galloped on.

They were now passing through a forest, and the princess took out her handkerchief and threw it upward, so that it stuck in one of the topmost branches of a tree.

"Dear me; how stupid! I have let my handkerchief blow away," she said. "Will you climb up and get it for me?" But José answered:

HJFORD

"We shall find plenty of handkerchiefs where we are going." And the horse galloped on.

After the wood they reached a river, and the princess slipped a ring off her finger and let it roll into the water.

"How careless of me," she gasped, beginning to sob. "I have lost my favorite ring; *do* stop for a moment and look if you can see it." But José answered:

"You will find plenty of rings where we are going." And the horse galloped on.

At last they entered the palace gates, and the king's heart bounded with joy at beholding his beloved Bella-Flor. But the princess brushed him aside as if he had been a fly, and locked herself into the nearest room, which she would not open for all his entreaties.

"Bring me the three things I lost on the way, and perhaps I may think about it," was all she would say. And in despair the king was driven to take counsel of José.

"There is no remedy that I can see," said his majesty, "but that you, who know where they are, should go and bring them back. And if you return without them, I will have you drowned."

Poor José was much troubled at these words. He thought that he had done all that was required of him, and that his life was safe. However, he bowed low, and went out to consult his friend the horse.

"Do not vex yourself," said the horse when he had heard the story. "Jump up, and we will go and look for the things." And José mounted at once.

They rode on till they came to the anthill, and then the horse asked:

"Would you like to have the bran?"

"What is the use of liking?" answered José.

"Well, call the ants, and tell them to fetch it for you; and if some of it has been scattered by the wind, to bring in its place the grains that were in the loaves you gave them." José listened in surprise. He did not much believe in the horse's plan; but he could not think of anything better, so he called to the ants, and bade them collect the bran as fast as they could.

Then he sat under a tree, and waited while his horse cropped the green turf.

"Look there!" said the animal, suddenly raising its head; and José looked behind him and saw a little mountain of bran, which he put into a bag that was hung over his saddle.

"Good deeds bear fruit sooner or later," observed the horse; "but mount again, as we have far to go."

When they arrived at the tree, they saw the handkerchief fluttering like a flag from the topmost branch, and José's spirits sank again.

"How am I to get that handkerchief?" he cried; "why, I should need Jacob's ladder!" But the horse answered:

"Do not be frightened. Call to the eagle you set free from the net; he will bring it to you."

So José called to the eagle, and the eagle flew to the top of the tree and brought back the handkerchief in its beak. José thanked him, and vaulting on his horse, they rode on to the river.

A great deal of rain had fallen in the night, and the river, instead of being clear as it was before, was dark and troubled.

"How am I to fetch the ring from the bottom of this river when I do not know exactly where it was dropped, and cannot even see it?" asked José. But the horse answered:

"Do not be frightened. Call the little fish whose life you saved, and she will bring it to you."

So José called to the fish, and the fish dived to the bottom and slipped behind big stones, and moved little ones with its tail till it found the ring, and brought it to José in its mouth.

Well pleased with all he had done, José returned to the palace. But when the king took the precious objects to Bella-Flor, she declared that she would never open her door until the bandit who had carried her off had been fried in oil.

"I am very sorry," said the king to José, "I really would rather not; but you see I have no choice."

While the oil was being heated in the great caldron, José went to the stables to inquire of his friend the horse if there was no way for him to escape.

"Do not be frightened," said the horse. "Get on my back and I will gallop until my whole body is wet with perspiration, then rub it all over your skin, and no matter how hot the oil may be, you will never feel it."

José did not ask any more questions, but did as the horse bade him; and men wondered at his cheerful face as they lowered him into the caldron of boiling oil. He was left there till Bella-Flor cried that he must be cooked enough. Then out came a youth so young and handsome, that everyone fell in love with him, and Bella-Flor most of all.

As for the old king, he saw that he had lost the game; and in despair he flung himself into the caldron, and was fried instead of José. Then José was proclaimed king, on the condition that he marry Bella-Flor, which he promised to do the next day. But first he went to the stables and sought out the horse, and said to him, "It is to you that I owe my life and my crown. Why have you done all this for me?" And the horse answered:

"I am the soul of that unhappy man for whom you spent all your fortune. And when I saw you in danger of death, I begged that I might help you, as you had helped me. For as I told you, good deeds bear their own fruit!"

The Two Caskets

SWEDEN

Far, far away, in the midst of a pine forest there lived a woman who had both a daughter and a stepdaughter. Ever since her own daughter was born the mother had given her all that she cried for, so she grew up to be as cross and disagreeable as she was ugly. The stepdaughter on the other hand had spent her childhood in working hard to keep house for her father, who died soon after his second marriage; and she was as much beloved by the neighbors for her goodness and industry as she was for her beauty.

As the years went on, the difference between the two girls grew more marked, and the old woman treated her stepdaughter worse than ever, and was always on the watch for some pretext for beating her, or depriving her of her food. Anything, however foolish, was good enough for this, and one day when she could think of nothing better, she set both the girls to spin while sitting on the low wall of the well.

"And you had better mind what you do," she said, "for the one whose thread breaks first shall be thrown to the bottom."

But of course she took good care that her own daughter's flax was fine and strong, while the stepsister had only some coarse thread that no one would have thought of using. As might be expected, in a very little while the poor girl's thread snapped, and the old woman, who had been watching from behind a door, seized her stepdaughter by her shoulders, and threw her into the well.

"That's the end of you!" she said. But she was wrong, for it was only the beginning.

Down, down, down went the girl — it seemed as if the well must reach to the very middle of the earth; but at last her feet touched the ground, and she found herself in a field more beautiful than even the summer pastures of her native mountains. Trees waved in the soft breeze, and flowers of the brightest colors danced in the grass. And though she was quite alone, the girl's heart danced too, for she felt happier than she had since before her father died. So she walked on through the meadow till she came to an old tumbledown fence — so old that it was a wonder it managed to stand up at all, and it looked as if it depended for support on the clematis vine that climbed all over it.

The girl paused for a moment as she came up, and gazed about for a place where she might safely cross. But before she could move, a voice cried from the fence:

"Do not hurt me, little maiden; I am so old, so old, I have not much longer to live."

And the maiden answered:

"No, I will not hurt you. Fear nothing." And then, seeing a spot where the clematis grew less thickly than in other places, she jumped lightly over.

"May all go well with you," said the fence as the girl walked on.

She soon left the meadow and turned onto a path that ran between two flowery hedges. Right in front of her stood an oven, and through its open door she could see a pile of white loaves.

"Eat as many loaves as you like, but do me no harm, little maiden," cried the oven. And the maiden told her to fear nothing, for she never hurt anything, and was very grateful for the oven's kindness in giving her such a beautiful white loaf. When she had finished it, down to the last crumb, she shut the oven door and said, "Good morning."

"May all go well with you," said the oven as the girl walked on.

By and by she became very thirsty, and seeing a cow with a milk pail hanging on her horn, turned toward her.

"Milk me and drink as much as you will, little maiden," cried the cow, "but be sure you spill none on the ground; and do me no harm, for I have never harmed anyone."

"Nor I," answered the girl. "Fear nothing." So she sat down and milked till the pail was nearly full. Then she drank it all up except a little drop at the bottom.

"Now throw any that is left over my hooves, and hang the pail on my horns again," said the cow. And the girl did as she was bid, and kissed the cow on her forehead, and went her way.

Many hours had now passed since the girl had fallen down the well, and the sun was setting.

Where shall I spend the night? she thought. And suddenly she saw before her a gate that she had not noticed before, and a very old woman leaning against it.

"Good evening," said the girl politely; and the old woman answered:

"Good evening, my child. Would that everyone was as polite as you. And what brings you to my garden gate?"

"I am in search of a position," replied the girl; and the woman smiled and said:

"Then stop a little while and comb my hair, and you shall tell me all the things you can do."

"Willingly, mother," answered the girl. And she began combing out the old woman's hair, which was long and white.

Half an hour passed in this way, and then the old woman said:

"As you did not think yourself too good to comb me, I will show you where you may take service. Be prudent and patient and all will go well."

So the girl thanked her, and set out for a farm at a little distance, where she was engaged to milk the cows and sift the corn.

As soon as it was light the next morning, the girl got up and went into the cowhouse. "I'm sure you must be hungry," she said, patting each cow in turn. And then she fetched hay from the barn, and while they were eating it, she swept out the cowhouse, and strewed clean straw upon the floor. The cows were so pleased with the care she took of them that they stood quite still while she milked them, and did not play any of the tricks on her that they had played on other dairymaids who were rough and rude. And when she had done, and was going to get up from her stool, she found sitting around her a whole circle of cats, black and white, tabby and tortoiseshell, who all cried with one voice:

"We are very thirsty, please give us some milk!"

"My poor little pussies," she said, "of course you shall have some." And she went into the dairy, followed by all the cats, and gave each one a little red saucerful. But before they drank, they all rubbed themselves against her knees and purred by way of thanks.

The next thing the girl had to do was to go to the storehouse and sift the corn through a sieve. While she was busy rubbing the corn, she heard a whirr of wings, and a flock of sparrows flew in at the window.

"We are hungry. Give us some corn! Give us some corn!" they cried; and the girl answered:

"You poor little birds, of course you shall have some!" and scattered

a fine handful over the floor. When they had finished, they flew onto her shoulders and flapped their wings by way of thanks.

Time went by, and no cows in the whole countryside were so fat and well tended as hers, and no dairy had so much milk to show. The farmer's wife was so well satisfied that she gave her higher wages, and treated her like her own daughter. At length one day the girl was bidden by her mistress to come into the kitchen, and when there, the old woman said to her, "I know you can tend cows and keep a dairy; now let me see what you can do besides. Take this sieve to the well, and fill it with water, and bring it home to me without spilling one drop by the way."

The girl's heart sank at this order; for how was it possible for her to do her mistress's bidding? However, she was silent, and taking the sieve, went down to the well with it. Stooping over the side, she filled it to the brim, but as soon as she lifted it the water all ran out of the holes. Again and again she tried, but not a drop would remain in the sieve, and she was just turning away in despair, when a flock of sparrows flew down from the sky.

"Ashes! Ashes!" they twittered; and the girl looked at them and said:

"Well, I can't be in a worse plight than I am already, so I will take your advice." And she ran back to the kitchen and filled her sieve with ashes. Then once more she dipped the sieve into the well, and, behold, this time not a drop of water disappeared!

"Here is the sieve, mistress," cried the girl, going to the room where the old woman was sitting.

"You are cleverer than I expected," she answered; "or else someone helped you who is skilled in magic." But the girl kept silent, and the old woman asked her no more questions.

Many days passed during which the girl went about her work as usual, but at length one day the old woman called her and said:

"I have something more for you to do. There are here two yarns, the one white, the other black. What you must do is to wash them in the river till the black one becomes white and the white black." And the girl took them to the river and washed hard for several hours, but wash as she would, they never changed one whit.

This is worse than the sieve, she thought, and was about to give up in despair, when there came a rush of wings through the air, and on every twig of the birch trees that grew by the bank was perched a sparrow.

"The black to the east, the white to the west!" they sang all at once; and the girl dried her tears and felt brave again. Picking up the black yarn, she stood facing the east and dipped it in the river, and in an instant it grew as white as snow. Then turning to the west, she held the white yarn in the water, and it became as black as a crow's wing. She looked back at the sparrows and smiled and nodded to them, and flapping their wings in reply, they flew swiftly away.

At the sight of the yarn the old woman was struck dumb; but when at length she found her voice, she asked the girl what magician had helped her to do what no one had done before. But she got no answer, for the maiden was afraid of bringing trouble on her little friends.

ASHES · ASHES · TWITTERED · THE · SPARROWS ·

For many weeks the mistress shut herself up in her room, and the girl went about her work as usual. She hoped that she would be given no more difficult tasks; but in this she was mistaken, for one day the old woman appeared suddenly in the kitchen, and said to her:

"There is one more trial to which I must put you, and if you do not fail in that, you will be left in peace forevermore. Here are the yarns that you washed. Take them and weave them into a web that is as smooth as a king's robe, and see that it is spun by the time that the sun sets."

This is the easiest thing I have been given to do, thought the girl, who was a good spinner. But when she began, she found that the yarn tangled and broke every moment.

"Oh, I can never do it!" she cried at last, and leaned her head against the loom and wept; but at that instant the door opened, and there entered, one behind another, a procession of cats.

"What is the matter, fair maiden?" they asked. And the girl answered:

"My mistress has given me this yarn to weave into a piece of cloth, which must be finished by sunset, and I have not even begun yet, for the yarn breaks whenever I touch it."

"If that is all, dry your eyes," said the cats; "we will manage it for you." And they jumped on the loom, and wove so fast and so skillfully that in a very short time the cloth was ready and was as fine as any king ever wore. The girl was so delighted at the sight of it that she gave each cat a kiss on his forehead as they left the room one behind the other as they had come.

"Who has taught you this wisdom?" asked the old woman, after she had passed her hands twice or thrice over the cloth, and could find no roughness anywhere. But the girl only smiled and did not answer. She had learned early the value of silence.

After a few weeks the old woman sent for her maid and told her that as her year of service was now up, she was free to return home, but that for her part the girl had served her so well, she hoped she might stay with her. But at these words the maid shook her head, and answered gently:

"I have been happy here, madam, and I thank you for your goodness to me; but I have left behind me a stepsister and a stepmother, and I would like to be with them once more." The old woman looked at her for a moment, and then she said:

"Well, that must be as you like; but as you have worked faithfully for me, I will give you a reward. Go now into the loft above the storehouse and there you will find many caskets. Choose the one that pleases you best, but be careful not to open it till you have set it in the place where you wish it to remain."

The girl left the room to go to the loft, and as soon as she got outside, she found all the cats waiting for her. Walking in procession as was their custom, they followed her into the loft, which was filled with caskets big and little, plain and splendid. She lifted one up and looked at it, and then put it down to examine another yet more beautiful. Which should she choose, the yellow or the blue, the red or the green, the gold or the silver? She hesitated long, and went first to one and then to another, when she heard the cats' voices calling, "Take the black! Take the black!"

The words made her look around — she had seen no black casket, but as the cats continued their cry, she peered into several corners that had remained unnoticed, and at length discovered a little black box, so small and so black that it might easily have been passed over.

TAKE THE BLACK TAKE THE BLACK cried the cats

"This is the casket that pleases me best, mistress," said the girl, carrying it into the house. And the old woman smiled, and nodded, and bade her go her way. So the girl set forth, after bidding farewell to the cows and the cats and the sparrows, who all wept as they said good-bye.

She walked on and on and on till she reached the flowery meadow, and there something happened. She never knew what, but suddenly she found herself sitting on the wall of the well in her stepmother's yard. Then she got up and entered the house.

The woman and her daughter stared as if they had been turned into stone; but at length the stepmother gasped out:

"So you are alive after all! Well, luck was ever against me! And where have you been this year past?" Then the girl told how she had taken service in the underworld, and besides her wages had brought home with her a little casket, which she would like to set up in her room.

"Give me the money, and take the ugly little box off to the hen-house," cried the woman, beside herself with rage, and the girl, quite frightened at her violence, hastened away, with her precious box clasped to her bosom.

The henhouse was in a very dirty state, as no one had been near it since the girl had fallen down the well; but she scrubbed and swept till everything was clean again, and then she placed the little casket on a small shelf in the corner.

"Now I may open it," she said to herself; and unlocking it with the key that hung to its handle, she raised the lid, but started back as she did so, almost blinded by the light that burst upon her. No one would ever have guessed that that little black box could have held such a quantity of beautiful things! Rings, crowns, girdles, necklaces — all made of wonderful stones; and they shone with such brilliance that not only the stepmother and her daughter but all the people around came running to see if the house was on fire. Of course the woman felt quite ill with greed and envy, and she would have certainly taken all the jewels for herself had she not feared the wrath of the neighbors, who loved her stepdaughter as much as they hated her.

But if she could not steal the casket and its contents for herself, at least she could get another like it, and perhaps a still richer one. So she bade her own daughter sit on the edge of the well, and threw her into the water exactly as she had done to the other girl; and exactly as before, the flowery meadow lay at the bottom.

Every inch of the way she trod the path that her stepsister had trodden, and saw the things that she had seen; but there the likeness ended. When the fence prayed her to do it no harm, she laughed rudely, and tore up some of the stakes so that she might get over it more easily; when the oven offered her bread, she scattered the loaves on the ground and stamped on them; and after she had milked the cow, and drunk as much as she wanted, she threw the rest on the grass, and kicked the pail to bits, and never heard them say, as they looked after her:

"You shall not have done this to me for nothing!"

Toward evening she reached the spot where the old woman was leaning against the gatepost, but she passed her by without a word.

"Have you no manners in your country?" asked the crone.

"I can't stop and talk; I am in a hurry," answered the girl. "It is getting late, and I have to find a position."

"Stop and comb my hair for a little," said the old woman, "and I will help you to get a position."

"Comb your hair, indeed! I have something better to do than that!" And slamming the gate in the crone's face, she went her way. And she never heard the words that followed her:

"You shall not have done this to me for nothing!"

By and by the girl arrived at the farm, and she was engaged to look after the cows and sift the corn as her stepsister had been. But it was only when someone was watching her that she did her work; at other times the cowhouse was dirty, and the cows ill-fed and beaten, so that they kicked over the pail, and tried to butt her; and everyone said that they had never seen such thin cows or such poor milk. As for the cats, she chased them away and ill-treated them, so that they had not even the spirit to chase the rats and mice, which nowadays ran about everywhere. And when the sparrows came to beg for some corn, they fared no better than the cows and the cats, for the girl threw her shoes at them till they flew in a fright to the woods, and took shelter among the trees.

Months passed in this manner, when one day the mistress called the girl to her.

"All that I have given you to do you have done ill," she said, "yet I will give you another chance. For though you cannot tend cows, or divide the grain from the chaff, there may be other things that you can do better. Therefore take this sieve to the well, and fill it with water, and see that you bring it back without spilling a single drop."

The girl took the sieve and carried it to the well as her sister had done; but no little birds came to help her, and after dipping it in the well two or three times she brought it back empty.

"I thought as much," said the old woman angrily; "she that is useless in one thing is useless in another."

Perhaps the mistress may have thought that the girl had learned a lesson, but if she did, she was quite mistaken, as the work was no better done than before. By and by she sent for her maid again, and gave her the black and white yarn to wash in the river; but there was no one to tell her the secret by which the black would turn white, and the white black; so she brought them back as they were. This time the old woman only looked at her grimly, but the girl was too well pleased with herself to care what anyone thought about her.

After some weeks her third trial came, and the yarn was given to her to spin as it had been given to her stepsister before her.

But no procession of cats entered the room to weave a web of fine cloth, and at sunset she only brought back to her mistress an armful of dirty, tangled wool.

"There seems nothing in the world you can do," said the old woman, and left her to herself.

Soon after this the year was up, and the girl went to her mistress to tell her that she wished to go home.

"Little desire have I to keep you," answered the old woman, "for no one thing have you done as you ought. Still, I will give you some payment, therefore go up into the loft, and choose for yourself one of the caskets that lies there. But see that you do not open it till you place it where you wish it to stay."

This was what the girl had been hoping for, and so rejoiced was she that, without even stopping to thank the old woman, she ran as fast as she could to the loft. There were the caskets, blue and red, green and yellow, silver and gold; and there in the corner stood a little black casket, just like the one her stepsister had brought home.

"If there are so many jewels in that little black thing, this big red one will hold twice the number," she said to herself; and snatching it up, she set off on her road home without even going to bid farewell to her mistress.

"See, Mother, see what I have brought!" she cried as she entered the cottage holding the casket in both hands.

"Ah! You have got something very different from that little black box," answered the old woman with delight. But the girl was so busy finding a place for it to stand that she took little notice of her mother.

"It will look best here — no, here," she said, setting it first on one piece of furniture and then on another. "No, after all it is too fine to live in a kitchen. Let us place it in the guest chamber."

So mother and daughter carried it proudly upstairs and put it on a shelf over the fireplace. Then, untying the key from the handle, they opened the box. As before, a bright light leaped out when the lid was raised, but it did not spring from the luster of jewels, but from hot flames, which darted along the walls and burnt up the cottage and all that was in it, and the mother and daughter as well.

As they had done when the stepdaughter came home, the neighbors all hurried to see what was the matter; but they were too late. Only the henhouse was left standing; and in spite of her riches, there the stepdaughter lived happily to the end of her days.

The Snake Prince

INDIA

Once upon a time there lived by herself, in a city, an old woman who was desperately poor. One day she found that she had only a handful of flour left in the house, and no money to buy more nor hope of earning it. Carrying her little brass pot, very sadly she made her way down to the river to bathe and to obtain some water, thinking afterward to come home and make herself an unleavened cake of what flour she had left; and after that she did not know what was to become of her.

While she was bathing, she left her little brass pot on the riverbank, covered with a cloth to keep the inside nice and clean; but when she came up out of the river and took the cloth off to fill the pot with water, she saw inside it the glittering folds of a deadly snake. At once she popped the cloth again into the mouth of the pot and held it there; and then she said to herself:

"Ah, kind death! I will take you home to my house, and there I will shake you out of my pot and you will bite me and I will die, and then all my troubles will be ended."

With these sad thoughts in her mind the poor old woman hurried home, holding her cloth carefully in the mouth of the pot; and when she got home, she shut all the doors and windows, and took away the cloth, and turned the pot upside down upon her hearthstone. What was her surprise to find that, instead of the deadly snake that she expected to see fall out of it, there fell out with a rattle and a clang a most magnificent necklace of flashing jewels!

For a few minutes she could hardly think or speak, but stood staring;

and then with trembling hands she picked the necklace up, and folding it in the corner of her veil, she hurried off to the king's hall of public audience.

"A petition, O king!" she said. "A petition for your private ear alone!" And when her prayer had been granted, and she found herself alone with the king, she shook out her veil at his feet, and there fell from it in glittering coils the splendid necklace. As soon as the king saw it, he was filled with amazement and delight; and the more he looked at it, the more he felt that he must possess it at once. So he gave the old woman five hundred silver pieces for it, and put it into his pocket immediately. Away she went full of happiness; for the money that the king had given her was enough to keep her for the rest of her life.

As soon as he could leave his business, the king hurried off and showed his wife his prize, with which she was as pleased as he, if not more so; and as soon as they had finished admiring the wonderful necklace, they locked it up in the great chest where the queen's jewelry was kept, the key of which always hung around the king's neck.

A short while afterward a neighboring king sent a message to say that a most lovely baby girl had been born to him; and he invited his neighbors to come to a great feast in honor of the occasion. The queen told her husband that of course they must be present at the banquet, and she would wear the new necklace that he had given her. They had only a short time to prepare for the journey, and at the last moment the king went to the jewel chest to take out the necklace for his wife to wear, but he could see no necklace at all, only in its place a fat little baby boy crowing and shouting. The king was so astonished that he nearly fell backward, but presently he found his voice, and called for his wife so loudly that she came running, thinking that the necklace must at least have been stolen.

"Look here! Look!" cried the king. "Haven't we always longed for a son? And now heaven has sent us one!"

"What do you mean?" cried the queen. "Are you mad?"

"Mad? No, I hope not," shouted the king, dancing in excitement around the open chest. "Come here, and look! Look what we've got instead of that necklace!"

Just then the baby let out a great cry of joy, as though he would like to jump up and dance with the king; and the queen gave a cry of surprise, and ran up and looked into the chest.

"Oh!" she gasped as she looked at the baby. "What a darling! Where could he have come from?"

"I'm sure I can't say," said the king. "All I know is that we locked up a necklace in the chest, and when I unlocked it just now there was no necklace, but a baby, and as fine a baby as ever was seen."

By this time the queen had the baby in her arms. "Oh, the blessed one!" she cried. "Fairer ornament for the bosom of a queen than any necklace that ever was made. Write," she continued, "write to our neighbor and say that we cannot come to his feast, for we have a feast of our own, and a baby of our own! Oh, happy day!"

So the visit was given up; and in honor of the new baby the bells of the city, and its guns, and its trumpets, and its people, small and great, had hardly any rest for a week; there was such a ringing, and banging, and blaring, and such fireworks, and feasting, and rejoicing, and merrymaking, as had never been seen before.

A few years went by; and as the king's baby boy and his neighbor's baby girl grew and throve, the two kings arranged that as soon as they were old enough, they should marry; and so with much signing of papers and agreements, and wagging of wise heads, and stroking of gray beards, the pact was made, and signed, and sealed, and lay waiting for its fulfillment. And this too came to pass, for as soon as the prince and princess were eighteen years of age, the kings agreed that it was time for the wedding; and the young prince journeyed away to the neighboring kingdom for his bride, and was there married to her with great and renewed rejoicings.

Now, I must tell you that the old woman who had sold the king the necklace had been called in by him to be the nurse of the young prince; and although she loved her charge dearly and was a most faithful servant, she could not help talking just a little, and so by and by it began to be rumored that there was some magic about the young prince's birth; and the rumor of course had come in due time to the ears of the parents of the princess. So now that she was going to marry the prince, her mother (who was curious, as many other people are) said to her daughter on the eve of the ceremony:

"Remember that the first thing you must do is to find out what this story is about the prince. And in order to do it, you must not speak a word to him whatever he says until he asks you why you are silent. Then you must ask him what the truth is about his magic birth; and until he tells you, you must not speak to him again."

And the princess promised that she would follow her mother's advice.

Therefore when they were married and the prince spoke to his bride, she did not answer him. He could not think what was the matter, but she would not utter a word even about her old home. At last he asked why she would not speak, and she said:

"Tell me the secret of your birth."

Then the prince was very sad and displeased, and although she pressed him sorely, he would not tell her, but would always reply:

"If I tell you, you will repent that you ever asked me."

For several months they lived together, and it was not such a happy time for either as it ought to have been, for the secret was still a secret, and lay between them like a cloud between the sun and the earth, making what should be fair, dull and sad.

At length the prince could bear it no longer, so he said to his wife one day, "At midnight I will tell you my secret if you still wish it, but you will repent it all your life." However, the princess was overjoyed that she had succeeded, and paid no attention to his warnings.

That night the prince ordered horses to be ready for the princess and himself a little before midnight. He placed her on one, and mounted the other himself, and they rode together down to the river to the place where the old woman had first found the snake in her brass pot. There the prince drew rein and said sadly, "Do you still insist that I should tell you my secret?" And the princess answered, "Yes." "If I do," answered the prince, "remember that you will regret it all your life." But the princess only replied, "Tell me!"

"Then," said the prince, "know that I am the son of the king of a far country, but by enchantment I was turned into a snake."

The word "snake" was hardly out of his lips when he disappeared, and the princess heard a rustle and saw a ripple on the water, and in the faint moonlight she beheld a snake swimming into the river. Soon it disappeared and she was left alone. In vain she waited with beating heart for something to happen, and for the prince to come back to her. Nothing happened and no one came; only the wind mourned through the trees on the riverbank, and the night birds cried, and a jackal howled in the distance, and the river flowed black and silent beneath her.

In the morning they found her, weeping and disheveled, on the riverbank; but no word could they learn from her or from anyone as to the fate of her husband. At her wish they built on the riverbank a little house of black stone; and there she lived in mourning, with a few servants and guards to watch over her.

A long, long time passed by, and still the princess lived in mourning for her prince, and saw no one, and went nowhere away from her house on the riverbank and the garden that surrounded it. One morning, when she woke up, she found a stain of fresh mud upon the carpet. She sent for the guards, who watched outside the house day and night, and asked them who had entered her room while she was asleep. They declared that no one *could* have entered, for they kept such careful watch that not even a bird could fly in without their knowledge; but none of them could explain the stain of mud. The next morning the princess found another stain of wet mud, and she questioned everyone most carefully; but none could say how the mud came there. The third night the princess determined to lie awake herself and watch; and for fear that she might fall asleep, she cut her finger with a dagger and rubbed salt into the cut, that the pain of it might keep her from sleeping. So she lay awake, and at midnight she saw a snake come wriggling along the ground with some mud from the river in its mouth; and when it came near the bed, it reared up its head and dropped its muddy head on the bedclothes. She was very frightened, but tried to control her fear, and called out:

The Snake Prince visits his wife

"Who are you, and what are you doing here?"

And the snake answered:

"I am the prince, your husband, and I am come to visit you."

Then the princess began to weep, and the snake continued:

"Alas! Did I not say that if I told you my secret you would repent it? And have you not repented?"

"Oh, indeed!" cried the poor princess. "I have repented it, and shall repent it all my life! Is there nothing I can do?"

And the snake answered:

"Yes, there is one thing, if you dare to do it."

"Only tell me," said the princess, "and I will do *anything*!"

"Then," replied the snake, "on a certain night you must put a large bowl of milk and sugar in each of the four corners of this room. All the snakes in the river will come out to drink the milk, and the one that leads the way will be the queen of the snakes. You must stand in her way at the door and say, 'Oh, Queen of Snakes, Queen of Snakes, give me back my husband!' and perhaps she will do it. But if you are frightened, and do not stop her, you will never see me again." And he glided away.

On the night of which the snake had told her, the princess got four large bowls of milk and sugar, and put one in each corner of the room, and stood in the doorway waiting. At midnight there was a great hissing and rustling from the direction of the river, and presently the ground appeared to be alive with horrible writhing forms of snakes whose eyes glittered and forked tongues quivered as they moved on in the direction of the princess's house. Foremost among them was a huge, repulsive scaly creature that led the dreadful procession. The guards were so terrified that they all ran away; but the princess stood in the doorway, as white as death, and with her hands clasped tight together for fear she should scream or faint, and fail to do her part. As they came closer and saw her in the way, all the snakes raised their horrid heads and swayed them to-and-fro, and looked at her with wicked beady eyes, while their breath seemed to poison the very air. Still the princess stood firm, and when the leading snake was within a few feet of her, she cried, "Oh, Queen of Snakes, Queen of Snakes, give me back my husband!" Then all the rustling, writhing crowd of snakes seemed to whisper to one another, "Her husband? Her husband?" But the queen of snakes moved on until her head was almost in the princess's face, and her little eyes seemed to flash fire. And still the princess stood in the doorway and never moved, but cried again, "Oh, Queen of Snakes, Queen of Snakes, give me back my husband!" Then the queen of snakes replied, "Tomorrow you shall have him — tomorrow!" When she heard these words and knew that she had conquered, the princess staggered from the door, and sank upon her bed and fainted. As in a dream she saw that her room was full of snakes, all jostling and squabbling over the bowls of milk until it was finished. And then they went away.

In the morning the princess was up early, and took off the mourning dress that she had worn for five whole years, and put on gay and beautiful clothes. And she swept the house and cleaned it, and adorned it with garlands and nosegays of sweet flowers and ferns, and prepared it as though she were making ready for her wedding. And when night fell, she lit up the woods and gardens with lanterns, and spread a table as for a feast, and lit in the house a thousand wax candles. Then she waited for her husband, not knowing in what shape he would appear. And at midnight there came striding from the river the prince, laughing, but with tears in his eyes; and she ran to meet him, and threw herself into his arms, crying and laughing too.

QUEEN OF SNAKES GIVE ME BACK MY HUSBAND

So the prince came home; and the next day they two went back to the palace, and the old king wept with joy to see them. And the bells, so long silent, were set ringing again, and the guns firing, and the trumpets blaring, and there was fresh feasting and rejoicing.

And the old woman who had been the prince's nurse became nurse to the prince's children — at least she was called so; though she was far too old to do anything for them but love them. Yet she still thought that she was useful, and knew that she was happy. And happy, indeed, were the prince and princess, who in due time became king and queen, and lived and ruled long and prosperously.

The Story of the Seven Simons

HUNGARY

Far, far away, beyond all sorts of countries, seas, and rivers, there stood a splendid city where lived King Archidej, who was as good as he was rich and handsome. His great army was made up of men ready to obey his slightest wish; he owned forty times forty cities, and in each city he had ten palaces with silver doors, golden roofs, and crystal windows. His council consisted of the twelve wisest men in the country, whose long beards flowed down over their breasts, each of whom was as learned as a whole college. This council always told the king the exact truth.

Now the king had everything to make him happy, but he did not enjoy anything because he could not find a bride to his mind.

One day as he sat in his palace looking out to sea, a great ship sailed into the harbor and several merchants came onshore. Said the king to himself, "These people have traveled far and beheld many lands. I will ask them if they have seen any princess who is as clever and as handsome as I am."

So he ordered the merchants to be brought before him, and when they came he said, "You have traveled much and visited many wonders. I wish to ask you a question, and I beg you to answer truthfully."

"Have you anywhere seen or heard of the daughter of an emperor, king, or a prince, who is as clever and as handsome as I am, and who would be worthy to be my wife and the queen of my country?"

The merchants considered for some time. At last the eldest of them said, "I have heard that across many seas, on the Island of Busan, there is a mighty king, whose daughter, the Princess Helena, is so lovely that she can certainly not be plainer than Your Majesty, and so clever that the wisest graybeard cannot guess her riddles."

"Is the island far off, and which is the way to it?"

"It is not near," was the answer. "The journey would take ten years, and we do not know the way. And even if we did, what use would that be? The princess is no bride for you."

"How dare you say so?" cried the king angrily.

"Your Majesty must pardon us; but just think for a moment. Should you send an envoy to the island, he will take ten years to get there and ten more to return — twenty years in all. Will not the princess have grown old in that time and have lost all her beauty?"

The king reflected gravely. Then he thanked the merchants, gave them leave to trade in his country without paying any duties, and dismissed them.

After they were gone, the king remained deep in thought. He felt puzzled and anxious; so he decided to ride into the country to distract his mind, and sent for his huntsmen and falconers. The huntsmen blew their horns, the falconers took their hawks on their wrists, and off they all set out across country till they came to a green hedge. On the other side of the hedge stretched a great field of maize as far as the eye could reach, and the yellow ears swayed to-and-fro in the gentle breeze like a rippling sea of gold.

The king drew rein and admired the field. "Upon my word," he said, "whoever dug and planted it must be good workmen. If all the fields in my kingdom were as well cared for as this, there would be more bread than my people could eat." And he wished to know to whom the field belonged.

Off rushed all his followers at once to do his bidding, and found a nice, tidy farmhouse, in front of which sat seven peasants, lunching on rye bread and drinking water. They wore red shirts bound with gold braid, and were so much alike that one could hardly be told from another.

The messengers asked, "Who owns this field of golden maize?" And the seven brothers answered, "The field is ours."

"And who are you?"

"We are King Archidej's laborers."

These answers were repeated to the king, who ordered the brothers to be brought before him at once. On being asked who they were, the eldest said, bowing low:

"We, King Archidej, are your laborers, children of one father and mother, and we all have the same name, for each of us is called Simon. Our father taught us to be true to our king, and to till the ground, and to be kind to our neighbors. He also taught each of us a different trade that he thought might be useful to us, and he bade us not neglect our mother earth, which would be sure to amply repay our labor."

The king was pleased with the honest peasant, and said, "You have done well, good people, in planting your field, and now you have a golden harvest. But I should like each of you to tell me what special trades your father taught you."

"My trade, O King!" said the first Simon, "is not an easy one. If you will give me some workmen and materials, I will build you a great white pillar that shall reach far above the clouds."

"Very good," replied the king. "And you, Simon the second, what is your trade?"

"Mine, Your Majesty, needs no great cleverness. When my brother has built the pillar, I can mount it and from the top, far above the clouds, I can see what is happening in every country under the sun."

"Good," said the king; "and Simon the third?"

"My work is very simple, Sire. You have many ships built by learned men, with all sorts of new and clever improvements. If you wish it I will build you quite a simple boat — one, two, three, and it's done! But my plain little homemade ship is not grand enough for a king. Where other ships take a year, mine makes the voyage in a day, and where they would require ten years, mine will do the distance in a week."

"Good," said the king again; "and what has Simon the fourth learned?"

"My trade, O King, is really of no importance. Should my brother build you a ship, then let me embark in it. If we should be pursued by an enemy, I can seize our boat by the prow and sink it to the bottom of the sea. When the enemy has sailed off, I can draw it up to the top again."

"That is very clever of you," answered the king; "and what does Simon the fifth do?"

"My work, Your Majesty, is mere blacksmith's work. Allow me to build a workshop and I will make you a crossbow, but from which neither the eagle in the sky nor the wild beast in the forest is safe. The arrow hits whatever the eye sees."

"That sounds very useful," said the king. "And now, Simon the sixth, tell me your trade."

"Sire, it is so simple I am almost ashamed to mention it. If my brother hits any creature, I catch it quicker than any dog can. If it falls into the water, I pick it up out of the greatest depths; and if it is in a dark forest, I can find it even at midnight."

The king was much pleased with the trades and talk of the six brothers, and said, "Thank you, good people; your father did well to teach you all these things. Now follow me to the town, as I want to see what you can do. I need such people as you about me; but when harvest time comes, I will send you home with royal presents."

The brothers bowed and said, "As the king wills." Suddenly the king remembered that he had not questioned the seventh Simon, so he turned to him and said, "Why are you silent? What is your handicraft?"

And the seventh Simon answered, "I have no handicraft, O King; I have learned nothing. I could not manage it. And if I *do* know how to do anything, it is not what might properly be called a real trade — it is rather a sort of performance; but it is one which no one — not the king himself — must watch me doing, and I doubt whether this performance of mine would please Your Majesty."

"Come, come," cried the king; "I will have no excuses. What is this trade?"

"First, Sire, give me your royal word that you will not kill me when I have told you. Then you shall hear."

"So be it then; I give you my royal word."

Then the seventh Simon stepped back a little, cleared his throat, and said, "My trade, King Archidej, is of such a kind that the man who follows it in your kingdom generally loses his life and has no hopes of pardon. There is only one thing I can do really well, and that is — to steal, and to hide the smallest scrap of anything I have stolen. Not the deepest vault, even if its lock were enchanted, could prevent my stealing anything out of it that I wished to have."

When the king heard this, he fell into a passion. "I will *not* pardon you, you rascal," he cried; "I will shut you up in my deepest dungeon on bread and water till you have forgotten such a trade. Indeed, it would be better to put you to death at once, and I've a good mind to do so."

"Don't kill me, O King! I am really not as bad as you think. Why, had I chosen, I could have robbed the royal treasury, bribed your judges to let me off, and built a white marble palace with what was left. But though I know how to steal, I don't do it. You yourself asked me my trade. If you kill me, you will break your royal word."

"Very well," said the king, "I will not kill you. I pardon you. But from this hour you shall be shut up in a dark dungeon. Here, guards! away with him to the prison. But you six Simons follow me and be assured of my royal favor."

So the six Simons followed the king. The seventh Simon was seized by the guards, who put him in chains and threw him in prison with only bread and water for food. The next day the king gave the first Simon carpenters, masons, smiths, and laborers, with great stores of iron, mortar, and the like, and Simon began to build. And he built his great white pillar far, far up into the clouds, as high as the nearest stars; but the other stars were higher still.

Then the second Simon climbed up the pillar and saw and heard all that was going on through the whole world. When he came down he had all sorts of wonderful things to tell. How one king was marching in battle against another, and which was likely to be the victor. How, in another place, great rejoicings were going on; while in a third, people were dying of famine. In fact there was not the smallest event going on over the earth that was hidden from him.

Next the third Simon began. He stretched out his arms, once, twice, thrice, and the wonder-ship was ready. At a sign from the king it was launched, and floated proudly and safely like a bird on the waves. Instead of ropes it had wires for rigging, and musicians played on them with fiddle bows and made lovely music. As the ship swam around, the fourth Simon seized the prow with his strong hand, and in a moment it was gone — sunk to the bottom of the sea. An hour passed, and then the ship floated again, drawn up by Simon's left hand, while in his right he brought a gigantic fish from the depth of the ocean for the royal table.

While this was going on, the fifth Simon had built his forge and hammered out his iron, and when the king returned from the harbor, the magic crossbow was made.

His Majesty went out into an open field at once, looked up into the sky and saw, far, far away, an eagle flying up toward the sun and looking like a little speck.

"Now," said the king, "if you can shoot that bird, I will reward you."

Simon only smiled; he lifted his crossbow, took aim, fired, and the eagle fell. As it was falling, the sixth Simon ran with a dish, caught the bird before it fell to earth and brought it to the king.

"Many thanks, my brave lads," said the king; "I see that each of you is indeed a master of his trade. You shall be richly rewarded. But now rest and have your dinner."

The six Simons bowed and went to dinner. But they had hardly begun before a messenger came to say that the king wanted to see them. They obeyed at once and found him surrounded by all his court and men of state.

"Listen, my good fellows," cried the king as soon as he saw them. "Hear what my wise counselors have thought of. As you, Simon the second, can see the whole world from the top of the great pillar, I want you to climb up to see and hear. For I am told that, far away, across many seas, is the great kingdom of the Island of Busan, and that the daughter of the king is the beautiful Princess Helena."

Off ran the second Simon and clambered quickly up the pillar. He gazed around, listened on all sides, then slid down to report to the king.

THE SIXTH SIMON CATCHES THE EAGLE

"Sire, I have obeyed your orders. Far away I saw the Island of Busan. The king is a mighty monarch, but full of pride, harsh, and cruel. He sits on his throne and declares that no prince or king on earth is good enough for his lovely daughter, that he will give her to none, and that if any king asks for her hand, he will declare war against him and destroy his kingdom."

"Has the king of Busan a great army?" asked King Archidej. "Is his country far off?"

"As far as I could judge," replied Simon, "it would take you nearly ten years in fair weather to sail there. But if the weather were stormy, we might say twelve. I saw the army being reviewed. It is not *so* very large — a hundred thousand men at arms and a hundred thousand knights. Besides these, he has a strong bodyguard and a good many crossbowmen. Altogether you may say another hundred thousand, and there is a picked body of heroes who reserve themselves for great occasions requiring particular courage."

The king sat for some time lost in thought. At last he said to the nobles and courtiers standing around, "I am determined to marry the Princess Helena, but how shall I do it?"

The nobles, courtiers, and counselors said nothing, but tried to hide behind each other. Then the third Simon said:

"Pardon me, Your Majesty, if I offer my advice. You wish to go to the Island of Busan? What can be easier? In my ship you will get there in a week instead of ten years. But ask your council to advise you what to do when you arrive — in one word, whether you will win the princess peacefully or by war?"

But the wise men were as silent as ever.

The king frowned, and was about to say something sharp, when the Court Fool pushed his way to the front and said:

"Dear me, what are all you clever people so puzzled about? The matter is quite clear. As it seems it will not take long to reach the island, why not send the seventh Simon? He will steal the fair maiden fast enough, and then the king, her father, may consider how he is going to bring his army over here — it will take him ten years to do it! — no less! What do you think of my plan?"

"What do I think? Why, that your idea is capital, and you shall be rewarded for it. Come, guards, hurry as fast as you can and bring the seventh Simon before me."

Not many minutes later, Simon the seventh stood before the king, who explained to him what he wished done, and also that to steal for the benefit of his king and country was by no means a wrong thing, though it was very wrong to steal for his own advantage.

The youngest Simon, who looked very pale and hungry, only nodded his head.

"Come," said the king, "tell me truly. Do you think you could steal the Princess Helena?"

"Why should I not steal her, Sire? The thing is easy enough. Let my brother's ship be laden with rich stuffs, brocades, Persian carpets, pearls, and jewels. Send me in the ship. Give me my four middle brothers as companions, and keep the two others as hostages."

When the king heard these words, his heart became filled with longing, and he ordered all to be done as Simon wished. Everyone ran about to do his bidding; and in next to no time the wonder-ship was laden and ready to start.

The five Simons took leave of the king, went on board, and had no sooner set sail than they were almost out of sight. The ship cut through the waters like a falcon through the air, and just a week after starting, sighted the Island of Busan. The coast appeared to be strongly guarded, and from afar the watchman on a high tower called out, "Halt and anchor! Who are you? Where do you come from, and what do you want?"

The seventh Simon answered from the ship, "We are peaceful people. We come from the country of the great and good King Archidej, and we bring foreign wares — rich brocades, carpets, and costly jewels, which we wish to show to your king and the princess. We desire to trade — to sell, to buy, and to exchange."

The brothers launched a small boat, took some of their valuable goods with them, rowed to shore, and went up to the palace. The princess sat in a rose-red room, and when she saw the brothers coming near, she called her nurse and other women, and told them to inquire who these people were, and what they wanted.

The seventh Simon answered the nurse, "We come from the country of the wise and good King Archidej," he said, "and we have brought all sorts of goods for sale. We trust the king of this country may condescend to welcome us, and to let his servants take charge of our wares. If he considers them worthy to adorn his followers, we shall be content."

THE SHIP ARRIVES

This speech was repeated to the princess, who ordered the brothers to be brought to the red-room at once. They bowed respectfully to her and displayed some splendid velvets and brocades, and opened cases of pearls and precious stones. Such beautiful things had never been seen on the island, and the nurse and waiting women stood bewildered by all the magnificence. They whispered together that they had never beheld anything like it. The princess too saw and wondered, and her eyes could not weary of looking at the lovely things, or her fingers of stroking the rich soft stuffs, and of holding up the sparkling jewels to the light.

"Fairest of princesses," said Simon. "Be pleased to order your waiting-maids to accept the silks and velvets, and let your women trim their headdresses with the jewels; these are no special treasures. But permit me to say that they are as nothing, to the many colored tapestries, the gorgeous stones, and ropes of pearls in our ship. We did not like to bring more with us, not knowing what your royal taste might be; but if it seems good to you to honor our ship with a visit, you might condescend to choose such things as were pleasing in your eyes."

This polite speech pleased the princess very much. She went to the king and said, "Dear father, some merchants have arrived with the most splendid wares. Pray allow me to go to their ship and choose out what I like."

The king thought and thought, frowned hard and rubbed his ear. At last he gave consent, and ordered out his royal yacht, with one hundred crossbows, one hundred knights, and one thousand soldiers, to escort the Princess Helena.

Off sailed the yacht with the princess and her escort. The brothers Simon came on board to conduct the princess to their ship, and, led by the brothers and followed by her nurse and other women, she crossed the crystal plank from one vessel to another.

The seventh Simon spread out his goods, and had so many curious and interesting tales to tell about them, that the princess forgot everything else in looking and listening, so that she did not know that the fourth Simon had seized the prow of the ship, and that all of a sudden it had vanished from sight, and was racing along in the depths of the sea.

The crew of the royal yacht shouted aloud, the knights stood still with terror, the soldiers were struck dumb and hung their heads. There was nothing to be done but to sail back and tell the king of his loss.

How he wept and stormed! "Oh, light of my eyes," he sobbed, "I am indeed punished for my pride. I thought no one was good enough to be your husband, and now you are lost in the depths of the sea, and have left me alone! As for all of you who saw this thing — away with you! Let them be put in irons and lock them up in prison, while I think how I can best put them to death!"

While the King of Busan was raging and lamenting in this fashion, Simon's ship was swimming like any fish under the sea, and when the island was well out of sight he brought it up to the surface again. At that moment the princess recollected herself. "Nurse," she said, "we have been gazing at these wonders only too long. I hope my father won't be vexed at our delay."

She tore herself away and stepped on deck. Neither the yacht nor the island was in sight! Helena wrung her hands and beat her breast. Then she changed herself into a white swan and flew off. But the fifth Simon seized his bow and shot the swan, and the sixth Simon did not let it fall into the water, but caught it in the ship, and the swan turned into a silver fish, but Simon lost no time and caught the fish, when, quick as thought, the fish turned into a black mouse and ran about the ship. It darted toward a hole, but before it could reach it, Simon sprang upon it more swiftly than any cat, and then the little mouse turned once more into the beautiful Princess Helena.

Early one morning King Archidej sat thoughtfully at his window gazing out to sea. His heart was sad and he would neither eat nor drink. His thoughts were full of the Princess Helena, who was as lovely as a dream. Is that a white gull he sees flying toward the shore, or is it a sail? No, it is no gull, it is the wonder-ship flying along with billowing sails. Its flags wave, the fiddlers play on the wire rigging, the anchor is thrown out, and the crystal plank laid from the ship to the pier. The

The lovely Helena comes ashore

lovely Helena steps across the plank. She shines like the sun, and the stars of heaven seem to sparkle in her eyes.

Up sprang King Archidej in haste. "Hurry, hurry," he cried. "Let us hasten to meet her! Let the bugles sound and the joy bells be rung!"

And the whole court swarmed with courtiers and servants. Golden carpets were laid down and the great gates thrown open to welcome the princess.

King Archidej went out himself, took her by the hand, and led her into the royal apartments.

"Madam," he said, "the fame of your beauty had reached me, but I had not dared to expect such loveliness. Still I will not keep you here against your will. If you wish it, the wonder-ship shall take you back to your father and your own country; but if you will consent to stay here, then reign over me and my country as our queen."

What more is there to tell? It is not hard to guess that the princess listened to the king's wooing, and their betrothal took place with great pomp and rejoicings.

The brothers Simon were sent again to the Island of Busan with a letter to the king from his daughter to invite him to the wedding. And the wonder-ship arrived at the Island of Busan just as all the knights and soldiers who had escorted the princess were being led out to execution.

Then the seventh Simon cried out from the ship, "Stop! Stop! I bring a letter from the Princess Helena!"

The King of Busan read the letter over and over again, and ordered the knights and soldiers to be set free. He entertained King Archidej's ambassadors hospitably, and sent his blessing to his daughter, but he could not be brought to attend the wedding.

When the wonder-ship got home, King Archidej and Princess Helena were enchanted with the news it brought.

The king sent for the seven Simons. "A thousand thanks to you, my brave fellows," he cried. "Take what gold, silver, and precious stones you will out of my treasury. Tell me if there is anything else you wish for and I will give it to you, my good friends. Do you wish to be made nobles, or to govern towns? Only speak."

Then the eldest Simon bowed and said:

"We are plain folk, Your Majesty, and understand simple things best. What figures should we cut as nobles or governors? Nor do we desire gold. We have our fields that give us food, and as much money as we need. If you wish to reward us, then grant that our land may be free of taxes, and of your goodness pardon the seventh Simon. He is not the first who has been a thief by trade and he will certainly not be the last."

"So be it," said the king. "Your land shall be free of all taxes, and Simon the seventh is pardoned."

Then the king gave each brother a goblet of wine and invited them to the wedding feast. And *what* a feast that was!

Peter Bull

DENMARK

There once lived in Denmark a peasant and his wife who owned a very good farm, but had no children. They often lamented to each other that they had no one of their own to inherit all the wealth that they possessed. They continued to prosper, and became rich people, but there was no heir to it all.

One year it happened that they owned a pretty little bull-calf, which they called Peter. It was the prettiest little creature they had ever seen — and so wise that it seemed to understand everything that was said to it, and so gentle and so full of play that both the man and his wife came to be as fond of it as if it had been their own child.

One day the man said to his wife, "I wonder, now, whether our parish clerk could teach Peter to talk; in that case we could not do better than adopt him as our son, and let him inherit all that we possess."

"Well, I don't know," said his wife, "our clerk is tremendously learned, and knows much more than his Paternoster, and I could almost believe that he might be able to teach Peter to talk, for Peter has a wonderfully good head too. You might at least ask him about it."

Off went the man to the clerk, and asked him whether he thought he could teach a bull-calf that they had to speak, for they wished so much to have it as their heir.

The clerk was no fool; he looked around to see that no one could overhear them, and said, "Oh, yes, I can easily do that, but you must not speak to anyone about it. It must be done in all secrecy, and the priest must not know of it, otherwise I shall get into trouble, as it is forbidden. It will also cost you something, as some very expensive books are required."

That did not matter at all, the man said; they would not care so very much what it cost. The clerk could have a hundred coins to begin with to buy the books. He also promised to tell no one about it, and to bring the calf around in the evening.

He gave the clerk the hundred coins on the spot, and in the evening took the calf around to him, and the clerk promised to do his best with it. In a week's time he came back to the clerk to hear about the calf and see how it was thriving. The clerk, however, said that he could not get a sight of it, for then Peter would long after him and forget all that he had already learned. He was getting on well with his learning, but another hundred coins were needed, as they must have more books. The peasant had the money with him, so he gave it to the clerk, and went home again with high hopes.

In another week the man came again to learn what progress Peter had made now.

"He is getting on very well," said the clerk.

"I suppose he can't say anything yet?" said the man.

"Oh, yes," said the clerk, "he can say 'Moo' now."

"Do you think he will get on with his learning?" asked the peasant.

"Oh, yes," said the clerk, "but I shall want another hundred coins for books. Peter can't learn well out of the ones that he has now."

"Well, well," said the man, "what must be spent *shall* be spent."

So he gave the clerk the third hundred coins for books, and a cask of good old ale for Peter. The clerk drank the ale himself, and gave the calf milk, which he thought would be better for it.

Some weeks passed, during which the peasant did not come around to ask after the calf, fearing that it might cost him another hundred coins, for he had begun to squirm a little at having to part with so much money. Meanwhile the clerk decided that the calf was as fat as it could be, so he killed it. After he had got all the beef out of the way he went inside, put on his black clothes, and made his way to the peasant's house.

As soon as he had said "Good day," he asked, "Has Peter come home?"

"No, indeed, he hasn't," said the man; "surely he hasn't run away?"

"I hope," said the clerk, "that he would not behave so contemptibly after all the trouble I have had to teach him, and all that I have spent upon him. I have had to spend at least a hundred coins of my own money to buy books to bring him so far along. He could say anything he liked now, so he said today that he longed to see his parents again. I was willing to give him that pleasure, but I was afraid that he wouldn't be able to find the way here by himself, so I made myself ready to go with him. But when we got outside the house, I remembered that I had left my stick inside and went in again to get it. When I came out again, Peter had gone off on his own. I thought he would be here, and if he isn't, I don't know where he is."

The peasant and his wife began to lament bitterly that Peter had run away in this fashion just when they were to gain so much happiness from him, and after they had spent so much on his education. The worst of it was that now they had no heir after all. The clerk comforted them as best he could; he also was greatly distressed that Peter should have behaved in such a way just when he should have gained fame from his pupil. Perhaps he had only gone astray, and he would inquire at church next Sunday, and find out if anyone had seen him. Then he bade them good-bye, and went home and dined on a good fat veal roast.

Now it so happened that the clerk took in a newspaper, and one day he chanced to read in its columns of a new merchant who had settled in a town at some distance, and whose name was "Peter Bull." He put the newspaper in his pocket, and went around to the sorrowing couple who had lost their heir. He read the paragraph to them, and added, "I wonder, now, whether that could be your bull-calf Peter?"

"Yes, of course it is," said the man; "who else would it be?"

His wife then spoke up and said, "You must set out, good husband, and see about him, for it *is* him, I am perfectly certain. Take a good sum of money with you too; for who knows but what he may want some cash now that he has become a merchant!"

The next day the man put a bag of money on his back and a sandwich in his pocket, and his pipe in his mouth, and set out for the town where the new merchant lived. It was no short way, and he traveled for many days before he finally arrived there. He reached it one morning, just at daybreak, found out the right place, and asked if the merchant was at home. Yes, he was, said the people, but he was not up yet.

"That doesn't matter," said the peasant, "for I am his father. Just show me up to his bedroom."

He was shown up to the room, and as soon as he entered it, and caught sight of the merchant, he recognized him at once. He had the same broad forehead, the same thick neck, the same red hair, but in other respects he was now like a human being. The peasant rushed straight up to him and took a firm hold of him. "O Peter," he said, "what a sorrow you have caused us, both myself and your mother, by running off like this just as we had got you so well educated! Get up, now, so that I can see you properly, and have a talk with you."

The merchant thought that it was a lunatic who had made his way in to him, and thought it best to take things quietly.

"All right," he said, "I shall do so at once." He got out of bed and made haste to dress himself.

"Ay," said the peasant, "now I can see how clever our clerk is. He has done well by you, for now you look just like a human being. If one didn't know it, one would never think that it was you we got from the red cow; will you come home with me now?"

"No," said the merchant, "I can't find time just now. I have a big business to look after."

"You could have the farm at once, you know," said the peasant, "and we old people would retire. But if you would rather stay in business, of course you may do so. Are you in want of anything?"

"Oh, yes," said the merchant; "I want nothing so much as money. A merchant always has a use for that."

"I can well believe that," said the peasant, "for you had nothing at all to start with. I have brought some with me for that very end." With that he emptied his bag of money out upon the table, so that it was all covered with bright coins.

When the merchant saw what kind of man he had before him, he began to speak kindly to him, and invited him to stay with him for some days, so that they might have some more talk together.

"Very well," said the peasant, "but you must call me 'Father.'"

"I have neither father nor mother alive," said Peter Bull.

"I know that," said the man; "your real father was sold at Hamburg last Michaelmas, and your real mother died while calving in the spring; but my wife and I have adopted you as our own, and you are our only heir, so you must call me 'Father.'"

Peter Bull was quite willing to do so, and it was settled that he should keep the money, while the peasant made his will and left to him all that he had, before he went home to his wife, and told her the whole story.

She was delighted to hear that it was true enough about Peter Bull — that he was no other than their own bull-calf.

"You must go at once and tell the clerk," said she, "and pay him the hundred coins of his own money that he spent upon our son. He has earned them well, and more besides, for all the joy he has given us in having such a son and heir."

The man agreed with this, and thanked the clerk for all he had done, and gave him two hundred coins. Then he sold the farm, and moved with his wife to the town where their dear son and heir was living. To him they gave all their wealth, and lived with him till their dying day.

The King of the Waterfalls

SCOTLAND

When the young king of the waterfalls came into his kingdom, the first thing he thought of was how he could amuse himself best. The sports that all his life had pleased him best suddenly seemed to have grown dull, and he wanted to do something he had never done before. At last his face brightened.

"I know!" he said. "I will go and play a game with the Gruagach." Now the Gruagach was a kind of wicked fairy, with long curly brown hair, and his house was not very far from the king's house.

But though the king was young and eager, he was also prudent, and his father had told him on his deathbed to be very careful in his dealings with the "good people," as the fairies were called. Therefore, before going to the Gruagach the king sought out a wise man of the countryside.

"I am wanting to play a game with the curly-haired Gruagach," he said.

"Are you, indeed?" replied the wizard. "If you will take my counsel, you will play with someone else."

"No. I will play with the Gruagach," persisted the king.

"Well, if you must, you must, I suppose," answered the wizard. "But if you win that game, ask as a prize the ugly crop-headed girl that stands behind the door."

"I will," said the king.

So before the sun rose, he got up and went to the house of the Gruagach, who was sitting outside.

"O King, what has brought you here today?" asked the Gruagach. "But right welcome you are, and more welcome will you be still if you will play a game with me."

"That is just what I want," said the king, and they played; and sometimes it seemed as if one would win, and sometimes the other, but in the end it was the king who was the winner.

"And what is the prize that you will choose?" inquired the Gruagach.

"The ugly crop-headed girl that stands behind the door," replied the king.

"Why, there are twenty others in the house, and each fairer than she!" exclaimed the Gruagach.

"Fairer they may be, but it is she whom I wish for my wife, and none other," and the Gruagach saw that the king's mind was set upon her, so he entered his house, and bade all the maidens in it come out one by one, and pass before the king.

One by one they came — tall and short, dark and fair, plump and thin — and each said, "I am she whom you want. You will be foolish indeed if you do not take me."

But he took none of them — neither short nor tall, dark nor fair, plump nor thin — till at last the crop-headed girl came out.

"This is mine," said the king, though she was so ugly that most men would have turned from her. "We will be married at once, and I will carry you home." And married they were, and they set forth across a meadow to the king's house. As they went, the bride stooped and picked a sprig of shamrock, which grew among the grass, and when she stood upright again her ugliness had all gone, and the most beautiful woman that ever was seen stood by the king's side.

The next day before the sun rose, the king sprang from his bed and told his wife he must have another game with the Gruagach.

"If my father loses that game, and you win it," she said, "accept nothing for your prize but the shaggy young horse with the stick saddle."

"I will do that," answered the king, and he went.

"Does your bride please you?" asked the Gruagach, who was standing at his own door.

"Ah! she does," answered the king quickly. "Otherwise I should be hard indeed to please. But will you play a game today?"

"I will," replied the Gruagach, and they played, and sometimes it seemed as if one would win, and sometimes the other, but in the end the king was the winner.

"What is the prize that you will choose?" asked the Gruagach.

"The shaggy young horse with the stick saddle," answered the king, but he noticed that the Gruagach held his peace, and his brow was dark as he led out the horse from the stable. Rough was its mane and dull was its skin, but the king cared nothing for that, and throwing his leg over the stick saddle, rode away like the wind.

On the third morning the king got up as usual before dawn, and as soon as he had eaten food, he prepared to go out, when his wife stopped him. "I would rather," she said, "that you did not go to play with the Gruagach, for though twice *you* have won, yet someday *he* will win, and then he will put trouble upon you."

"Oh! I *must* have one more game," cried the king. "Just this one." And he went off to the house of the Gruagach.

Joy filled the heart of the Gruagach when he saw him coming, and without waiting to talk they played their game. Somehow or other, the king's strength and skill had departed from him, and soon the Gruagach was the victor.

"Choose your prize," said the king when the game was ended. "But do not be too hard on me, or ask what I cannot give."

"The prize I choose," answered the Gruagach "is that the crop-headed creature should take your head and your neck, if you do not get for me the Sword of Light that hangs in the house of the king of the oak windows."

" I will get it," replied the young man bravely. But as soon as he was out of sight of the Gruagach, he pretended no more, and his face grew dark and his steps lagged.

"You have brought nothing with you tonight," said the queen, who was standing on the steps awaiting him. She was so beautiful that the king smiled when he looked at her, but then he remembered what had happened, and his heart grew heavy again.

"What is it? What is the matter? Tell me your sorrow that I may bear it with you, or, it may be, help you!" Then the king told her everything that had befallen him, and she stroked his hair all the while.

"That is nothing to grieve about," she said when the tale was finished. "You have the best wife in Erin, and the best horse in Erin. Only do as I bid you, and all will go well." And the king allowed himself to be comforted.

He was still sleeping when the queen rose and dressed herself to make everything ready for her husband's journey; and the first place she went to was the stable, where she fed and watered the shaggy brown horse and put the saddle on it. Most people thought the saddle was of wood, and did not see the little sparkles of gold and silver that were hidden in it. She strapped it lightly on the horse's back, and then led the horse down before the house, where the king waited.

"Good luck to you, and victories in all your battles," she said as she kissed him before he mounted. "I need not be telling you anything. Take the advice of the horse, and see you obey it."

So he waved his hand and set out on his journey, and the wind was not swifter than the brown horse — no, not even the March wind that raced it could catch it. But the horse never stopped nor looked behind, till in the dark of the night he reached the castle of the king of the oak windows.

"We are at the end of the journey," said the horse, "and you will find the Sword of Light in the king's own chamber. If it comes to you without scrape or sound, the token is a good one. At this hour the king is eating his supper, and the room is empty, so none will see you. The sword has a knob at the end, and take heed that when you grasp it, you draw it softly out of its sheath. Now go! I will be under the window."

Stealthily the young man crept along the passage pausing now and then to make sure that no man was following him, and entered the king's chamber. A strange white line of light told him where the sword was, and crossing the room on tiptoe, he seized the knob, and drew it

slowly out of the sheath. The king could hardly breathe with excitement lest it should make some noise and bring all the people in the castle running to see what was the matter. But the sword slid swiftly and silently along the case till only the point was left touching it. Then a low sound was heard, as of the edge of a knife touching a silver plate, and the king was so startled that he nearly dropped the knob.

"Quick! Quick!" cried the horse, and the king scrambled hastily through the small window, and leapt into the saddle.

"He has heard and he will follow," said the horse, "but we have a good start." And on they sped, on and on, leaving the winds behind them.

At length the horse slackened its pace. "Look and see who is behind you," it said; and the young man looked.

"I see a swarm of brown horses racing madly after us," he answered.

"We are swifter than those," said the horse, and flew on again.

"Look again, O King! Is anyone coming now?"

"A swarm of black horses, and one has a white face, and on that horse a man is seated. He must be the king of the oak windows."

"That horse is my brother, and swifter still than I," said the horse, "and he will fly past me with a rush. Then you must have your sword ready, and take off the head of the man who sits on him, as he turns and looks at you. And there is no sword in the world that will cut off his head, save only that one."

"I will do it," replied the king; and he listened with all his might, till he judged that the white-faced horse was close to him. Then he sat up very straight and made ready.

The next moment there was a rushing noise as of a mighty tempest, and the young man caught a glimpse of a face turned toward him. Almost blindly he struck, not knowing whether he had killed or only wounded the rider. But the head rolled off, and was caught in the brown horse's mouth.

"Jump on my brother, the black horse, and go home as fast as you can, and I will follow as quickly as I may," cried the brown horse; and leaping forward the king alighted on the back of the black horse, but so near the tail that he almost fell off again. But he stretched out his arm and clutched wildly at the mane and pulled himself into the saddle.

Before the sky was streaked with red he was at home again, and the queen was sitting waiting till he arrived, for sleep was far from her eyes. Glad was she to see him enter, but she said little, only took her harp and sang softly the songs that he loved, till he went to bed, soothed and happy.

It was broad day when he woke, and he sprang up saying:

"Now I must go to the Gruagach, to find out if the spells he laid on me are loose."

"Have a care," answered the queen, "for it is not with a smile as on the other days that he will greet you. Furiously he will meet you, and will ask you in his wrath if you have got the sword, and you will reply that you have got it. Next he will want to know how you got it, and to this you must say that but for the knob you had not got it at all. Then he will raise his head to look at the knob, and you must stab him in the mole that is on the right side of his neck; but take heed, for if you miss the mole with the point of the sword, then my death and your death are certain. He is brother to the king of the oak windows, and sure will he be that the king must be dead, or the sword would not be in your hands." After that she kissed him, and wished him success.

"Did you get the sword?" asked the Gruagach, when they met in the usual place.

"I got the sword."

"And how did you get it?"

"If it had not had a knob on the top, I could not have got it," answered the king.

"Give me the sword to look at," said the Gruagach, peering forward; but like a flash the king had drawn it from under his nose and pierced the mole, so that the Gruagach rolled over on the ground.

Now I shall be at peace, thought the king. But he was wrong, for when he reached home he found his servants tied together back to back, with cloths bound around their mouths so that they could not speak. He hastened to set them free, and he asked who had treated them in so evil a manner.

"No sooner had you gone than a great giant came, and dealt with us as you see, and carried off your wife and your two horses," said the men.

"Then my eyes will not close nor will my head lay itself down till I fetch my wife and horses home again," he answered, and he stooped and noted the tracks of the horses on the grass, and followed after them till he arrived at the wood, when the darkness fell.

"I will sleep here," he said to himself, "but first I will make a fire." And he gathered some twigs that were lying about, and then took two dry sticks and rubbed them together till the fire came, and he sat by it.

The twigs crackled and the flame blazed up, and a slim yellow dog pushed through the bushes and laid his head on the king's knee, and the king stroked his head.

"Wuf, wuf," said the dog. "Sore was the plight of your wife and your horses when the giant drove them last night through the forest."

"That is why I have come," answered the king; and suddenly his heart seemed to fail him and he felt that he could not go on.

"I cannot fight that giant," he cried, looking at the dog with a white face. "I am afraid, let me turn homeward."

"No, don't do that," replied the dog. "Eat and sleep, and I will watch over you." So the king ate and lay down, and slept till the sun waked him.

"It is time for you to start on your way," said the dog, "and if danger presses, call on me, and I will help you."

"Farewell, then," answered the king; "I will not forget that promise," and on he went, and on, and on, till he reached a tall cliff with many sticks lying about.

It is almost night, he thought; I will make a fire and rest, and thus he did, and when the flames blazed up, the hoary hawk of the gray rock flew onto a bough above him.

"Sore was the plight of your wife and your horses when they passed here with the giant," said the hawk.

"Never shall I find them," answered the king, "and nothing shall I get for all my trouble."

"Oh, take heart," replied the hawk. "Things are never so bad but what they might be worse. Eat and sleep and I will watch you," and the king did as he was bidden by the hawk, and by morning he felt brave again.

"Farewell," said the bird, "and if danger presses, call to me and I will help you."

On and on he walked, and on and on, till as the dusk was falling he came to a great river, and on the bank there were sticks lying about.

I will make myself a fire, he thought, and thus he did, and by and by a smooth brown head peered at him from the water, and a long body followed it.

"Sore was the plight of your wife and your horses when they passed the river last night," said the otter.

"I have sought them and not found them," answered the king, "and nothing shall I get for my trouble."

"Be not so downcast," replied the otter. "Before noon tomorrow you shall behold your wife. But eat and sleep and I will watch over you." So the king did as the otter bid him, and when the sun rose, he woke and saw the otter lying on the bank.

"Farewell," cried the otter as he jumped into the water, "and if danger presses, call to me and I will help you."

For many hours the king walked, and at length he reached a high rock, which was rent in two by a great earthquake. Throwing himself on the ground he looked over the side, and right at the very bottom he saw his wife and his horses. His heart gave a great bound, and all his fears left him, but he was forced to be patient, for the sides of the rock were smooth, and not even a goat could find a foothold. So he got up again, and made his way through the wood, pushing by trees, scrambling over rocks, wading through streams, till at last he was on flat ground again, close to the mouth of the cavern.

His wife gave a shriek of joy when he came in, and then burst into tears, for she was tired and very frightened. But her husband did not understand why she wept, and he was tired and bruised from his climb, and a little cross too.

"You give me but a sorry welcome," he grumbled, "when I have half-killed myself to get to you."

"Do not heed him," said the horses to the weeping woman. "Put him in front of us, where he will be safe, and give him food, for he is weary." And she did as the horses told her, and he ate and rested, till by and by, a long shadow fell over them, and their hearts beat with fear, for they knew that the giant was coming.

"I smell a stranger," cried the giant as he entered; but it was dark inside the chasm, and he did not see the king who was crouching down between the feet of the horses.

"A stranger, my lord! No stranger ever comes here, not even the sun!" and the king's wife laughed gaily as she went up to the giant and stroked the huge hand that hung down by his side.

"Well, I perceive nothing, certainly," he answered, "but it is very odd. However, it is time that the horses were fed;" and he lifted down

THE GIANT'S SHADOW

an armful of hay from a shelf of rock and held out a handful to each animal who moved forward to meet him, leaving the king behind. As soon as the giant's hands were near their mouths they each made a snap and began to bite them, so that his groans and shrieks might have been heard a mile off. Then they wheeled around and kicked him till they could kick no more. At length the giant crawled away, and lay quivering in a corner, and the queen went up to him.

"Poor thing! Poor thing!" she said. "They seem to have gone mad; it was awful to behold."

"If I had had my soul in my body they would certainly have killed me," groaned the giant.

"It was lucky indeed," answered the queen; "but tell me, where is your soul, that I may take care of it?"

"Up there, in the Bonnach stone," answered the giant, pointing to a stone that was balanced loosely on the edge of rock. "But now leave me that I may sleep, for I have far to go tomorrow."

Soon snores were heard from the corner where the giant lay, and then the queen lay down too, and the horses, and the king was hidden between them, so that none could see him.

Before the dawn the giant rose and went out, and immediately the queen ran up to the Bonnach stone, and tugged and pushed at it till it was quite steady on its ledge, and could not fall over. And so it was in the evening when the giant came home; and when they saw his shadow, the king crept down in front of the horses.

"Why, what have you done to the Bonnach stone?" asked the giant.

"I feared it would fall over, and be broken, with your soul in it," said the queen, "so I put it farther back on the ledge."

"It is not there that my soul is," he answered, "it is on the threshold. But it is time the horses were fed;" and he fetched the hay, and gave it to them, and they bit and kicked him as before, till he lay half dead on the ground.

The next morning he rose and went out, and the queen ran to the threshold of the cave, and washed the stones, and pulled up some moss and little flowers that were hidden in the crannies, and by and by when dusk had fallen, the giant came home.

"You have been cleaning the threshold," he said.

"And was I not right to do it, seeing that your soul is in it?" asked the queen.

"It is not there that my soul is," answered the giant. "Under the threshold is a stone, and under the stone is a sheep, and in the sheep's body is a duck, and in the duck is an egg, and in the egg is my soul. But it is late, and I must feed the horses"; and he brought them the hay, but they only bit and kicked him as before, and if his soul had been within him, they would have killed him outright.

It was still dark when the giant got up and went his way, and then the king and queen ran forward to take up the threshold, while the horses looked on. But sure enough, just as the giant had said, underneath the threshold was the flagstone, and they pulled and tugged till the stone gave way. Then something jumped out so suddenly, that it nearly knocked them down, and as it fled past, they saw it was a sheep.

"If the slim yellow dog of the greenwood were only here, he would soon have that sheep," cried the king; and as he spoke, the slim yellow dog appeared from the forest, with the sheep in his mouth. With a blow from the king, the sheep fell dead, and they opened its body, only to be blinded by a rush of wings as the duck flew past.

"If the hoary hawk of the rock were only here, he would soon have that duck," cried the king; and as he spoke the hoary hawk was seen hovering above them, with the duck in his mouth. They cut off the duck's head with a swing of the king's sword, and took the egg out of its body, but in his triumph the king held it carelessly, and it slipped from his hand, and rolled swiftly down the hill right into the river.

"If the brown otter of the stream were only here, he would soon have that egg," cried the king; and the next minute there was the brown otter, dripping with water, holding the egg in his mouth. But beside the brown otter, a huge shadow came stealing along — the shadow of the giant.

The king stood staring at it, as if he were turned into stone, but the queen snatched the egg from the otter and crushed it between her two hands. And after that the shadow suddenly shrank and was still, and they knew that the giant was dead, because they had found his soul.

The next day they mounted the two horses and rode home again, visiting their friends the brown otter and the hoary hawk and the slim yellow dog along the way.

The Knights of the Fish

SPAIN

Once upon a time there lived an old cobbler who worked hard at his trade from morning till night, and scarcely gave himself a moment to eat. But industrious as he was, he could hardly buy bread and cheese for himself and his family, and they grew thinner and thinner daily.

For a long while they pretended to each other that they had no appetite, and that a few blackberries from the hedges were a great deal nicer than a good strong bowl of soup. But at length there came a day when the cobbler could bear it no longer, and he threw away his last berries, and borrowing a rod from a neighbor, he went out to fish.

Now the cobbler was as patient about fishing as he had been about cobbling. From dawn to dark he stood on the banks of the little stream without hooking anything better than an eel, or a few old shoes that even he, clever though he was, felt were not worth mending. At length his patience began to give way, and as he undressed one night he said to himself, "Well, I will give it one more chance; and if I don't catch a fish tomorrow, I will go and hang myself."

He had not cast his line for ten minutes the next morning before he drew from the river the most beautiful fish he had ever seen in his life. But he nearly fell into the water from surprise when the fish began to speak to him in a small, squeaky voice:

"Take me back to your hut and cook me; then cut me up into six pieces, and sprinkle me over with pepper and salt. Give two of the pieces to your wife, one each to your children, and bury the remaining two in the garden."

The cobbler did not know what to make of these strange words; but he was wiser than many people, and when he did not understand, he thought it was well to obey. His children wanted to eat all the fish themselves, and begged their father to tell them what to do with the pieces he had put aside; but the cobbler only laughed, and told them it was no business of theirs. And when they were safe in bed, he stole out and buried the two pieces in the garden.

The next morning, in the spot where he had buried the fish, the cobbler found two tall plants, each topped with a brilliant gold shield. And in the cool shadows cast by the shields two babies, exactly alike, lay in a cradle. "Wife!" rejoiced the cobbler. "Behold our Knights of the Fish, and enough gold to keep us all well-fed!"

Years passed, and the babies were now strong young men, still known as the Knights of the Fish. They had cared for their parents until they had died and were now tired of living quietly at home, being mistaken for each other by everybody they saw. And so they determined to set off in different directions to seek adventures.

One fine morning the two brothers left the hut, and walked together to the place where the great road divided. There they embraced and parted, promising that if anything remarkable had happened to either, he would return to the crossroad and wait till his brother came.

The youth who took the path that ran eastward arrived presently at a large city, where he found everybody standing at the doors, wringing their hands and weeping bitterly.

"What is the matter?" he asked, pausing and looking around. And a man replied, in a faltering voice, that each year a beautiful girl was chosen by lot to be offered up to a dreadful fiery dragon who had a mother even worse than himself, and this year the lot had fallen on their peerless princess.

"But where *is* the princess?" said the young man once more, and again the man answered him, "She is standing under a tree, a mile away, waiting for the dragon."

This time the Knight of the Fish did not stop to hear more, but ran off as fast as he could, and found the princess bathed in tears, and trembling from head to foot.

She turned as she heard the sound of his sword, and removed her handkerchief from her eyes.

"Fly," she cried. "Fly while you have yet time, before that monster sees you."

She said it, and she meant it; yet when he had turned his back, she felt more forsaken than before. But in reality it was not more than a few minutes before he came back, galloping furiously on a horse he had borrowed, and carrying a huge mirror across its neck.

"I am in time, then," he cried, dismounting very carefully, and placing the mirror against the trunk of a tree.

"Give me your veil," he said hastily to the princess. And when she had unwound it from her head, he covered the mirror with it.

"The moment the dragon comes near you, you must tear off the veil," he cried, "and be sure you hide behind the mirror. Have no fear; I shall be at hand."

He and his horse had scarcely found shelter among some rocks, when the flap of the dragon's wings could be plainly heard. He tossed his head with delight at the sight of her, and approached slowly to the place where she stood, a little in front of the mirror. Then, still looking the monster steadily in the face, she passed one hand behind her back and snatched off the veil, stepping swiftly behind the tree as she did so.

The princess had not known when she obeyed the orders of the Knight of the Fish what she expected to happen. Would the dragon with snaky locks be turned to stone, she wondered, like the dragon in an old story her nurse had told her; or would some fiery spark dart from the heart of the mirror, and strike him dead? Neither of these things occurred, but instead the dragon stopped short with surprise and rage when he saw a monster before him as big and strong as himself. He shook his mane with rage and fury; the enemy in front did exactly the same. He lashed his tail, and rolled his red eyes, and the dragon opposite him did the same. Opening his mouth to its very widest, he gave an awful roar; but the other dragon only roared back. This was too much, and with another roar that made the princess shake in her shoes, he flung himself upon his foe. In an instant the mirror lay at his

THE DRAGON AND THE MIRROR

feet broken into a thousand pieces, but as every piece reflected part of himself, the dragon thought that he too had been smashed into atoms.

It was the moment for which the Knight of the Fish had watched and waited, and before the dragon could find out that he was not hurt at all, the young man's lance was down his throat, and he was rolling, dead, on the grass.

Oh! What shouts of joy rang through the great city when the youth came riding back with the princess sitting behind him, and dragging the horrible monster by a rope. Everybody cried out that the king must give the victor the hand of the princess; and so he did, and no one had ever seen such balls and feasts and sports before. And when they were all over, the young couple went to the palace prepared for them, which was so large that it was three miles around.

The first wet day after their marriage the bridegroom begged the bride to show him all the rooms in the palace, and it was so big and took so long that the sun was shining brightly again before they stepped onto the roof to see the view.

"What castle is that out there?" asked the knight. "It seems to be made of black marble."

"It is called the castle of Albatroz," answered the princess. "It is enchanted, and no one that has tried to enter it has ever come back."

Her husband said nothing, and began to talk of something else. But the next morning he ordered his horse, took his spear, called his bloodhound, and set off for the castle.

It needed a brave man to approach it, for it made one's hair stand on end merely to look at it. It was as dark as the night of a storm, and as silent as the grave. But the Knight of the Fish knew no fear, and had never turned his back on an enemy, so he drew out his horn, and blew a blast.

The sound awoke all the sleeping echoes in the castle, and was repeated now loudly, now softly; now near, and now far. But nobody stirred for all that.

"Is there anyone inside?" cried the young man in his loudest voice. "Anyone who will give a knight hospitality? Neither governor, nor squire, not even a page?"

"Not even a page!" answered the echoes. But the young man did not heed them, and only struck a furious blow at the gate.

Then a small grating opened, and there appeared the tip of a huge nose, which belonged to the ugliest old woman that ever was seen.

"What do you want?" she said.

"To enter," he answered shortly. "Can I rest here tonight? Yes or no?"

"No, No, No!" repeated the echoes.

Between the fierce sun and his anger at being kept waiting, the Knight of the Fish had grown so hot that he lifted his visor, and when the old woman saw how handsome he was, she began fumbling with the lock of the gate.

"Come in, come in," she said. "So fine a gentleman will do us no harm."

"Harm!" repeated the echoes, but again the young man paid no heed.

"Let us go in, ancient dame," but she interrupted him.

"You must call me the Lady Berberisca," she answered sharply, "and this is my castle, to which I bid you welcome. You shall live here with me and be my husband." But at these words the knight let his spear fall, so surprised was he.

"I marry *you*? Why you must be a hundred at least!" he cried. "You are mad! All I desire is to inspect the castle and then go." As he spoke, he heard the voices give a mocking laugh; but the old woman took no notice, and only bade the knight follow her.

Old though she was, it seemed impossible to tire her. There was no room, however small, she did not lead him into, and each room was full of curious things he had never seen before.

At length they came to a stone staircase, which was so dark that you could not see your hand if you held it up before your face.

"I have kept my most precious treasure till the last," said the old woman. "But let me go first, for the stairs are steep, and you might easily break your leg." So on she went, now and then calling back to the young man in the darkness. But he did not know that she had slipped aside into a recess, till suddenly he put his foot on a trapdoor that gave way under him, and he fell down, down, as many good knights had done before him, and his voice joined the echoes of theirs.

"So you would not marry me!" chuckled the old witch. "Ha! ha! Ha! ha!"

Meanwhile his brother had wandered far and wide, and at last he wandered back to the same great city where the other young knight had met with so many adventures. He noticed with amazement that as he walked through the streets, the guards drew themselves up in line, and saluted him, and the drummers played the royal march. But he was still more bewildered when several servants in livery ran up to him and told him that the princess was sure something terrible had befallen him, and had made herself ill with weeping. At last it occurred to him that once more he had been taken for his brother. I had better say nothing, he thought. Perhaps I shall be able to help him after all. So he allowed himself to be taken in triumph to the palace, where the princess threw herself into his arms.

"And so you did go to the castle?" she asked.

"Yes, of course I did," he answered.

"And what did you see there?"

"I am forbidden to tell you anything about it, until I have returned there once more," he replied.

"Must you really go back to that dreadful place?" she asked wistfully. "You are the only man who has ever come back from it."

"I must," was all he answered. And the princess, who was a wise woman, only said, "Well, go to bed now, for I am sure you must be very tired."

But the knight shook his head. "I have sworn never to lie in a bed as long as my work in the castle remains standing." And the princess again sighed, and was silent.

Early the next day the young man started for the castle, feeling sure that some terrible thing must have happened to his brother.

At the blast of his horn the long nose of the old woman appeared at the grating, but the moment she caught sight of his face, she nearly fainted from fright, as she thought it was the ghost of the youth whose bones were lying in the dungeon of the castle.

"Lady of all the ages," cried the newcomer, "did you not give hospitality to a young knight but a short time ago?"

"A short time ago!" wailed the voices.

"And how have you ill-treated him?" he went on.

"Ill-treated him!" answered the voices. The woman did not stop to hear more; she turned to fly, but the knight's sword entered her body.

"Where is my brother, cruel hag?" he asked sternly.

"I will tell you," she said; "but as I feel that I am going to die, I shall keep that piece of news to myself, until you have brought me to life again."

The young man laughed scornfully. "How do you propose that I should work that miracle?"

"Oh, it is quite easy. Go into the garden and gather the flowers of the everlasting plant and some of dragon's blood. Crush them together and boil them in a large tub of water, and then put me into it."

The knight did as the old witch bade him, and sure enough, she came out quite whole, but uglier than ever. She then told the young man what had become of his brother, and he went down into the dungeon, and brought up his body and the bodies of the other victims who lay there, and when they were all washed in the magic water, their strength was restored to them.

And, besides these, he found in another cavern the bodies of the girls who had been sacrificed to the dragon, and brought them back to life also.

As to the old witch, in the end she died of rage at seeing her prey escape her; and at the moment she drew her last breath, the castle of Albatroz fell into ruins with a great noise.

The Prince and the Three Fates

ANCIENT EGYPT

Once upon a time a little boy was born to a king who ruled over a great country through which a wide river ran. The king was nearly beside himself with joy, for he had always longed for a son to inherit his crown, and he sent messages to beg all the most powerful fairies to come and see this wonderful baby. In an hour or two so many were gathered around the cradle that the child seemed in danger of being smothered; but the king, who was watching the fairies eagerly, was disturbed to see them looking grave. "Is there anything the matter?" he asked anxiously.

The fairies looked at him, and all shook their heads at once.

"He is a beautiful boy, and it is a great pity; but what *is* to happen *will* happen," they said. "It is written in the book of fate that he must die, either by a crocodile, or a serpent, or by a dog. If we could save him, we would; but that is beyond our power."

And so saying, they vanished.

For a time the king stood where he was, horror-stricken at what he had heard; but being of a hopeful nature, he began at once to invent plans to save the prince from the dreadful doom that awaited him. He instantly sent for his master builder, and bade him construct a strong castle on the top of a mountain, which should be fitted with the most precious things from the king's own palace, and every kind of toy a child could wish to play with. And, besides, he gave the strictest orders that a guard should walk around the castle night and day.

For four or five years the baby lived in the castle alone with his nurses, going out of doors only on the broad terraces, which were surrounded by walls, with a moat beneath them, and only a drawbridge to connect them with the outer world.

One day when the prince was old enough to run quite fast by himself, he looked from the terrace across the moat, and saw a little soft fluffy ball of a dog jumping and playing on the other side. Now, of course, all dogs had been kept from him for fear that the fairies' prophecy should come true, and he had never even beheld one before. So he turned to the page who was walking behind him, and said:

"What is that funny little thing which is running so fast over there?"

"That is a dog, prince," answered the page.

"Well, bring me one like it, and we will see which can run the faster." And he watched the dog till it had disappeared around the corner.

The page was much puzzled to know what to do. He had strict orders to refuse the prince nothing; yet he remembered the prophecy, and felt that this was a serious matter. At last he thought he had better tell the king the whole story, and let him decide the question.

"Oh, get him a dog if he wants one," said the king. "He will only cry his heart out if he does not have it." So a puppy was found, exactly like the other; they might have been twins, and perhaps they were.

Years went by, and the boy and the dog played together till the boy grew tall and strong. The time came at last when he sent a message to his father, saying:

"Why do you keep me shut up here, doing nothing? I know all about the prophecy that was made at my birth, but I would far rather be killed at once than live an idle, useless life here. So give me arms, and let me go, I pray you; me and my dog too."

And again the king listened to his wishes, and he and his dog were carried in a ship to the other side of the river, which was so broad here it might almost have been the sea. A black horse was waiting for him, tied to a tree, and he mounted and rode away wherever his fancy took him, the dog always at his heels. Never was any prince so happy as he, and he rode and rode till at length he came to a king's palace.

The king who lived in it did not care about looking after his country, and seeing that his people lived cheerful and contented lives. He spent his whole time in making riddles, and inventing plans which he had much better have let alone. At the period when the young prince reached the kingdom, he had just completed a wonderful house for his only child, a daughter. It had seventy windows, each seventy feet from the ground, and he had sent the royal herald around the borders of the neighboring kingdoms to proclaim that whoever could climb up the walls to the window of the princess should win her for his wife.

The fame of the princess's beauty had spread far and wide, and there was no lack of princes who wished to try their fortune. Very funny the palace must have looked each morning, with the dabs of different color on the white marble as the princes were climbing up the walls. But though some managed to get farther than others, nobody was anywhere near the top.

They had already been spending several days in this manner when the young prince arrived, and as he was pleasant to look upon, and civil to talk to, they welcomed him to the house which had been given to them, and saw that his bath was properly perfumed after his long journey. "Where do you come from?" they said at last. "And whose son are you?"

But the young prince had reasons for keeping his own secret, and he answered:

"My father was master of the horse to the king of my country, and after my mother died, he married another wife. At first all went well, but as soon as she had babies of her own, she hated me, and I fled, lest she should do me harm."

The hearts of the other young men were touched as soon as they heard this story, and they did everything they could think of to make him forget his past sorrows.

"What are you doing here?" said the youth one day.

"We spend our whole time climbing up the walls of the palace, trying to reach the windows of the princess," answered the young men. "But, as yet, no one has reached within ten feet of them."

"Oh, let me try too," cried the prince. "Tomorrow I will wait and see what you do before I begin."

So the next day he stood where he could watch the young men go up, and he noted the places on the wall that seemed most difficult, and made up his mind that when his turn came, he would go up some other way.

Day after day he was to be seen watching the wooers, till one morning he felt that he knew the plan of the walls by heart, and took his place by the side of the others. Thanks to what he had learned from the failure of the rest, he managed to grasp one little rough projection after another, till at last, to the envy of his friends, he stood on the sill of the princess's window. Looking up from below, they saw a white hand stretched forth to draw him in.

Then one of the young men ran straight to the king's palace, and said, "The wall has been climbed, and the prize is won!"

"By whom?" cried the king, starting up from his throne. "Which of the princes may I claim as my son-in-law?"

"The youth who succeeded in climbing to the princess's window is not a prince at all," answered the young man. "He is the son of the master of the horse to the great king who dwells across the river, and he fled from his own country to escape from the hatred of his stepmother."

At this news the king was very angry, for it had never entered his head that anyone *but* a prince would seek to woo his daughter.

"Let him go back to the land from which he came," he shouted in anger. "Does he expect me to give my daughter to an exile?" And he began to smash the drinking vessels in his fury; indeed, he quite frightened the young man, who ran hastily home to his friends, and told the youth what the king had said.

Now the princess, who was leaning from her window, heard his words and bade the messenger go back to the king her father and tell him that she had sworn a vow never to eat or drink again if the youth was taken from her. The king was more angry than ever when he received this message, and ordered his guards to go at once to the palace and put the successful wooer to death; but the princess threw herself between him and his murderers.

"Lay a finger on him, and I shall be dead before sunset," she said;

and as they saw that she meant it, they left the palace, and carried the tale to her father.

By this time the king's anger was dying away, and he began to consider what his people would think of him if he broke the promise he had publicly given. So he ordered the princess to be brought before him, and the young man also, and when they entered the throne room he was so pleased with the noble air of the victor that his wrath quite melted away, and he ran to him and embraced him.

"Tell me who you are," he said when he had recovered himself a little, "for I will never believe that you do not have royal blood in your veins."

But the prince still had his reasons for being silent, and only told the same story. However, the king had taken such a fancy to the youth that he said no more, and the marriage took place the following day, and great herds of cattle and a large estate were given to the young couple.

After a little while the prince said to his wife: "My life is in the hands of three creatures — a crocodile, a serpent, and a dog."

"Ah, how rash you are!" cried the princess, throwing her arms around his neck. "If you know that, how can you have that horrid beast about you? I will give orders to have him killed at once."

But the prince would not listen to her.

"Kill my dear little dog, who has been my playfellow since he was a puppy?" he exclaimed. "Oh, never would I allow that." And all that the princess could get from him was that he would always wear a sword, and have somebody with him when he left the palace.

When the prince and princess had been married a few months, the prince heard that his stepmother was dead, and his father was old and ill, and longing to have his eldest son by his side again. The young man could not remain deaf to such a message, and he took a tender farewell of his wife, and set out on his journey home. It was a long way, and he was forced to rest often on the road, and so it happened that one night when he was sleeping in a city on the banks of the great river, a huge crocodile came silently up and made its way along a passage to the prince's room. Fortunately one of his guards woke up as it was trying to steal past them, and shut the crocodile up in a large hall, where a giant watched over it, never leaving the spot except during the night when the crocodile slept. And this went on for more than a month.

Now, when the prince found that he was not likely to leave his father's kingdom again, he sent for his wife, and bade the messenger tell her that he would await her coming in the town on the banks of the great river. This was the reason why he delayed his journey so long, and narrowly escaped being eaten by the crocodile. During the weeks that followed, the prince amused himself as best he could, though he counted the minutes to the arrival of the princess, and when she did come, he at once prepared to start for the court. That very night, however, while he was asleep, the princess noticed something strange in one of the corners of the room. It was a dark patch, and seemed, as she looked, to grow longer and longer, and to be moving slowly toward the cushions on which the prince was lying. She shrank in terror, but, slight as was the noise, the thing heard it, and raised its head to listen. Then she saw it was the long flat head of a serpent, and the recollection of the prophecy rushed into her mind. Without waking her husband, she glided out of bed, and taking up a heavy bowl of milk which stood on a table, laid it on the floor in the path of the serpent — for she knew that no serpent in the world can resist milk. She held her breath as the snake drew near and watched it throw up its head again as if it was smelling something nice, while its forky tongue darted out greedily. At length its eyes fell upon the milk, and in an instant it was lapping it so fast that it was a wonder the creature did not choke, for it never took its head from the bowl as long as a drop was left in it. After that it dropped on the ground and slept heavily. This was what the princess had been waiting for, and taking up her husband's sword, she severed the snake's head from its body.

The morning after this adventure the prince and princess set out for the king's palace, but found when they reached it that he was already dead. They gave him a magnificent burial, and then the prince had to examine the new laws which had been made in his absence, and do a

The Princess and the Snake

great deal of business besides, till he grew quite ill from fatigue, and was obliged to go away to one of his palaces on the banks of the river in order to rest. Here he soon got better, and began to hunt, and to shoot wild duck with his bow; and wherever he went, his dog, now grown very old, went with him.

One morning the prince and his dog were out as usual, and in chasing their game they drew near the bank of the river. The prince was running at full speed after his dog when he almost fell over something that looked like a log of wood which was lying in his path. To his surprise a voice spoke to him, and he saw that the thing which he had taken for a branch was really a crocodile.

"You cannot escape from me," it was saying, when he had gathered his senses again. "I am your fate, and wherever you go, and whatever you do, you will always find me before you. There is only one means of shaking off my power. If you can dig a pit in the dry sand which will remain full of water, my spell will be broken. If not, death will come to you speedily. I give you this one chance. Now go."

The young man walked sadly away, and when he reached the palace, he shut himself into his room, and for the rest of the day refused to see anyone, even his wife. At sunset, however, as no sound could be heard through the door, the princess grew quite frightened, and made such a noise that the prince was forced to draw back the bolt and let her come in. "How pale you look," she cried. "Has anything hurt you? Tell me, I pray you, what is the matter, for perhaps I can help!"

So the prince told her the whole story, and of the impossible task given him by the crocodile.

"How can a sand hole remain full of water?" he asked. "Of course it will all run through. The crocodile called it a 'chance,' but he might as well have dragged me into the river at once. He said truly that I cannot escape him."

"Oh, if *that* is all," cried the princess, "I can set you free myself, for my fairy godmother taught me to know the use of plants and in the desert not far from here there grows a little four-leaved herb which will keep the water in the pit for a whole year. I will go in search of it at dawn, and you can begin to dig the hole as soon as you like."

To comfort her husband the princess had spoken lightly and gaily, but she knew very well she had no light task before her. Still, she was full of courage and energy, and determined that one way or another her husband should be saved.

It was still starlight when she left the palace on a snow-white donkey, and rode away from the river straight to the west. For some time she could see nothing before her but a flat waste of sand, which became hotter and hotter as the sun rose higher and higher. Then a dreadful thirst seized her and the donkey, but there was no stream to quench it, and if there had been, she would hardly have had time to stop, for she still had far to go, and must be back before evening, or else the crocodile might declare that the prince had not fulfilled his conditions. So she spoke cheering words to her donkey, who brayed in reply, and the two pushed steadily on.

Oh! How glad they both were when they caught sight of a tall rock in the distance. They forgot that they were thirsty, and that the sun was hot; and the ground seemed to fly under their feet, till the donkey stopped of its own accord in the rock's cool shadow. But though the donkey might rest the princess could not, for the plant, as she knew, grew on the very top of the rock, and a wide chasm ran around the foot of it. Luckily she had brought a rope with her, and making a noose at one end, she flung it across with all her might. The first time it slid back slowly into the ditch, and she had to draw it up, and throw it again, but at length the noose caught on something, the princess could not see what, and had to trust her whole weight to this little bridge, which might snap and let her fall deep down among the rocks. And in that case her death was as certain as that of the prince.

But nothing so dreadful happened. The princess got safely to the other side, and then came the worst part of her task. As fast as she put her foot on a ledge of the rock, the stone broke away from under her, and left her in the same place as before. Meanwhile the hours were passing, and it was nearly noon.

The heart of the poor princess was filled with despair, but she would not give up the struggle. She looked around till she saw a small stone above her which seemed rather stronger than the rest, and by only poising her foot lightly on those that lay between, she managed by a great effort to reach it. In this way, with torn and bleeding hands, she gained the top; but here such a violent wind was blowing that she was almost blinded with dust, and was obliged to throw herself on the ground, and feel about after the precious herb.

For a few terrible moments she thought that the rock was bare, and that her journey had been to no purpose. Feel where she would, there was nothing but grit and stones, when suddenly her fingers touched something soft in a crevice. It was a plant, that was clear; but was it the right one? She could not see, for the wind was blowing more fiercely than ever, so she lay where she was and counted the leaves. One, two, three — yes! yes! there were four! And plucking a leaf, she held it safe in her hand while she turned, almost stunned by the wind, to go down the rock.

When once she was safely over the side, all became still in a moment, and she slid down the rock so fast that it was only a wonder that she did not land in the chasm. However, by good luck, she stopped quite close to her rope bridge and was soon across it. The donkey brayed joyfully at the sight of her, and set off home at his best speed, never seeming to know that the earth under his feet was nearly as hot as the sun above him. On the bank of the great river he halted, and the princess rushed up to where the prince was standing by the pit he had dug in the dry sand, with a huge water pot beside it. A little way off the crocodile lay blinking in the sun, with his jaws wide open and sharp glistening teeth.

At a signal from the princess the prince poured the water in the hole, and the moment it reached the brim the princess flung in the four-leaved plant. Would the charm work, or would the water trickle away slowly through the sand, and the prince fall a victim to that horrible monster? For half an hour they stood with their eyes rooted to the spot, but the hole remained as full as at the beginning, with the little green leaf floating on the top. Then the prince turned to the crocodile and shouted triumphantly, "Behold, the pool in the sand!" The defeated crocodile plunged sulkily into the river.

The prince had escaped forever the second of his three fates!

He stood there looking after the crocodile, and rejoicing that he was free, when he was startled by a wild duck which flew past them, seeking shelter among the rushes that bordered the edge of the stream. In another instant his dog dashed by in hot pursuit and knocked heavily against his master's legs. The prince staggered, lost his balance and fell backward into the river, where the mud and the rushes caught him and held him fast. He shrieked for help to his wife, who came running; and luckily brought her rope with her. The poor old dog was drowned, but the prince was pulled to shore. "My wife," he said, "was stronger than my fate."

THE POOL IN THE SAND

The Story of the Hero Makóma

ZIMBABWE

Once upon a time, in the town in Senna on the banks of the Zambesi, was born a child. He was not like other children, for he was very tall and strong; over his shoulder he carried a big sack, and in his hand an iron hammer. He could also speak like a grown man, but usually he was very silent.

One day his mother said to him, "My child, by what name shall we know you?"

And he answered, "Call all the head men of Senna here to the river's bank." And his mother called the head men of the town, and when they had come, he led them down to a deep black pool in the river where all the fierce crocodiles lived.

"O great men!" he said while they all listened, "which of you will leap into the pool and overcome the crocodiles?" But no one would come forward. So he turned and sprang into the water and disappeared.

The people held their breath, for they thought, surely the boy is bewitched and throws away his life, for the crocodiles will eat him! Then suddenly the ground trembled, and the pool, heaving and swirling, became red with blood, and presently the boy rising to the surface swam onshore.

But he was no longer just a boy! He was stronger than any man and very tall and handsome, so that the people shouted with gladness when they saw him.

"Now, O my people!" he cried waving his hand, "you know my

MAKOMA LEAPS INTO THE POOL OF CROCODILES

name — I am Makóma, 'the Greater'; for have I not slain the crocodiles in the pool where none would venture?"

Then he said to his mother, "Rest gently, my mother, for I go to make a home for myself and become a hero." Then entering his hut, he took Nu-éndo, his iron hammer, and throwing the sack over his shoulder, he went away.

Makóma crossed the Zambesi, and for many moons he wandered toward the north and west until he came to a very hilly country where one day he met a huge giant making mountains.

"Greetings," shouted Makóma. "Who are you?"

"I am Chi-éswa-mapíri, who makes the mountains," answered the giant. "And who are you?"

"I am Makóma, which signifies 'greater,'" he answered.

"Greater than who?" asked the giant.

"Greater than you!" answered Makóma.

The giant gave a roar and rushed upon him. Makóma said nothing, but swinging his great hammer Nu-éndo, he struck the giant upon the head.

He struck him so hard a blow that the giant shrank into quite a little man, who fell upon his knees saying, "You are indeed greater than I, O Makóma; take me with you to be your slave!" So Makóma picked him up and dropped him into the sack that he carried upon his back.

He was greater than ever now, for all the giant's strength had gone into him; and he resumed his journey, carrying his burden with as little difficulty as an eagle might carry a hare.

Before long he came to a country broken up with huge stones and immense clods of earth. Looking over one of the heaps, he saw a giant wrapped in dust dragging out the very earth and hurling it in handfuls on either side of him.

"Who are you," cried Makóma, "that pulls up the earth in this way?"

"I am Chi-dúbula-táka," he said, "and I am making the riverbeds."

"Do you know who I am?" said Makóma. "I am he that is called 'greater'!"

"Greater than who?" thundered the giant.

"Greater than you!" answered Makóma.

With a shout Chi-dúbula-táka seized a great clod of earth and launched it at Makóma. But the hero had his sack held over his left arm and the stones and earth fell harmlessly upon it, and tightly gripping his iron hammer, he rushed in and struck the giant to the ground. Chi-dúbula-táka groveled before him, all the while growing smaller and smaller; and when he had become a convenient size, Makóma picked him up and put him into the sack beside Chi-éswa-mapíri.

He went on his way even greater than before, as all the river-maker's power had become his; and at last he came to a forest of baobabs and thorn trees. He was astonished at their size, for every one was full grown and larger than any trees he had ever seen, and close by he saw Chi-gwísa-míti, the giant who was planting the forest.

Chi-gwísa-míti was taller than either of his brothers, but Makóma was not afraid, and called out to him, "Who are you, O Big One?"

"I," said the giant, "am Chi-gwísa-míti, and I am planting these baobabs and thorns as food for my children the elephants."

"Leave off!" shouted the hero. "For I am Makóma, and would like to exchange a blow with you!"

The giant, plucking up a monster baobab by the roots, struck heavily at Makóma; but the hero sprang aside, and as the weapon sank deep into the soft earth, whirled Nu-éndo the hammer around his head and felled the giant with one blow.

So terrible was the stroke that Chi-gwísa-míti shriveled up as the other giants had done; and when he had got back his breath, he begged Makóma to take him as his servant. "For," he said, "it is honorable to serve a man so great as you."

Makóma, after placing him in his sack, proceeded upon his journey, and traveling for many days, he at last reached a country so barren and rocky that not a single living thing grew upon it — everywhere reigned grim desolation. And in the midst of this dead region he found a man eating fire.

"What are you doing?" demanded Makóma.

"I am eating fire," answered the man, laughing; "and my name is Chi-ídea-móto, for I am the flame-spirit and can waste and destroy what I like."

"You are wrong," said Makóma; "for I am Makóma, who is 'greater' than you — and you cannot destroy me!"

The fire-eater laughed again, and blew a flame at Makóma. But the hero sprang behind a rock — just in time, for the ground upon which he had been standing was turned to molten glass, like an overbaked pot, by the heat of the flame-spirit's breath.

MAKÓMA throws his hammer at the FIRE-EATER

Then the hero flung his iron hammer at Chi-ídea-móto, and striking him, it knocked him helpless; so Makóma placed him in the sack with the other great men that he had overcome.

And now, truly, Makóma was a very great hero; for he had the strength to make hills, the industry to lead rivers over dry wastes, foresight and wisdom in planting trees, and the power of producing fire when he wished.

Wandering on, he arrived one day at a great plain, well watered and full of game; and in the very middle of it, close to a large river, was a grassy spot, very pleasant to make a home upon.

Makóma was so delighted with the little meadow that he sat down under a large tree, and removing the sack from his shoulder, took out all the giants and set them before him. "My friends," he said, "I have traveled far and am weary. Is not this such a place as would suit a hero for his home? Let us then go tomorrow to bring in timber to make a village."

So the next day Makóma and the giants set out to get poles to build the village, leaving only Chi-éswa-mapíri to look after the place and cook some venison that they had killed. In the evening when they returned, they found the giant helpless and tied to a tree by one enormous hair!

"How is it," said Makóma, astonished, "that we find you thus bound and helpless?"

"O Chief," answered Chi-éswa-mapíri, "at midday a man came out of the river; he was of immense stature, and his gray mustache hairs were of such length that I could not see where they ended! He demanded of me, 'Who is your master?' And I answered, 'Makóma, the greatest of heroes.' Then the man seized me, and pulling a hair from his mustache, tied me to this tree — even as you see me."

Makóma was very angry, but he said nothing, and drawing his fingernail across the hair (which was as thick and strong as palm rope), cut it, and set free the mountain-maker.

The three following days exactly the same thing happened, only each time with a different one of the party; and on the fourth day Makóma stayed in camp when the others went to cut poles, saying that he would see for himself what sort of man this was that lived in the river and whose mustache hairs were so long that they extended beyond men's sight.

So when the giants had gone, he swept and tidied the camp and put some venison on the fire to roast. At midday when the sun was right overhead, he heard a rumbling noise from the river, and looking up, he saw the head and shoulders of an enormous man emerging from it. And behold! right down the riverbed and up the riverbed, till it faded into the blue distance, stretched the giant's gray mustache!

"Who are you?" bellowed the giant as soon as he was out of the water.

"I am he that is called Makóma," answered the hero; "and before I slay you, tell me also what is your name and what you are doing in the river."

"My name is Chin-débou Máu-giri," said the giant. "My home is in the river, for my mustache is the gray fever-mist that hangs above the water, and with which I bind all those that come unto me so that they die."

"You cannot bind me!" shouted Makóma, rushing upon him and striking with his hammer. But the river giant was so slimy that the blow slid harmlessly off his green chest, and as Makóma stumbled and tried to regain his balance, the giant swung one of his long hairs around him and tripped him up.

For a moment Makóma was helpless, but remembering the power of the flame-spirit that had entered into him, he breathed a fiery breath

upon the giant's hair and cut himself free.

As Chin-débou Máu-giri leaned forward to seize him, the hero flung his sack over the giant's slippery head, and gripping his iron hammer, struck him again; this time the blow alighted upon the dry sack and Chin-débou Máu-giri fell dead.

When the four giants returned at sunset with the poles, they rejoiced to find that Makóma had overcome the fever-spirit, and they feasted on the roast venison till far into the night; but in the morning when they awoke, Makóma was already warming his hands at the fire, and his face was gloomy.

"In the darkness of the night, O my friends," he said presently, "the white spirits of my fathers came unto me and spoke, saying, 'Go, Makóma, for you shall have no rest until you have found and fought with Sákatirína, who has five heads, and is very great and strong; so take leave of your friends, for you must go alone.'"

Then the giants were very sad, and bewailed the loss of their hero; but Makóma comforted them, and gave back to each the gifts he had taken from them. Then bidding them farewell, he went on his way.

Makóma traveled far toward the west; over rough mountains and waterlogged morasses, fording deep rivers, and tramping for days across dry deserts where most men would have died, until at length he arrived at a hut standing near some large peaks, and inside the hut were two beautiful women.

"Greetings!" said the hero. "Is this the country of Sákatirína of five heads, whom I am seeking?"

"We greet you, O Great One!" answered the women. "We are the wives of Sákatirína; your search is at an end, for there stands he whom you seek!" And they pointed to what Makóma had thought were two tall mountain peaks. "Those are his legs," they said. "His body you cannot see, for it is hidden in the clouds."

Makóma was astonished when he beheld how tall the giant was; but never daunted, he went forward until he reached one of Sákatirína's legs, which he struck heavily with Nu-éndo. Nothing happened, so he hit again and then again until, presently, he heard a tired, faraway voice saying, "Who is it that scratches my feet?"

And Makóma shouted as loud as he could, answering, "It is I, Makóma, who is called 'Greater'!" And he listened, but there was no answer.

Then Makóma collected all the dead brushwood and trees that he could find, and making an enormous pile around the giant's legs, set a light to it.

This time the giant spoke; his voice was very terrible, for it was the rumble of thunder in the clouds. "Who is it," he said, "making that fire smoulder around my feet?"

"It is I, Makóma!" shouted the hero. "And I have come from

faraway to see you, O Sákatirína, for the spirits of my fathers bade me go seek and fight with you lest I should grow fat, and weary of myself."

There was silence for a while, and then the giant spoke softly, "It is good, O Makóma!" he said. "For I too have grown weary. There is no man so great as I, therefore I am all alone. Guard yourself!" And bending suddenly, he seized the hero in his hands and dashed him

MAKOMA IN THE HANDS OF SAKATIRINA

upon the ground. And lo! instead of death, Makóma had found life, for he sprang to his feet mightier in strength and stature than before, and rushing in, he gripped the giant by the waist and wrestled with him.

Hour by hour they fought, and mountains rolled beneath their feet like pebbles in a flood; now Makóma would break away, and summoning up his strength, strike the giant with Nu-éndo his iron hammer, and Sákatirína would pluck up the mountains and hurl them upon the hero, but neither one could slay the other. At last, upon the second day, they grappled so strongly that they could not break away; but their strength was failing, and just as the sun was sinking, they fell together to the ground, insensible.

In the morning when they awoke, Mulímo the Great Spirit was standing by them; and he said, "O Makóma and Sákatirína! You are heroes so great that no man may come against you. Therefore you will leave the world and take up your home with me in the clouds." And as he spoke, the heroes became invisible to the people of the Earth, and were no longer seen among them.

Hábogi

ICELAND

Once upon a time there lived two peasants who had three daughters, and as generally happens, the youngest was the most beautiful and the best tempered, and when her sisters wanted to go out, she was always ready to stay at home and do their work.

Years passed quickly with the whole family, and one day the parents suddenly perceived that all three girls were grown up, and that very soon they would be thinking of marriage.

"Have you decided what your husband's name is to be?" said the father laughingly to his eldest daughter one evening when they were all sitting at the door of their cottage. "You know that is a very important point!"

"Yes; I will never wed any man who is not called Sigmund," she answered.

"Well, it is lucky for you that there are a great many Sigmunds in this part of the world," replied her father, "so that you can take your choice! And what do *you* say?" he added, turning to the second.

"Oh, *I* think that there is no name so beautiful as Sigurd," she cried.

"Then you won't be an old maid either," he answered. "There are seven Sigurds in the next village alone! And you, Helga?"

Helga, who was still the prettiest of the three, looked up. She also had her favorite name, but just as she was going to say it, she seemed to hear a voice whisper, "Marry no one who is not called Hábogi."

The girl had never heard of such a name, and did not like it, so she determined to pay no attention; but as she opened her mouth to tell her father that her husband must be called Njal, she found herself answering instead, "If I do marry, it will be to no one except Hábogi."

"Who *is* Hábogi?" asked her father and sisters. "We never heard of such a person."

"All I can tell you is that he will be my husband, if ever I have one," returned Helga; and that was all she would say.

Before very long the young men who lived in the neighboring villages or on the sides of the mountains, had heard of this talk of the three girls, and Sigmunds and Sigurds in scores came to visit the little cottage. There were other young men too, who bore different names, though not one of them was called "Hábogi," and these thought that they might perhaps gain the heart of the youngest. But though there was more than one "Njal" among them, Helga's eyes seemed always turned another way.

At length the two elder sisters made their choice from out of the Sigurds and the Sigmunds, and it was decided that both weddings should take place at the same time. Invitations were sent out to the friends and relations, and when on the morning of the great day they were all assembled, a rough, coarse old peasant left the crowd and came up to the brides' father.

"My name is Hábogi, and Helga must be my wife," was all he said. And though Helga stood pale and trembling with surprise, she did not try to run away.

"I cannot talk of such things just now," answered the father, who could not bear the thought of giving his favorite daughter to this horrible old man, and hoped by putting it off that something might happen. But the sisters, who had always been rather jealous of Helga, were secretly pleased that their bridegrooms should outshine hers.

When the feast was over, Hábogi led up a beautiful horse from a field where he had left it to graze, and bade Helga jump up on its splendid saddle, all embroidered in scarlet and gold. "You shall come back again," he said; "but now you must see the house that you are to live in." And though Helga was very unwilling to go, something inside her forced her to obey.

The old man settled her comfortably, then sprang up in front of her as easily as if he had been a boy, and shaking the reins, they were soon out of sight.

After some miles they rode through a meadow, with grass so green that Helga's eyes felt quite dazzled; and feeding on the grass were a quantity of large fat sheep, with the curliest and whitest wool in the world.

"What lovely sheep! Whose are they?" cried Helga.

"Your Hábogi's," he answered. "All that you see belongs to him; but the finest sheep in the whole herd, which has little golden bells hanging between its horns, you shall have for yourself."

This pleased Helga very much, for she had never had anything of her own; and she smiled quite happily as she thanked Hábogi for his present.

They soon left the sheep behind them, and entered a large field with a river running through it, where a number of beautiful gray cows were standing by a gate waiting for a milkmaid to come and milk them.

"Oh, what lovely cows!" cried Helga again; "I am sure their milk must be sweeter than any other cows'. How I should like to have some! I wonder to whom they belong?"

"To your Hábogi," he replied. "Some day you shall have as much milk as you like, but we cannot stop now. Do you see that big gray one, with the silver bells between her horns? That is to be yours, and you can have her milked every morning the moment you wake."

And Helga's eyes shone, and though she did not say anything, she thought that she would learn to milk the cow herself.

A mile farther on they came to a wide pasture, with short, springy turf, where horses of all colors, with skins of satin, were kicking up their heels in play. The sight of them so delighted Helga that she nearly sprang from her saddle with a shriek of joy.

"Whose are they? Oh! Whose are they?" she asked. "How happy any man must be who is the master of such lovely creatures!"

"They are your Hábogi's," he replied, "and the one which you think the most beautiful of all you shall have for yourself, and learn to ride him."

At this Helga quite forgot the sheep and the cow.

"Oh do stop for a minute" said HELGA · HABOGI'S HORSES · But HABOGI would not stop or listen

"A horse of my own!" she said. "Oh, stop one moment, and let me see which I will choose. The white one? No. The chestnut? No. I think, after all, I like the coal-black one best, with the little white star on his forehead. Oh, do stop, just for a minute."

But Hábogi would not stop or listen. "When we are married, you will have plenty of time to choose one," was all he answered, and they rode on two or three miles farther.

At length Hábogi drew rein before a small house, very ugly and mean looking, and that seemed on the point of tumbling to pieces.

"This is my house, and is to be yours," said Hábogi, as he jumped down and held out his arms to lift Helga from the horse. The girl's heart sank a little, as she thought that the man who possessed such wonderful sheep, and cows, and horses might have built himself a prettier place to live in; but she did not say so. And taking her arm he led her up the steps.

But when she got inside, she stood quite bewildered at the beauty of all around her. None of her friends owned such things, not even the miller, who was the richest man she knew. There were carpets everywhere, thick and soft, and of deep rich colors; and the cushions were of silk, and made you sleepy even to look at them; and curious little figures in china were scattered about. Helga felt as if it would take her all her life to see everything properly, and it only seemed a second since she had entered the house, when Hábogi came up to her.

"I must begin the preparations for our wedding at once," he said, "but my foster brother will take you home, as I promised. In three days he will bring you back here, with your parents and sisters, and any guests you may invite, in your company. By that time the feast will be ready."

Helga had so much to think about, that the ride home appeared very short. Her father and mother were delighted to see her, as they did not feel sure that so ugly and cross looking a man as Hábogi might not have played her some cruel trick. And after they had given her some supper, they begged her to tell them all she had done. But Helga only told them that they should see for themselves on the third day, when they would come to her wedding.

It was very early in the morning when the party set out, and Helga's two sisters grew green with envy as they passed the flocks of sheep, and cows, and horses, and heard that the best of each was given to Helga herself; but when they caught sight of the poor little house which was to be her home, their hearts grew light again.

"I should be ashamed of living in such a place," whispered each to the other; and the eldest sister spoke of the carved stone over *her* doorway, and the second boasted of the number of rooms *she* had. But the moment they went inside, they were struck dumb with rage at the splendor of everything, and their faces grew white and cold with fury

The Jealous sisters spell-bound in the Ashpit

when they saw the dress which Hábogi had prepared for his bride — a dress that glittered like sunbeams dancing upon ice.

"She *shall* not look so much finer than us," they cried passionately to each other as soon as they were alone; and when night came, they stole out of their rooms, and taking out the wedding dress, they laid it in the ash pit, and heaped ashes upon it. But Hábogi, who knew a little magic, and had guessed what they would do, changed the ashes into roses, and cast a spell over the sisters, so that they could not leave the spot for a whole day, and everyone who passed by mocked at them.

The next morning when they all awoke, the ugly little tumbledown house had disappeared, and in its place stood a splendid palace. The guests' eyes sought in vain for the bridegroom, but could only see a handsome young man, with a coat of blue velvet and silver and a gold crown upon his head.

"Who is that?" they asked Helga.

"That is my Hábogi," she said.

The Fairy of the Dawn

ROMANIA

Once upon a time what should happen *did* happen; and if it had not happened, this tale would never have been told.

There was once an emperor, very great and mighty, and he ruled over an empire so large that no one knew where it began and where it ended. But if nobody could tell the exact extent of his sovereignty, everybody was aware that the emperor's right eye laughed, while his left eye wept. A few men of valor had had the courage to ask him the reason for this strange fact, but the question brought such a fit of rage from the emperor that no one dared ask it again. And so for many years the reason for the deadly enmity between his two eyes remained a secret known only to the monarch himself.

And all the while the emperor's sons were growing up. And such sons! All three like the morning stars in the sky!

Florea, the eldest, was so tall and broad-shouldered that no man in the kingdom could approach him.

Costan, the second, was quite different. Small of stature, and slightly built, he had a strong arm and stronger wrist.

Petru, the third and youngest, was tall and thin, more like a girl than a boy. He spoke very little, but laughed and sang, sang and laughed, from morning till night. He was very seldom serious, but then he had a way when he was thinking of stroking his hair over his forehead, which made him look old enough to sit in his father's council!

"You are grown up, Florea," said Petru one day to his eldest brother. "Go and ask father why one eye laughs and the other weeps."

THE EMPEROR WHOSE RIGHT EYE LAUGHED WHILE HIS LEFT EYE WEPT

But Florea would not go. He had no desire to experience the emperor's rage.

Petru next went to Costan, but did not succeed any better with him.

"Well, well, as everyone else is afraid, I suppose I must do it myself," said Petru at length. No sooner said than done; the boy went straight to his father and put his question:

"May you go blind!" exclaimed the emperor in wrath; "what business is it of yours?" and boxed Petru's ears soundly.

Petru returned to his brothers, and told them what had befallen him; but not long after, it struck him that his father's left eye seemed to weep less, and the right to laugh more.

I wonder if it has anything to do with my question, he thought. I'll try again! After all, what do two boxes on the ear matter?

So he put his question for the second time, and had the same answer; but the left eye only wept now and then, while the right eye looked ten years younger.

It really *must* be true, thought Petru. Now I know what I have to do. I shall have to go on putting that question, and getting boxes on the ear, till both eyes laugh together.

No sooner said than done. Petru never, never forswore himself.

"Petru, my dear boy," cried the emperor, both his eyes laughing together, "I see you have got this on the brain. Well, I will let you in on the secret. My right eye laughs when I look at my three sons, and see how strong and handsome you all are, and the other eye weeps because I fear that after I die, you will not be able to keep the empire together and to protect it from its enemies. But if you can bring me water from the well of the Fairy of the Dawn to bathe my eyes, then they will laugh forevermore; for I shall know that my sons are brave enough to overcome any foe."

Thus spoke the emperor, and Petru picked up his hat and went to find his brothers.

The three young men took counsel together, and talked the subject over well, as brothers should do. And the end of it was that Florea, as the eldest, went to the stables, chose the best and handsomest horse they contained, saddled him, and took leave of the court.

"I am starting at once," he said to his brothers, "and if after a year, a month, a week, and a day I have not returned with the water from the well of the Fairy of the Dawn, you, Costan, had better come after me." So saying, he disappeared around a corner of the palace.

For three days and three nights he never drew rein. Like a spirit the horse flew over mountains and valleys till he came to the borders of the empire. Here was a deep, deep trench that girdled it the whole way around, and there was only a single bridge by which the trench could be crossed. Florea made instantly for the bridge, and there pulled up to look around him once more, to take leave of his native land. Then he turned, but before him was standing a dragon — oh! *such* a dragon! — a dragon with three heads and three horrible faces, all with their mouths wide open, one jaw reaching to heaven and the other to earth.

At this awful sight Florea did not wait to give battle. He put spurs to his horse and dashed off, *where* he neither knew nor cared.

The dragon heaved a sigh and vanished without leaving a trace behind him.

A week went by. Florea did not return home. Two passed; and nothing was heard of him. After a month Costan began to haunt the stables and to pick out a horse for himself. And the moment the year, the month, the week, and the day were over, Costan mounted his horse and took leave of his youngest brother.

"If I fail, then you come," he said, and followed the path that Florea had taken.

The dragon on the bridge was more fearful and his three heads more terrible than before, and the young hero rode away still faster than his brother had done.

Nothing more was heard either of him or Florea; and Petru remained alone.

"I must go after my brothers," said Petru one day to his father.

"Go, then," said his father, "and may you have better luck than they"; and he bade farewell to Petru, who rode straight to the borders of the kingdom.

The dragon on the bridge was yet more dreadful than the one Florea and Costan had seen, for this one had seven heads instead of only three.

Petru stopped for a moment when he caught sight of this terrible creature. Then he found his voice.

"Get out of the way!" he cried. "Get out of the way!" he repeated again as the dragon did not move. "Get out of the way!" and with this last summons he drew his sword and rushed upon him. In an instant the heavens seemed to darken around him and he was surrounded by fire — fire to the right of him, fire to the left of him, fire to the front of him, fire to the rear of him; nothing but fire whichever way he looked, for the dragon's seven heads were vomiting flame.

The horse neighed and reared at the horrible sight, and Petru could not use the sword he had in readiness.

"Be quiet! This won't do!" he said, dismounting hastily, but holding the bridle firmly in his left hand and grasping his sword in his right.

But even so, he got on no better, for he could see nothing but fire and smoke.

"There is no help for it; I must go back and get a better horse," he said, and mounted again and rode homeward.

At the gate of the palace his nurse, old Birscha, was waiting for him eagerly.

PETRU HAS TO TURN BACK

"Ah, Petru, my son, I knew you would have to come back," she cried. "You did not set about the matter properly."

"How ought I to have set about it?" asked Petru, half angrily, half sadly.

"Look here, my boy," replied old Birscha. "You can never reach the well of the Fairy of the Dawn unless you ride the horse that your father, the emperor, rode in his youth. Go and ask where it is to be found, and then mount it and be off with you."

Petru thanked her heartily for her advice, and went at once to make inquiries about the horse.

"By the light of my eyes!" exclaimed the emperor when Petru had put his question. "Who has told you anything about that? It must have been that old witch of a Birscha. Have you lost your wits? Fifty years have passed since I was young, and who knows where the bones of my horse may be rotting, or whether a scrap of his reins still lies in his stall? I have forgotten all about him long ago."

Petru turned away in anger, and went back to his old nurse.

"Do not be cast down," she said with a smile. "If that is how the affair stands, all will go well. Go and fetch the scrap of the reins; I shall soon know what must be done."

The place was full of saddles, bridles, and bits of leather. Petru picked out the oldest, and blackest, and most decayed pair of reins, and brought them to the old woman, who murmured something over them and sprinkled them with incense, and held them out to the young man.

"Take the reins," she said, "and strike them violently against the pillars of the house."

Petru did what he was told, and scarcely had the reins touched the pillars when something happened — *how* I have no idea — that made Petru stare with surprise. A horse stood before him — a horse whose equal in beauty the world had never seen; with a saddle on him of gold and precious stones, and with such a dazzling bridle, you hardly dared to look at it, lest you should lose your sight. A splendid horse, a splendid saddle, and a splendid bridle, all ready for the splendid young prince!

"Jump on the back of the brown horse," said the old woman, and she turned around and went into the house.

The moment Petru was seated on the horse, he felt his arm three times as strong as before, and even his heart felt braver.

"Sit firmly in the saddle, my lord, for we have a long way to go and no time to waste," said the brown horse, and Petru soon saw that they were riding as no man and horse had ever ridden before.

On the bridge stood a dragon, but not the same one as he had tried to fight with, for this dragon had twelve heads, each more hideous and shooting forth more terrible flames than the other. But horrible though he was, he had met his match. Petru showed no fear, but rolled up his sleeves so that his arms might be free.

"Get out of the way!" he said when he had done, but the dragon's heads only breathed forth more flames and smoke. Petru wasted no more words, but drew his sword and prepared to throw himself on the bridge.

"Stop a moment; be careful, my lord," put in the horse, "and be sure you do what I tell you. Dig your spurs in my body up to the rowel, draw your sword, and keep yourself ready, for we shall have to leap over both bridge and dragon. When you see that we are right above the dragon, cut off his biggest head, wipe the blood off the sword, and put it back clean in the sheath before we touch earth again."

So Petru dug in his spurs, drew his sword, cut off the head, wiped the blood, and put the sword back in the sheath before the horse's hoofs touched the ground again.

And in this fashion they passed the bridge.

"But we have got to go farther still," said Petru after he had taken a farewell glance at his native land.

"Yes, forward," answered the horse; "but you must tell me, my lord, at what speed you wish to go. Like the wind? Like thought? Like desire? Or like a curse?"

Petru looked about him, up at the heavens and down again to the earth. A desert lay spread out before him, whose aspect made his hair stand on end.

"We will ride at different speeds," he said, "not so fast as to grow tired nor so slow as to waste time."

And so they rode, one day like the wind, the next like thought, the third and fourth like desire and like a curse, till they reached the borders of the desert.

"Now walk, so that I may look about, and see what I have never seen before," said Petru, rubbing his eyes like one who wakes from sleep, or like him who beholds something strange. . . . Before Petru lay a wood made of copper, with copper trees and copper leaves, with bushes and flowers of copper also.

Petru stood and stared as a man does when he sees something that he has never seen, and of which he has never heard.

Then he rode right into the wood. On each side of the way the rows of flowers began to praise Petru, and to try and persuade him to pick some of them and make himself a wreath.

"Take me, for I am lovely, and can give strength to whoever plucks me," said one.

"No, take me, for whoever wears me in his hat will be loved by the most beautiful woman in the world," pleaded the second; and then one after another stirred itself, each more charming than the last, all promising, in soft sweet voices, wonderful things to Petru, if only he would pick them.

Petru was not deaf to their persuasions, and was just stooping to pick one when the horse sprang to one side.

"Why don't you stay still?" asked Petru roughly.

"Do not pick the flowers; it will bring you bad luck," answered the horse.

"Why should it do that?"

"These flowers are under a curse. Whoever plucks them must fight the Welwa of the woods."

"What kind of a goblin is the Welwa?"

"Oh, do leave me in peace! But listen. Look at the flowers as much as you like, but pick none," and the horse walked on slowly.

Petru knew by experience that he would do well to attend to the horse's advice, so he made a great effort and tore his mind away from the flowers.

But it was in vain! If a man is fated to be unlucky, unlucky he will be, whatever he may do!

The flowers went on beseeching him, and his heart grew ever weaker and weaker.

"What must come will come," said Petru at length. "At any rate I shall see the Welwa of the woods, what she is like, and which way I had best fight her. If she is ordained to be the cause of my death, well, then it will be so; but if not, I shall conquer her though she were twelve hundred Welwas," and once more he stooped down to gather the flowers.

"You have done very wrong," said the horse sadly. "But it can't be helped now. Get yourself ready for battle, for here is the Welwa!"

Hardly had he done speaking, scarcely had Petru twisted his wreath, when a soft breeze arose on all sides at once. Out of the breeze came a storm wind, and the storm wind swelled and swelled till everything around was blotted out in darkness, and darkness covered them as with a thick cloak, while the earth swayed and shook under their feet.

"Are you afraid?" asked the horse, shaking his mane.

"Not yet," replied Petru stoutly, though cold shivers were running down his back. "What must come will come, whatever it is."

"Don't be afraid," said the horse. "I will help you. Take the bridle from my neck, and try to catch the Welwa with it."

The words were hardly spoken, and Petru had no time even to unbuckle the bridle, when the Welwa herself stood before him; and Petru could not bear to look at her, so horrible was she.

She had not exactly a head, yet neither was she without one. She did not fly through the air, but neither did she walk upon the earth. She had a mane like a horse, horns like a deer, a face like a bear, eyes like a polecat; while her body had something of each. And that was the Welwa.

Petru planted himself firmly in his stirrups, and began to lay about him with his sword, but could feel nothing.

A day and a night went by, and the fight was still undecided, but at last the Welwa began to pant for breath.

"Let us wait a little and rest," she gasped.

THE BATTLE WITH THE WELWA IN THE COPPER WOOD

Petru stopped and lowered his sword.

"You must not stop an instant," said the horse, and Petru gathered up all his strength, and laid about him harder than ever.

The Welwa gave a neigh like a horse and a howl like a wolf, and threw herself afresh on Petru. For another day and night the battle raged more furiously than before. And Petru grew so exhausted, he could scarcely move his arm.

"Let us wait a little and rest," cried the Welwa for the second time, "for I see you are as weary as I am."

"You must not stop an instant," said the horse.

And Petru went on fighting, though he barely had strength to move his arm. But the Welwa had ceased to throw herself upon him, and began to deliver her blows cautiously, as if she no longer had power to strike.

And on the third day they were still fighting, but as the morning sky began to redden, Petru somehow managed — how I cannot tell — to throw the bridle over the head of the tired Welwa. In a moment, from the Welwa sprang a horse — the most beautiful horse in the world.

"Sweet be your life, for you have delivered me from my enchantment," he said, and began to rub his nose against his brother's. And he told Petru all his story, and how he had been bewitched for many years.

So Petru tied the Welwa to his own horse and rode on. Where did he ride? That I cannot tell you, but he rode on fast till he got out of the copper wood.

"Stay still, and let me look about, and see what I never have seen before," said Petru again to his horse. For in front of him stretched a forest that was far more wonderful, as it was made of glistening trees and shining flowers. It was the silver wood.

As before, the flowers began to beg the young man to gather them.

"Do not pluck them," warned the Welwa, trotting beside him, "for my brother is seven times stronger than I." But though Petru knew by experience what this meant, it was no use, and after a moment's hesitation he began to gather the flowers and to twist himself a wreath.

Then the storm wind howled louder, the earth trembled more violently, and the night grew darker than the first time, and the Welwa of the silver wood came rushing on with seven times the speed of the other. For three days and three nights they fought, but at last Petru cast the bridle over the head of the second Welwa.

"Sweet be your life, for you have delivered me from enchantment," said the second Welwa, and they all journeyed on as before.

But soon they came to a gold wood far more lovely than the other two, and again Petru's companions pleaded with him to ride through it quickly, and to leave the flowers alone. But Petru turned a deaf ear to all they said, and before he had woven his golden crown, he felt that something terrible that he could not see was coming near him right out of the earth. He drew his sword and made himself ready for the fight. "I will die!" he cried. "Or she shall have my bridle over her head."

He had hardly said the words when a thick fog wrapped itself around him, and so thick was it that he could not see his own hand, or hear the sound of his voice. For a day and a night he fought with his sword, without ever once seeing his enemy. Then suddenly the fog began to lighten. By dawn of the second day it had vanished altogether, and the sun shone brightly in the heavens. It seemed to Petru that he had been born again.

"You had better take breath now while you can, for the fight will have to begin all over again," said the horse.

"What was it?" asked Petru.

"It was the Welwa," replied the horse, "changed into a fog! Listen! She is coming back!"

And Petru had hardly drawn a long breath when he felt something approaching from the side, though *what* he could not tell. A river, yet not a river, for it seemed not to flow over the earth, but to go where it liked, and to leave no trace of its passage.

"Woe be to me!" cried Petru, frightened at last.

"Beware, and never stand still," called the brown horse, and more he could not say, for the water was choking him.

The battle began anew. For a day and a night Petru fought on, without knowing at whom or what he struck. At dawn on the second day he felt that both his feet were lame.

Now I am done for, he thought, and his blows fell thicker and harder in his desperation. And the sun came out and the water disappeared, without his knowing how or when.

"Take breath," said the horse, "for you have no time to lose. The Welwa will return in a moment."

Petru made no reply, only wondered how, exhausted as he was, he should ever be able to carry on the fight. But he settled himself in his saddle, grasped his sword, and waited.

And then something came to him — *what* I cannot tell you. Perhaps in his dreams a man may see a creature that has what it has not got, and has not got what it has. At least, that was what the Welwa seemed like to Petru. She flew with her feet, and walked with her wings; her head was in her back, and her tail was on top of her body; her eyes were in her neck, and her neck in her forehead, and how to describe her further I do not know.

Petru felt for a moment as if he was wrapped in a garment of fear; then he shook himself and took heart, and fought as he had never yet fought before.

As the day wore on, his strength began to fail, and when darkness fell, he could hardly keep his eyes open. By midnight he knew he was no longer on his horse, but standing on the ground, though he could not have told how he got there. When the gray light of morning came, he was past standing on his feet, but fought now upon his knees.

"Make one more struggle; it is nearly over now," said the horse, seeing that Petru's strength was waning fast.

Petru wiped the sweat from his brow with his gauntlet, and with a desperate effort rose to his feet.

"Strike the Welwa on the mouth with the bridle," said the horse, and Petru did it.

The Welwa uttered a neigh so loud that Petru thought he would be deaf for life, and then, though she too was nearly spent, flung herself upon her enemy; but Petru was on the watch and threw the bridle over her head as she rushed on, so that when the day broke, there were three horses trotting beside him.

"May your wife be the most beautiful of women," said the Welwa, "for you have delivered me from my enchantment." So the four horses galloped fast, and by nightfall they were at the borders of the golden forest.

Then Petru began to think of the crowns that he wore, and what they had cost him.

After all, what do I want with so many? I will keep the best, he said to himself; and taking off first the copper crown and then the silver, he threw them away.

"Stop!" cried the horse. "Do not throw them away! Perhaps we shall find them of use. Get down and pick them up." So Petru got down and picked them up, and they all went on.

In the evening when the sun was getting low, Petru saw a wide heath stretching before him.

At the same instant the horse stood still itself.

"What is the matter?" asked Petru.

"I am afraid that something evil will happen to us," answered the horse.

"But why should it?"

"We are going to enter the kingdom of the goddess Mittwoch, and the farther we ride into it, the colder we shall get. But all along the road there are huge fires, and I dread lest you should stop and warm yourself at them."

"And why should I not warm myself?"

"Something fearful will happen to you if you do," replied the horse.

"Well, forward!" cried Petru lightly. "And if I have to bear cold, I must bear it!"

With every step they went into the kingdom of Mittwoch, the air grew colder and more icy, till even the marrow in their bones was frozen. But Petru was no coward; the fight he had gone through had strengthened his powers of endurance, and he stood the test bravely.

Along the road on each side were great fires with men standing by them who spoke pleasantly to Petru as he went by, and invited him to join them. The breath froze in his mouth, but he took no notice, only bade his horse ride on the faster.

How long Petru may have waged battle silently with the cold, one cannot tell, for everybody knows that the kingdom of Mittwoch is not to be crossed in a day, but he struggled on, though the frozen rocks burst around, and though his teeth chattered, and even his eyelids were frozen.

At length they reached the dwelling of Mittwoch herself, and jumping from his horse, Petru threw the reins over his horse's neck and entered the hut.

"Good day, little mother!" he said.

"Very well, thank you, my frozen friend!"

Petru laughed, and waited for her to speak.

"You have borne yourself bravely," the goddess went on, tapping him on the shoulder. "Now you shall have your reward," and she opened an iron chest, out of which she took a little box.

"Look!" she said; "this little box has been lying here for ages, waiting for the man who could win his way through the Ice Kingdom. Take it, and treasure it, for someday it may help you. If you open it, it will tell you anything you want, and give you news of your fatherland."

Petru thanked her gratefully for her gift, mounted his horse, and rode away.

When he was some distance from the hut, he opened the casket.

"What are your commands?" asked a voice inside.

"Give me news of my father," he replied rather nervously.

"He is sitting in council with his nobles," answered the casket.

"Is he well?"

"Not particularly, for he is furiously angry."

"What has angered him?"

"Your brothers Costan and Florea," replied the casket. "They finally returned home after their unsuccessful attempts to bring back water from the Fairy of the Dawn. They are now trying to rule your father and the kingdom as well, and the old man says they are not fit to do it."

"Push on, good horse, for we have no time to lose!" cried Petru; then he shut the box, and put it in his pocket.

They rushed on as fast as ghosts, as whirlwinds, as vampires when they hunt at midnight, and how long they rode no man can tell, for the way is far.

"Stop! I have some advice to give you," said the horse at last.

"What is it?" asked Petru.

"You have known what it is to suffer cold; you will have to endure heat, such as you have never dreamed of. Be as brave now as you were then. Let no one tempt you to try to cool yourself, or evil will befall you."

"Forward!" answered Petru. "Do not worry yourself. If I have escaped without being frozen, there is no chance of my melting."

"Why not? This is a heat that will melt the marrow in your bones — a heat that is only to be felt in the kingdom of the Goddess of Thunder."

And it *was* hot. The very iron of the horse's shoes began to melt, but Petru gave no heed. The sweat ran down his face, but he dried it with his gauntlet. What heat could be he never knew before, and on the way, not a stone's throw from the road, lay the most delicious valleys, full of shady trees and bubbling streams. When Petru looked at them, his heart burned within him and his mouth grew parched. And standing among the flowers were lovely maidens who called to him in soft voices, till he had to shut his eyes against their spells.

"Come, my hero, come and rest; the heat will kill you," they said.

Petru shook his head and said nothing, for he had lost the power of speech.

Long he rode in this awful state, how long none can tell. Suddenly the heat seemed to become less, and in the distance he saw a little hut on a hill. This was the dwelling of the Goddess of Thunder, and when he drew rein at her door, the goddess herself came out to meet him.

She welcomed him, and kindly invited him in, and bade him tell her all his adventures. So Petru told her all that had happened to him, and why he was there, and then took farewell of her, as he had no time to lose. "For," he said, "who knows how far the Fairy of the Dawn may yet be?"

"Stay for one moment, for I have a word of advice to give you. You are about to enter the kingdom of Venus. Go and tell her, as a message from me, that I hope she will not tempt you to delay. On your way back, come to me again, and I will give you something that may be of use to you."

So Petru mounted his horse, and had hardly ridden three steps when he found himself in a new country. Here it was neither hot nor cold, but the air was warm and soft like spring, though the way ran through a heath covered with sand and thistles.

"What can that be?" asked Petru, when he saw a long, long way off, at the very end of the heath, something resembling a house.

"That is the house of the goddess Venus," replied the horse, "and if

Among the Flowers were lovely maidens calling to him with soft voices

we ride hard, we may reach it before dark"; and he darted off like an arrow, so that as twilight fell, they found themselves nearing the house. Petru's heart leaped at the sight, for all the way along he had been followed by a crowd of shadowy figures who danced about him from right to left, and from back to front, and Petru, though a brave man, felt now and then a thrill of fear.

"They won't hurt you," said the horse. "They are just the daughters of the whirlwind amusing themselves while they are waiting for the ogre of the moon."

Then he stopped in front of the house, and Petru jumped off and went to the door.

"Do not be in such a hurry," cried the horse. "There are several things I must tell you first. You cannot enter the house of the goddess Venus like that. She is always watched and guarded by the whirlwind."

"What am I to do then?"

"Take the copper wreath, and go with it to that little hill over there. When you reach it, say to yourself, 'Were there ever such lovely maidens! Such angels! Such fairy souls!' Then hold the wreath high in the air and cry, 'Oh! if I knew whether anyone would accept this wreath from me. . . . If I knew! If I knew!' and throw the wreath from you!"

"And why should I do all this?" said Petru.

"Ask no questions, but go and do it," replied the horse. And Petru did.

Scarcely had he flung away the copper wreath than the whirlwind flung himself upon it, and tore it in pieces.

Then Petru turned once more to the horse.

"Stop!" cried the horse again. "I have other things to tell you. Take the silver wreath and knock at the windows of the goddess Venus. When she says, 'Who is there?' answer that you have come on foot and lost your way on the heath. She will then tell you to find your way back again; but take care not to stir from the spot. Instead, be sure you say to her, 'No, indeed I shall do nothing of the sort, as from my childhood I have heard stories of the beauty of the goddess Venus, and it was not for nothing that I had shoes made of leather with soles of steel, and have traveled for nine years and nine months, and have won in battle the silver wreath, which I hope you may allow me to give you, and have done and suffered everything to be where I now am.' This is what you must say. What happens after is your affair."

Petru asked no more, but went toward the house.

By this time it was pitch dark, and there was only the ray of light that streamed through the windows to guide him, and at the sound of his footsteps two dogs began to bark loudly.

"Which of those dogs is barking? Is he tired of life?" asked the goddess Venus.

The Whirlwind seizes the Wreath

"It is I, O goddess!" replied Petru rather timidly. "I have lost my way on the heath, and do not know where I am to sleep this night."

"Go away, my son, there is no place for you here," she continued, drawing back from the window.

Then Petru repeated hastily what the horse had told him to say, and no sooner had he done so than the goddess opened the window, and in gentle tones she asked him:

"Let me see this wreath, my son," and Petru held it out to her.

"Come into the house," the goddess went on. "Do not fear the dogs, they always know my will." And so they did, for as the young man passed, they wagged their tails to him.

"Good evening," said Petru as he entered the house, and seating himself near the fire, listened comfortably to whatever the goddess might choose to talk about, which was for the most part the wickedness of men, with whom she was evidently very angry. But Petru agreed with her in everything as he had been taught was only polite.

But was anybody ever so old as she! I do not know why Petru devoured her so with his eyes, unless it was to count the wrinkles on her face; but if so he would have had to live seven lives, and each life seven times the length of an ordinary one, before he could have reckoned them up.

But Venus was joyful in her heart when she saw Petru's eyes fixed upon her.

"Nothing was that is, and the world was not a world when I was born," she said. "When I grew up and the world came into being, everyone thought I was the most beautiful girl that ever was seen, though many hated me for it. But every hundred years there came a wrinkle on my face. And now I am old." Then she went on to tell Petru that she was the daughter of an emperor, and their nearest neighbor was the Fairy of the Dawn, with whom she had a violent quarrel, and with that she broke out into loud abuse of her.

Petru did not know what to do. He listened in silence for the most part, but now and then he would say, "Yes, yes, you must have been badly treated," just for politeness' sake; what more could he do?

"I will give you a task to perform, for you are brave, and will carry it through," continued Venus, when she had talked a long time, and both of them were getting sleepy. "In the Fairy's house is a well, and whoever drinks from it will blossom again like a rose. Bring me a bottle of it, and I will do anything to prove my gratitude. It is not easy! No one knows that better than I do — the kingdom is guarded on every side by wild beasts and horrible dragons. But I will tell you more about that, and I also have something to give you." Then she rose and lifted the lid of an iron-bound chest, and took out of it a very tiny flute.

"Do you see this?" she asked. "An old man gave it to me when I was young. Whoever listens to this flute goes to sleep, and nothing can wake him. Take it and play on it as long as you remain in the kingdom of the Fairy of the Dawn, and you will be safe."

At this Petru told her that he had another task to fulfill at the well of the Fairy of Dawn, and Venus was still better pleased when she heard his tale.

So Petru bade her good night, put the flute in its case, and laid himself down in the lowest chamber to sleep.

Before the dawn he was awake again, and his first care was to give to each of his horses as much corn as they could eat, and then to lead them to the well to water. Then he dressed himself and made ready to start.

"Stop," cried Venus from her window, "I have still a piece of advice to give you: Leave one of your horses here, and only take three. Ride slowly till you get to the fairy's kingdom, then dismount, and go on foot. When you return, see that all your three horses remain on the road, while you walk. But above all beware never to look the Fairy of the Dawn in the face, for she has eyes that will bewitch you, and glances that will befool you. She is hideous, more hideous than anything you can imagine, with owl's eyes, a foxy face, and cat's claws. Do you hear? Do you hear? Be sure you never look at her."

Petru thanked her, and managed to get off at last.

Far, far away, where the heavens touch the earth, where the stars kiss the flowers, a soft red light was seen, such as the sky sometimes has in spring, only lovelier, more wonderful.

That light was behind the palace of the Fairy of the Dawn, and it took Petru two days and nights through flowery meadows to reach it. And besides, it was neither hot nor cold, bright nor dark, but something of them all, and Petru did not find the way a step too long.

After some time Petru saw something white rise up out of the red of the sky, and when he drew nearer, he saw it was a castle so splendid that his eyes were dazzled when they looked at it. He did not know there was such a beautiful castle in the world.

But no time was to be lost, so he shook himself, jumped down from his horse, and leaving him on the dewy grass, began to play on his flute as he walked along.

He had hardly gone many steps when he stumbled over a huge giant, who had been lulled to sleep by the music. This was one of the guards of the castle! As he lay there on his back, he seemed so big that in spite of Petru's haste he stopped to measure him.

The farther Petru went, the more strange and terrible were the sights he saw — lions, tigers, dragons with seven heads, all stretched out in the sun fast asleep. It is needless to say what the dragons were like, for nowadays everyone knows, and dragons are not things to joke about. Petru ran through them like the wind.

At last he came to a river, but let nobody think for a moment that this river was like other rivers. Instead of water there flowed milk, and instead of pebbles and sand the bottom was of precious stones and pearls. And it ran neither fast nor slow, but both fast and slow together. The river flowed around the castle, and on its banks slept lions with iron teeth and claws; and beyond were gardens such as only the Fairy of the Dawn can have, and on the flowers slept a fairy! All this Petru saw from the other side.

But how was he to get over? To be sure there was a bridge, but even if it had not been guarded by sleeping lions, it was plainly not meant for anyone to walk on. Who could tell what it was made of? It looked like soft little woolly clouds!

So he stood thinking what was to be done, for get across he must. After a while he determined to take the risk, and strode back to the sleeping giant. "Wake up, my brave man!" he cried, giving him a shake.

The giant woke and stretched out his hand to pick up Petru, just as we should catch a fly. But Petru played on his flute, and the giant fell back again. Petru tried this three times, and when he was satisfied that the giant was really in his power, he took out a handkerchief, bound the two little fingers of the giant together, drew his sword, and cried for the fourth time, "Wake up, my brave man."

When the giant saw the trick that had been played on him, he said to Petru, "Do you call this a fair fight? Fight according to rules, if you really are a hero!"

"I will by and by, but first I want to ask you a question! Will you swear that you will carry me over the river if I fight honorably with you?" And the giant swore.

When his hands were freed, the giant flung himself upon Petru, hoping to crush him by his weight. But he had met his match. It was not yesterday, nor the day before, that Petru had fought his first battle, and he bore himself bravely.

For three days and three nights the battle raged, and sometimes one had the upper hand, and sometimes the other, till at length they both lay struggling on the ground, but Petru was on top, with the point of his sword at the giant's throat.

"Let me go! Let me go!" the giant shrieked. "I admit that I am beaten!"

"Will you take me over the river?" asked Petru.

"I will," gasped the giant.

"What shall I do to you if you break your word?"

"Kill me, any way you like! But let me live now."

"Very well," said Petru, and he bound the giant's left hand to his right foot, tied one handkerchief around his mouth to prevent him from crying out, another around his eyes, and led him to the river.

Once they had reached the bank, the giant stretched one leg over to the other side, and catching up Petru in the palm of his hand, set him down on the farther shore.

"Thank you," said Petru. Then he played a few notes on his flute, and the giant went to sleep again. Even the fairies who had been bathing a little lower down heard the music and fell asleep among the flowers on the bank. Petru saw them as he passed, and thought, If they are so beautiful, why should the Fairy of the Dawn be so ugly? But he dared not linger, and pushed on.

And now he was in the wonderful gardens, which seemed more wonderful still than they had done from afar. But Petru could see no faded flowers, nor any birds, as he hastened through them to the castle. No one was there to bar his way, for all were asleep. Even the leaves had ceased to move.

He passed through the courtyard, and entered the castle itself.

What he beheld there need not be told, for all the world knows that the palace of the Fairy of the Dawn is no ordinary place. Gold and precious stones were as common as wood with us, and the stables where the horses of the sun were kept were more splendid than the palace of the greatest emperor in the world.

Petru went up the stairs and walked quickly through forty-eight rooms, hung with silken stuffs, and all empty. In the forty-ninth he found the Fairy of the Dawn herself.

In the middle of this room, which was as large as a church, Petru saw the celebrated well that he had come so far to seek. It was a well just like other wells, and it seemed strange that the Fairy of the Dawn should have it in her own chamber; yet anyone could tell it had been there for hundreds of years. And by the well slept the Fairy of the Dawn — the Fairy of the Dawn — herself!

And as Petru looked at her, the magic flute dropped by his side and he held his breath.

Near the well was a table, on which stood bread made with does' milk, and a bottle of wine. It was the bread of strength and the wine of youth, and Petru longed for them. He looked once at the bread and once at the wine, and then at the Fairy of the Dawn, still sleeping on her silken cushions.

As he looked, a mist came over his senses. The fairy opened her eyes slowly and looked at Petru, who lost his head still further; but he just managed to remember his flute, and a few notes of it sent the Fairy to sleep again, and he kissed her thrice. Then he stooped and laid his golden wreath upon her forehead, ate a piece of the bread, and drank a cupful of the wine of youth, and this he did three times over. Then he filled two flasks with water from the well, and vanished swiftly.

As he passed through the garden, it seemed quite different from what it was before. The flowers were lovelier, the streams ran quicker, the sunbeams shone brighter, and the fairies seemed gayer. And all this had been caused by the three kisses Petru had given the Fairy of the Dawn.

He passed everything safely by, and was soon seated in his saddle again. Faster than the wind, faster than thought, faster than longing, faster than hatred rode Petru. At length he dismounted, and leaving his horses at the roadside, went on foot to the house of Venus.

The goddess Venus knew that he was coming, and went to meet him, bearing with her white bread and red wine.

"Welcome back, my prince," she said.

"Good day, and many thanks," replied the young man, holding out

MORNING-GLORY THE FAIRY OF THE DAWN

one flask containing the magic water. She received it with joy, and after a short rest Petru set forth, for he had no time to lose.

He stopped a few minutes, as he had promised, with the Goddess of Thunder, and was taking a hasty farewell of her, when she called him back.

"Stay, I have a warning to give you," she said. "Beware for your life; make friends with no one; do not ride fast, or let the water go out of your hand; believe no one, and flee flattering tongues. Go and take care, for the way is long, the world is bad, and you hold something very precious. But I will give you this cloth to help you. It is not much to look at, but it is enchanted, and whoever carries it will never be struck by lightning, pierced by a lance, or smitten with a sword, and the arrows will glance off his body."

Petru thanked her and rode off, and taking out his treasure box, inquired how matters were going at home. Not well, it said. The emperor was blind altogether now, and Florea and Costan had begged him to give the government of the kingdom into their hands; but he would not, saying that he did not mean to resign the government till he had washed his eyes with water from the well of the Fairy of the Dawn. Then the brothers had gone to consult old Birscha, who told them that Petru was already on his way home bearing the water. They had set out to meet him, and would try to take the magic water from him, and then claim as their reward the government of the emperor.

"You are lying!" cried Petru angrily, throwing the box on the ground, where it broke into a thousand pieces.

It was not long before he began to catch glimpses of his native land, and he drew rein near a bridge, the better to look at it. He was still gazing, when he heard a sound in the distance as if someone was calling him by his name.

"You, Petru!" it said.

"On! On!" cried the horse. "It will fare ill with you if you stop."

"No, let us stop, and see who and what it is!" answered Petru, turning his horse around, and coming face to face with his two brothers. When Costan and Florea drew near with soft and flattering words, he jumped straight off his horse, and rushed to embrace them. He had a thousand questions to ask, and a thousand things to tell.

"Petru, our dear brother," said Florea at length, "would it not be better if we carried the water for you? Someone might try to take it from you on the road, while no one would suspect us."

"So it would," added Costan. "Florea is right."

But the horse neighed, and Petru knew what it meant. He remembered the Goddess of Thunder's warning, and told his brothers of the cloth she had given him.

At this the brothers understood there was no way to kill Petru, or to get the water from him. And so they left, never to return again, while Petru went home to his father, and washed his eyes with water from the well of the Fairy of the Dawn. The emperor's sight was restored and both of his eyes would laugh together forevermore, for he now knew he had a son who could surely overcome any foe to keep the empire together.

The King Who Wanted to See Paradise

PAKISTAN

Once upon a time there was a king who, one day out hunting, came upon a *fakir*, or holy man, in a lonely place in the mountains. The fakir was seated on a little old bedstead reading the Koran, with his patched cloak thrown over his shoulders.

The king asked him what he was reading; and he said he was reading about Paradise, and praying that he might be worthy to enter there. Then they began to talk, and by and by the king asked the fakir if he could show him a glimpse of Paradise, for he found it very difficult to believe in what he could not see. The fakir replied that he was asking a very difficult, and perhaps a very dangerous, thing; but that he would pray for him, and perhaps he might be able to do it; only he warned the king both against the dangers of his disbelief, and against the curiosity which prompted him to ask this thing. However, the king was not to be turned from his purpose, and he promised the fakir always to provide him with food, if he in return would pray for him. To this the fakir agreed, and so they parted.

Time went on, and the king always sent the old fakir his food according to his promise; but whenever he sent to ask him when he was going to show him Paradise, the fakir always replied, "Not yet, not yet!"

After a year or two had passed by, the king heard one day that the fakir was very ill — indeed, he was believed to be dying. Instantly he hurried off himself, and found that it was really true, and that the fakir was even then breathing his last. There and then the king begged him to remember his promise, and to show him a glimpse of Paradise. The dying fakir replied that if the king would come to his funeral, and when the grave was filled in, and everyone else was gone away, he would come and lay his hand upon the grave, he would keep his word, and show him a glimpse of Paradise. At the same time he implored the king not to do this thing, but to be content to see Paradise when Allah called him there. Still the king's curiosity was so aroused that he would not give way.

Accordingly, after the fakir was dead, and had been buried, the king stayed behind when all the rest went away; and then when he was quite alone, he stepped forward, and laid his hand upon the grave! Instantly the ground opened, and the astonished king, peeping in, saw

NO ONE KNOWS WHAT WAS THERE SHOWN TO THE KING

a flight of rough steps, and at the bottom of them the fakir sitting, just as he used to sit, on his rickety bedstead, reading the Koran!

At first the king was so surprised and frightened that he could only stare; but the fakir beckoned to him to come down, so mustering up his courage, he boldly stepped down into the grave.

The fakir rose, and making a sign to the king to follow, walked a few paces along a dark passage. Then he stopped, turned solemnly to his companion, and with a movement of his hand, drew aside a heavy curtain, and revealed — what? No one knows what was shown there to the king, nor did he ever tell anyone; but when the fakir at length dropped the curtain, and the king turned to leave the place, he had had his glimpse of Paradise! Trembling in every limb, he staggered back along the passage, and stumbled up the steps out of the tomb into the fresh air again.

The dawn was breaking. It seemed odd to the king that he had been so long in the grave. It appeared but a few minutes ago that he had descended, passed along a few steps to the place where he had peeped beyond the veil, and returned again after perhaps five minutes of that wonderful view! And what *was* it he had seen? He racked his brains to remember, but he could not call to mind a single thing! How curious everything looked too! Why, his own city, which by now he was entering, seemed changed and strange to him! The sun was already up when he turned into the palace gate and entered the public durbar hall. It was full; and there upon the throne sat another king! The poor king, all bewildered, sat down and stared about him. Presently a chamberlain came across and asked him why he sat unbidden in the king's presence. "But *I* am the king!" he cried.

"What king?" said the chamberlain.

"The true king of this country," he said indignantly.

Then the chamberlain went away, and spoke to the king who sat on the throne, and the old king heard words like "mad," "age," "pity." Then the king on the throne called him to come forward, and as he went, he caught sight of himself reflected in the polished steel shields of the bodyguard, and started back in horror! He was old, decrepit, dirty, and ragged! His long white beard and locks were unkempt, and

straggled all over his chest and shoulders. Only one sign of royalty remained to him, and that was the signet ring upon his right hand. He dragged it off with shaking fingers and held it up to the king.

"Tell me who I am," he cried. "There is my signet, who once sat where you sit — even yesterday!"

The king looked at him compassionately, and examined the signet with curiosity. Then he commanded, and they brought out dusty records and archives of the kingdom, and old coins of previous reigns, and compared them faithfully. At last the king turned to the old man, and said: "Old man this ring belonged to a king who reigned seven hundred years ago, but he is said to have disappeared, no one knows where. Where did you get the ring?"

Then the old man struck his breast, and cried out with a loud lamentation; for he understood that he, who was not content to wait patiently to see the Paradise of the faithful, had been judged already. And he turned and left the hall without a word, and went into the jungle, where he lived for twenty-five years a life of prayer and meditation, until at last the Angel of Death came to him, and mercifully released him, purged and purified through his punishment.

Ian, the Soldier's Son

SCOTLAND

There dwelt a knight in Grianaig of the land of the West, who had three daughters, and for goodness and beauty they had not their like in all the isles. All the people loved them, and loud was the weeping when one day, as the three maidens sat on the rocks on the edge of the sea dipping their feet in the water, there arose a great beast from under the waves and swept them away beneath the ocean. And none knew where they had gone, or how to find them.

Now there lived in a town a few miles away a soldier who had three sons, fine youths and strong, and the best players at hockey in that country. At Christmastide that year, when families met together and great feasts were held, Ian, the youngest of the three brothers, said:

"Let us have a match at hockey on the lawn of the knight of Grianaig, for his lawn is wider and the grass smoother than ours."

But the others answered:

"No, he is in sorrow and will think of the games that we have played there when his daughters looked on."

"Let him be pleased or angry as he will," said Ian; "we will drive our ball on his lawn today."

And so it was done, and Ian won three games from his brothers. But the knight looked out of his window, and was angered; and had his men bring the youths before him. When he stood in his hall and beheld them, his heart was softened somewhat; but his face was stern as he asked:

"Why did you choose to play hockey in front of my castle when you

knew full well that the remembrance of my daughters would come back to me? The pain that you have made me suffer you shall suffer also."

"Since we have done you wrong," answered Ian the youngest, "build us a ship, and we will go and seek your daughters. Let them be to windward, or to leeward, or under the four brown boundaries of the sea, we will find them before a year and a day goes by, and will carry them back to Grianaig."

In seven days the ship was built, and a great store of food and wine placed in her. And the three brothers put her head to the sea and sailed away, and in seven days the ship ran herself onto a beach of white sand, and they all went ashore. None of them had ever seen that land before, and they looked about them. Then they saw that a short way from them a number of men were working on a rock, with one man standing over them.

"What place is this?" asked the eldest brother. And the man who was standing by answered:

"This is the place where the three daughters of the knight of Grianaig dwell. They are to be wedded tomorrow to three giants."

"How can we find them?" asked the young man again. And the overlooker answered:

"To reach the daughters of the knight of Grianaig you must get into this basket, and be drawn by a rope up the face of this rock."

"Oh, that is easily done," said the eldest brother, jumping into the basket, which at once began to move — up, and up, and up — till he had gone about halfway, when a fat black raven flew at him and pecked him till he was nearly blind, so that he was forced to go back the way he had come.

After that the second brother got into the basket; but he fared no better, for the raven flew upon him, and he returned as his brother had done.

"Now it is my turn," said Ian. But when he was halfway up, the raven set upon him also.

"Quick! Quick!" cried Ian to the men who held the rope. "Quick! Quick! Or I shall be blinded!" And the men pulled with all their

THE KNIGHT AND THE RAVEN

might, and in another moment Ian was on top, and the raven behind him.

"Will you give me a piece of tobacco?" asked the raven, who was now quite quiet.

"You rascal! Am I to give you tobacco for trying to peck my eyes out?" answered Ian.

"That was part of my duty," replied the raven; "but give it to me, and I will prove a good friend to you." So Ian broke off a piece of tobacco and gave it to him. The raven hid it under his wing, and then went on, "Now I will take you to the house of the big giant, where the knight's eldest daughter sits sewing, sewing, till even her thimble is wet with tears." And the raven hopped before him till they reached a large house, the door of which stood open. They entered and passed through one hall after the other, until they found the knight's daughter, as the bird had said.

"What brought you here?" she asked. And Ian answered:

"Why can I not go where you can go?"

"I was brought here by a giant," she replied.

"I know that," said Ian. "But tell me where can I find this giant."

"He is on the hunting hill," she answered; "and nothing will bring him home except a shake of the iron chain that hangs outside the gate. But, there, neither to leeward, nor to windward, nor in the four brown boundaries of the sea, is there any man that can hold battle against him, except Ian, the soldier's son, and he is now but sixteen years old, and how shall he stand against the giant?"

"In the land from which I have come there are many men with the strength of Ian," he answered. And he went outside and pulled at the chain, but he could not move it, and fell onto his knees. At that he rose swiftly, and gathering up his strength, he seized the chain, and this time he shook it so that the link broke. And the giant heard it on the hunting hill, and lifted his head, thinking —

"It sounds like the noise of Ian, the soldier's son," he said; "but he is only sixteen years old. Still, I had better look to it." And home he came.

"Are you Ian, the soldier's son?" he asked as he entered the castle.

"No, surely not," answered the youth, who had no wish that they should know him.

"Then who are you in the leeward, or in the windward, or in the four brown boundaries of the sea, who are able to move my battle chain?"

"That will be plain to you after wrestling with me as I wrestle with my mother. And one time she got the better of me, and two times she did not."

IAN BREAKS THE GIANT'S CHAIN

So they wrestled, and twisted and strove with each other till the giant forced Ian to his knee.

"You are the stronger," said Ian; and the giant answered:

"All men know that!" And they took hold of each other once more, and at last Ian threw the giant, and wished that the raven were there to help him. No sooner had he wished his wish than the raven came.

"Put your hand under my right wing and you will find a knife sharp enough to take off his head," said the raven. And the knife was so sharp that it cut off the giant's head with a blow.

"Now go and tell the daughter of the knight of Grianaig; but do not listen to her words, for she will try to keep you. Instead, seek the middle daughter, and when you have found her, you shall give me a piece of tobacco for reward."

"Well have you earned the half of all I have," answered Ian. But the raven shook his head.

"You know only what has passed, and nothing of what lies before you. If you do not want to fail, wash yourself in clean water, and take balsam from a vessel on top of the door, and rub it over your body, and to-morrow you will be as strong as many men, and I will lead you to the dwelling of the middle one.

Ian did as the raven bade him, and in spite of the eldest daughter's entreaties, he set out to seek her next sister. He found her where she was seated sewing, her very thimble wet from the tears that she had shed.

"What brought you here?" asked the second sister.

"Why can I not go where you can go?" he answered. "And why are you weeping?"

"Because in one day I will be married to the giant who is on the hunting hill."

"How can I get him home?" asked Ian.

"Nothing will bring him but a shake of that iron chain which hangs outside the gate. But there is neither to leeward, nor to windward, nor in the four brown boundaries of the sea, any man that can hold battle with him except Ian, the soldier's son, and he is now but sixteen years of age."

"In the land from which I have come there are many men with the strength of Ian," he said. And he went outside and pulled at the chain, but he could not move it, and fell on his knees. At that he rose to his feet, and gathering up his strength mightily, he seized the chain, and this time he shook it so that three links broke. And the second giant heard it on the hunting hill, and lifted his head:

"It sounds like the noise of Ian, the soldier's son," he said. "But he is only sixteen years old. Still, I had better look to it." And home he came.

"Are you Ian, the soldier's son?" he asked as he entered the castle.

"No, surely not," answered Ian, who had no wish that this giant should know him either; "but I will wrestle with you as if I were he."

Then they seized each other by the shoulder, and the giant threw him on his two knees. "You are the stronger," cried Ian; "but I am not beaten yet." And rising to his feet, he threw his arms around the giant.

Backward and forward they swayed, and first one was uppermost and then the other; but at length Ian worked his leg around the giant's and threw him to the ground. Then he called to the raven, and the raven came flapping toward him, and said, "Put your hand under my right wing, and you will find there a knife sharp enough to take off his head." And sharp indeed it was, for with a single blow, the giant's head rolled from his body.

"Now wash yourself with warm water, and rub yourself over with oil of balsam, and tomorrow you will be as strong as many men. But beware of the words of the knight's daughter, for she is cunning, and will try to keep you at her side. So farewell; but first give me a piece of tobacco."

"That I will gladly," answered Ian, breaking off a large piece.

He washed and rubbed himself that night, as the raven had told him, and the next morning he entered the chamber where the knight's daughter was sitting.

"Stay here with me," she said, "and be my husband. There is silver and gold in plenty in the castle." But he took no heed, and went on his way till he reached the castle where the knight's youngest daughter was sewing in the hall. And tears dropped from her eyes onto her thimble.

"What brought you here?" she asked. And Ian made answer:

"Why can I not go where you can go?"

"I was brought here by a giant."

"I know that full well," he said.

"Are you Ian, the soldier's son?" he was asked again. And this time he answered:

"Yes, I am; but tell me, why you are weeping?"

"Tomorrow the giant will return from the hunting hill, and I must

◇ IAN FINDS THE YOUNGEST SISTER ◇

marry him," she sobbed. And Ian took no heed, and only said, "How can I bring him home?"

"Shake the iron chain that hangs outside the gate."

And Ian went out, and gave such a pull to the chain that he fell down at full length from the force of the shake. But in a moment he was on his feet again, and seized the chain with so much strength that four links came off in his hand. And the giant heard him in the hunting hill, as he was putting the game he had killed into a bag.

"In the leeward, or the windward, or in the four brown boundaries of the sea, there is none who could give my chain a shake except Ian, the soldier's son. And if he has reached me, then he has left my two brothers dead behind him." With that he strode back to the castle, the earth trembling under him as he went.

"Are you Ian, the soldier's son?" he asked. And the youth answered:

"No, surely not."

"Then who are you in the leeward, or the windward, or in the four brown boundaries of the sea, who are able to shake my battle chain? There is only Ian, the soldier's son, who can do this, and he is but now sixteen years old."

"I will show you who I am when you have wrestled with me," said Ian. And they threw their arms around each other, and the giant forced Ian onto his knees; but in a moment he was up again, and crooking his leg around the shoulders of the giant, he threw him heavily to the ground. "Stumpy black raven, come quick!" he cried; and the raven came, and beat the giant about the head with his wings, so that he could not get up. Then the raven told Ian to take the sharp knife from under his right wing and strike off the giant's head with it. And so sharp was that knife that with one blow the giant's head rolled on the ground.

"Rest now this night also," said the raven, "and tomorrow you shall take the knight's three daughters to the edge of the rock that leads to the lower world. But take heed to go down first yourself, and let them follow after you. And before I go you shall give me a piece of tobacco."

"Take it all," answered Ian, "for well have you earned it."

"No; give me but a piece. You know what is behind you, but you have no knowledge of what is before you." And picking up the tobacco in his beak, the raven flew away.

So the next morning the knight's youngest daughter loaded donkeys with all the silver and gold to be found in the castle, and she set out with Ian, the soldier's son, for the house where her second sister was waiting to see what would befall. She also had donkeys laden with precious things to carry away, and so had the eldest sister, when they reached the castle where she had been kept a prisoner. Together they all rode to the edge of the rock, and then Ian lay down and shouted, and the basket was drawn up, and the donkeys got in it one by one, and were let down to the bottom. When the last one was gone, Ian should have gone also, and left the three sisters to come after him; but he had forgotten the raven's warning, and bade them go first, in case some accident should happen. Only, he begged the youngest sister to let him keep the little gold cap, which, like the others, she wore on her head; and then he helped them, each in her turn, into the basket.

Long he waited, but wait as he might, the basket never came back, for in their joy at being free the knight's daughters had forgotten all about Ian, and had set sail in the ship that had brought him and his brothers to the land of Grianaig.

At last he began to understand what had happened to him, and while he was taking counsel with himself what had best be done, the raven came to him.

"You did not heed my words," he said gravely.

"No, I did not, and therefore I am here," answered Ian, bowing his head.

"The past cannot be undone," the raven continued. "He that will not take counsel will take combat. This night, you will sleep in the giant's castle. And now you shall give me a piece of tobacco."

"I will. But I pray you, stay in the castle with me."

"That I may not do, but tomorrow I will come."

And he did, and he told Ian to go to the giant's stable where stood a horse to whom it mattered nothing if she journeyed over land or sea.

"But be careful," he added, "how you enter the stable, for the door swings without ceasing to-and-fro, and if it touches you, it will cause you to cry out. I will go first and show you the way."

"Go," said Ian. And the raven gave a bob and a hop, and thought he was quite safe, but the door slammed on a feather of his tail, and he screamed loudly.

Then Ian took a run backward, and a run forward, and made a spring; but the door caught one of his feet, and he fell fainting on the stable floor. Quickly the raven pounced on him, and picked him up in his beak and claws, and carried him back to the castle, where he laid ointments on his foot till it was as well as it ever was.

"Now come out to walk," said the raven, "but take care that you do not wonder at anything you may behold; nor touch anything. And first give me a piece of tobacco."

Many strange things did Ian behold on that island, more than he had thought for. In a glen lay three heroes stretched on their backs, done to death by three spears that still stuck in their breasts. But he kept his counsel and said nothing, only he pulled out the spears, and the men sat up and said:

"You are Ian, the soldier's son, and a spell is laid upon you to travel in our company, to the cave of the black fisherman."

So together they went till they reached the cave, and one of the men entered to see what should be found there. And he beheld a hag, horrible to look upon, seated on a rock, and before he could speak, she struck him with her club, and changed him into a stone; and in like manner she dealt with the other three. At the last Ian entered.

"These men are under spells," said the witch, "and alive they can never be till you have anointed them with the water that you must fetch from the island of Big Women. See that you do not tarry." And Ian turned away with a sinking heart, for he would rather have followed the youngest daughter of the knight of Grianaig.

"You did not obey my counsel," said the raven, hopping toward him, "and so trouble has come upon you. But sleep now, and tomorrow you shall mount the horse that is in the giant's stable, which can gallop over sea and land. When you reach the island of Big Women, sixteen boys will come to meet you, and will offer the horse food, and wish to take her saddle and bridle from her. But see that they touch her not, and give her food yourself, and yourself lead her into the stable, and shut the door. And be sure that for every turn of the lock given by the sixteen stable lads, you give one. And now you shall break me off a piece of tobacco."

The next morning Ian arose, and led the horse from the stable, without the door hurting him, and he rode her across the sea to the island of Big Women, where the sixteen stable lads met him, and each one offered to take his horse, and to feed her, and to put her into the stable. But Ian only answered:

"I myself will put her in and will see to her." And thus he did. And while he was rubbing her sides, the horse said to him:

"Every kind of drink will they offer you, but see you take none, except whey and water only." And so it fell out; and when the sixteen stable lads saw that he would drink nothing, they drank it all themselves, and one by one lay stretched around the board.

Then Ian felt pleased in his heart that he had withstood their fair words, and he forgot the counsel that the horse had likewise given him saying:

"Beware lest you fall asleep, and let slip the chance of getting home again"; for while the lads were sleeping, sweet music reached his ears, and he slept also.

When this came to pass, the steed broke through the stable door, and kicked him and woke him roughly.

"You did not heed my counsel," she said; "and who knows if it is not too late to win over the sea? But first take the sword that hangs on the wall, and cut off the heads of the sixteen grooms."

Filled with shame at being once more proved heedless, Ian arose and did as the horse bade him. Then he ran to the well and poured some of the water into a leather bottle, and jumping on the horse's back rode over the sea to the island where the raven was waiting for him.

"Lead the horse into the stable," said the raven, "and lie down yourself to sleep, for tomorrow you must bring the heroes to life again, and must slay the hag. And have a care not to be so foolish tomorrow as you were today."

"Stay with me for company," begged Ian; but the raven shook his head, and flew away.

In the morning Ian awoke, and hastened to the cave where the old hag was sitting, and he struck her dead as she was, before she could cast spells on him. Next he sprinkled the water over the heroes, who came to life again, and together they all journeyed to the other side of the island, and there the raven met them.

"At last you have followed the counsel that was given you," said the raven; "and now, having learned wisdom, you may go home again to

Grianaig. There you will find that the knight's two eldest daughters are to be wedded this day to your two brothers, and the youngest to the chief of the men at the rock. But her gold cap you shall give to me, and if you want it, you have only to think of me and I will bring it to you. And one more warning I give you. If anyone asks you where you came from, answer that you have come from behind you; and if anyone asks you where you are going, say that you are going before you."

So Ian mounted the horse and set her face to the sea and her back to the shore, and she was off, away and away till she reached the church of Grianaig, and there in a field of grass, beside a well of water, he leaped down from his saddle.

"Now," the horse said to him, "draw your sword and cut off my head." But Ian answered:

"Poor thanks would that be for all the help I have had from you."

"It is the only way that I can free myself from the spells that were laid by the giants on me and the raven; for I was a girl and he was a youth wooing me! So have no fears, but do as I have said."

Then Ian drew his sword as she bade him, and cut off her head, and went on his way without looking backward. As he walked, he saw a woman standing at her house door. She asked him where he had come from, and he answered as the raven had told him, that he came from behind. Next she inquired where he was going, and this time he made reply that he was going on before him, but that he was thirsty and would like a drink.

"You are an impudent fellow," said the woman; "but you shall have a drink." And she gave him some milk, which was all she had till her husband came home.

"Where is your husband?" asked Ian, and the woman answered him:

"He is at the knight's castle trying to fashion gold and silver into a cap for the youngest daughter, like unto the caps that her sisters wear, such as are not to be found in all this land. But see, he is returning; and now we shall hear how he has sped."

At that the man entered the gate, and beholding a strange youth, he said to him, "What is your trade, boy?"

"I am a blacksmith," replied Ian. And the man answered:

"Good luck has befallen me, then, for you can help me to make a cap for the knight's daughter."

"You cannot make that cap, and you know it," said Ian.

"Well, I must try," replied the man, "or I shall be hanged on a tree; so it would be a good deed to help me."

"I will help you if I can," said Ian; "but keep the gold and silver for yourself, and lock me into the shop tonight, and I will work my spells." So the man, wondering to himself, locked him in.

As soon as the key was turned in the lock, Ian wished for the raven, and the raven came to him, carrying the cap in his mouth.

"Now take my head off," said the raven. But Ian answered:

"Poor thanks were that for all the help you have given me."

"It is the only thanks you can give me," said the raven, "for I was a youth like yourself before spells were laid on me."

Then Ian drew his sword and cut off the head of the raven, and shut his eyes so that he might see nothing. After that he lay down and slept till morning dawned, and the man came and unlocked the door and shook the sleeper.

"Here is the cap," said Ian drowsily, drawing it from under his pillow. And he fell asleep again directly.

The sun was high in the heavens when he woke again, and this time he beheld a tall, brown-haired youth standing by him.

"I am the raven," said the youth, "and the spells are broken. But now get up and come with me."

Then the two went together to the place where Ian had left the dead horse; but no horse was there now, only a beautiful maiden.

"I am the horse," she said, "and the spells are broken"; and she and the youth went away together.

In the meantime the smith had carried the cap to the castle, and bade a servant belonging to the knight's youngest daughter bear it to her mistress. But when the girl's eyes fell on it, she cried out:

"He speaks false; and if he does not bring me the man who really made the cap, I will hang him on the tree beside my window."

The servant was filled with fear at her words, and hastened and told the smith, who ran as fast as he could to seek for Ian. And when he found him and brought him into the castle, the girl was first struck dumb with joy; then she declared that she would marry nobody else. At this someone fetched to her the knight of Grianaig, and when Ian had told his tale, the knight vowed that the maiden was right, and that his elder daughters should never wed with men who had not only taken glory to themselves that did not belong to them, but had left the real doer of the deeds to his fate.

And the wedding guests said that the knight had spoken well; and the two elder brothers were forced to leave the country, for no one would speak to them.

The Elf Maiden

LAPLAND

Once upon a time two young men living in a small village fell in love with the same girl. During the winter it was all night except for an hour or so about noon, when the darkness seemed a little less dark, and then they used to see which of them could tempt her out for a sleigh ride with the Northern Lights flashing above them, or which could persuade her to come to a dance in some neighboring barn. But when the spring began, and the light grew longer, the hearts of the villagers leaped at the sight of the sun, and a day was fixed for the boats to be brought out, and the great nets to be spread in the bays of some islands that lay a few miles to the north. Everybody went on this expedition, and the two young men and the girl went with them.

They all sailed merrily across the sea, chattering like a flock of magpies, or singing their favorite songs. And when they reached the shore, what an unpacking there was! For this was a noted fishing ground, and here they would live, in little wooden huts, till autumn and bad weather came around again.

The maiden and the two young men happened to share the same hut with some friends, and fished daily from the same boat. And as time went on, one of the youths remarked that the girl took less notice of him than she did of his companion. At first he tried to think that he was dreaming, and for a long while he kept his eyes shut very tight to what he did not want to see, but in spite of his efforts, the truth managed to wriggle through, and then the young man gave up trying to deceive himself, and set about finding some way to get the better of his rival.

The plan that he hit upon could not be carried out for some months; but the longer the young man thought of it, the more pleased he was with it, so he made no sign of his feelings, and waited patiently until the moment came. This was the very day that they were all going to leave the islands, and sail back to the mainland for the winter. In the bustle and hurry of departure, the cunning fisherman contrived that their boat should be the last to put off, and when everything was ready, and the sails about to be set, he suddenly called out:

"Oh, dear, what shall I do! I have left my best knife behind in the hut. Run, like a good fellow, and get it for me, while I raise the anchor and loosen the tiller."

Not thinking any harm, the youth jumped back onshore and made his way up the steep bank. At the door of the hut he stopped and looked back, then started and gazed in horror. The head of the boat stood out to sea, and he was left alone on the island.

Yes, there was no doubt of it — he was quite alone; and he had nothing to help him except the knife which his comrade had purposely dropped on the ledge of the window. For some minutes he was too stunned by the treachery of his friend to think about anything at all, but after a while he shook himself awake, and determined that he would manage to keep alive somehow, if it were only to revenge himself.

So he put the knife in his pocket and went off to a part of the island which was not so bare as the rest, and had a small grove of trees. From one of these he cut himself a bow, which he strung with a piece of cord that had been left lying about the huts.

When this was ready, the young man ran down to the shore and shot one or two seabirds, which he plucked and cooked for supper.

In this way the months slipped by, and Christmas came around again. The evening before, the youth went down to the rocks and into the thicket, collecting all the driftwood the sea had washed up or the gale had blown down, and he piled it up in a great stack outside the door, so that he might not have to fetch any all the next day. As soon as his task was done, he paused and looked out toward the mainland, thinking of Christmas Eve last year, and the merry dance they had had. The night was still and cold, and by the help of the Northern Lights he could almost see across to the opposite coast, when suddenly he noticed a boat, which seemed to be steering straight for the island. At first he could hardly stand for joy, the chance of speaking to another man was so delightful; but as the boat drew near, there was something, he could not tell what, that was different from the boats which he had been used to all his life, and when it touched the shore, he saw that the people that filled it were beings of another world than ours. Then he hastily stepped behind the wood stack, and waited for what might happen next.

The strange folk jumped onto the rocks one by one, each bearing a different bundle. Among the women he noticed two young girls, more beautiful and better dressed than any of the rest, carrying between them two great baskets full of provisions. The young man peeped out cautiously to see what all this crowd could be doing inside the tiny hut, but in a moment he drew back again, as the girls returned and looked about as if they wanted to find out what sort of a place the island was.

Their sharp eyes soon discovered the form of a man crouching behind the bundles of sticks, and at first they felt a little frightened, and started as if they would run away. But the youth remained so still, that they took courage and laughed gaily to each other. "What a strange creature, let us see what he is made of," said one, and she stooped down and gave him a pinch.

Now the young man had a pin sticking in the sleeve of his jacket, and the moment the girl's hand touched him she pricked it so sharply that the blood came. The girl screamed so loudly that the people all ran out of their huts to see what was the matter. But as soon as they caught sight of the man, they turned and fled in the other direction, and picking up the goods they had brought with them scampered as fast as they could down to the shore. In an instant, boat, people, and goods had vanished completely.

In their hurry they had, however, forgotten two things: a bundle of keys which lay on the table, and the girl whom the pin had pricked,

'You will have to make me your wife" said the Elf-maiden

and who now stood pale and helpless beside the wood stack.

"You will have to make me your wife," she said at last, "for you have drawn my blood, and I belong to you."

"Why not? I am quite willing," he answered. "But how do you suppose we can manage to live till summer comes around again?"

"Do not be anxious about that," said the girl; "if you will only marry me, all will be well. I am very rich, and all my family are rich also."

Then the young man gave her his promise to make her his wife. The girl fulfilled her part of the bargain, and food was plentiful on the island all through the long winter months, though the young man never knew how it got there. And by and by it was spring once more, and time for the fishing folk to sail from the mainland.

"Where are we to go now?" asked the girl one day, when the sun seemed brighter and the wind softer than usual.

"I do not care where I go," the young man answered. "What do you think?"

The girl replied that she would like to go somewhere right at the other end of the island, and build a house, far away from the huts of the fishing folk. And he agreed, and that very day they set off in search of a sheltered spot on the banks of a stream, so that it would be easy to get water.

In a tiny bay on the opposite side of the island, they found the very thing which seemed to have been made on purpose for them; and as they were tired with their long walk, they laid themselves down on a bank of moss among some birches and prepared to have a good night's rest, so as to be fresh for work the next day. But before she went to sleep, the girl turned to her husband and said, "If in your dreams you fancy that you hear strange noises, be sure you do not stir, or get up to see what it is."

"Oh, it is not likely we shall hear any noises in such a quiet place," he answered, and fell sound asleep.

Suddenly he was awakened by a great clatter about his ears, as if all the workmen in the world were sawing and hammering and building close to him. He was just going to spring up and go to see what it meant, when luckily he remembered his wife's words and lay still. But the time until morning seemed very long, and with the first ray of sun they both rose, and pushed aside the branches of the birch trees. There, in the very place they had chosen, stood a beautiful house — doors and windows, and everything all complete!

"Now you must choose a spot for your cow stalls," said the girl when they had breakfasted off wild cherries; "and take care it is the proper size, neither too large nor too small." And the husband did as he was bid, though he wondered what use a cowhouse could be, as they had no cows to put in it. But as he was a little afraid of his wife, who knew so much more than he, he asked no questions.

This night also he was awakened by the same sounds as before, and in the morning they found, near the stream, the most beautiful cowhouse that ever was seen, with stalls and milk pails and stools all complete; indeed, everything that a cowhouse could possibly want, except the cows. Then the girl bade him measure out the ground for a storehouse, and this, she said, might be as large as he pleased; and when the storehouse was ready she proposed that they should set off to pay her parents a visit.

The old people welcomed them heartily, and summoned their neighbors for many miles around to a great feast in their honor. In fact, for several weeks there was no work done on the farm at all; and at length the young man and his wife grew tired of so much play, and declared that they must return to their own home. But before they started on the journey, the wife whispered to her husband, "Take care to jump over the threshold as quick as you can, or it will be the worse for you."

The young man listened to her words, and sprang over the threshold like an arrow from a bow; and it was well he did, for no sooner was he on the other side, than his father-in-law threw a great hammer at him, which would have broken both his legs, if it had only touched them.

When they had gone some distance on the road home, the girl turned to her husband and said: "Till you step inside the house, be sure you do not look back, whatever you may hear or see."

And the husband promised, and for a while all was still; and he thought no more about the matter till he noticed at last that the nearer

THE ELF MAIDEN'S HOUSE

he drew to the house the louder grew the noise of the trampling of feet behind him. As he laid his hand upon the door he thought he was safe, and turned to look. There, sure enough, was a vast herd of cattle, which had been sent after him by his father-in-law when he found that his daughter had been cleverer than he. Half of the herd was already through the fence and cropping the grass on the banks of the stream, but half still remained outside and faded into nothing, even as he watched them.

However, enough cattle were left to make the young man rich, and he and his wife lived happily together, except that every now and then the girl vanished from his sight, and never told him where she had been. For a long time he kept silence about it; but one day when he had been complaining of her absence, she said to him, "Dear husband, I am bound to go, even against my will, and there is only one way to stop me. Drive a nail into the threshold, and then I can never pass in or out."

And so he did.

The Girl With the Wooden Helmet

JAPAN

In a little village in the country of Japan there lived long, long ago a man and his wife. For many years they were happy and prosperous, but bad times came, and at last nothing was left them but their daughter, who was as beautiful as the morning. The neighbors were very kind, and would have done anything they could to help their poor friends, but the old couple felt that since everything had changed, they would rather go elsewhere. So one day they set off to bury themselves in the country, taking their daughter with them.

Now the mother and daughter had plenty to do in keeping the house clean and looking after the garden, but the man would sit for hours at a time gazing straight in front of him, and thinking of the riches that once were his. Each day he grew more and more wretched, till at length he took to his bed and never got up again.

His wife and daughter wept bitterly for his loss, and it was many months before they could take pleasure in anything. Then one morning the mother suddenly looked at the girl, and found that she had grown still more lovely than before. Once her heart would have been glad at the sight, but now that they were alone in the world, she feared some harm might come of it. So, like a good mother, she tried to teach her daughter all she knew, and to bring her up to be always busy, so that she would never have time to think about herself. And the girl was a good girl, and listened to all her mother's lessons, and so the years passed away.

At last one wet spring the mother caught cold, and though in the beginning she did not pay much attention to it, she gradually grew more and more ill, and knew that she had not long to live. Then she called her daughter and told her that very soon she would be alone in the world; that she must take care of herself, as there would be no one to take care of her. And because it was more difficult for beautiful women to pass unheeded than for others, she bade her fetch a wooden helmet out of the next room, and put it on her head, and pull it low down over her brows, so that nearly the whole of her face should lie in its shadow. The girl did as she was bid, and her beauty was so hidden beneath the wooden cap, which covered up all her hair, that she might have gone through any crowd, and no one would have looked twice at her. And when she saw this, the heart of the mother was at rest, and she lay back in her bed and died.

The girl wept for many days, but by and by she felt that, being alone in the world, she must go and get work, for she had only herself to depend upon. There was none to be got by staying where she was, so she made her clothes into a bundle, and walked over the hills till she reached the house of the man who owned the fields in that part of the country. And she took service with him and labored for him early and late, and every night when she went to bed she was at peace, for she had not forgotten one thing that she had promised her mother; and however hot the sun might be, she always kept the wooden helmet on her head, and the people gave her the nickname of Hatsu Hime.

In spite of all her care, however, the fame of her beauty spread abroad. Many of the impudent young men that are always to be found in the world stole softly up behind her while she was at work, and tried to lift off the wooden helmet. But the girl would have nothing to say to them, and only bade them be off; then they began to talk to her, but she never answered them, and went on with what she was doing. Though her wages were low and food not very plentiful, she could still manage to live, and that was enough.

One day her master happened to pass through the field where she was working, and was struck by her industry and stopped to watch her. After a while he put one or two questions to her, then led her into his house, and told her that henceforward her only duty should be to tend

THE IMPVDENT YOVNG MEN

his sick wife. From this time the girl felt as if all her troubles were ended, but the worst of them was yet to come.

Not very long after Hatsu Hime had become maid to the sick woman, the eldest son of the house returned home from Kyoto, where he had been studying all sorts of things. He was tired of the splendors of the town and its pleasures, and was glad enough to be back in the green country, among the peach-blossoms and sweet flowers. Strolling about in the early morning, he caught sight of the girl with the odd wooden helmet on her head, and immediately he went to his mother to ask who she was, and where she came from, and why she wore that strange thing over her face. His mother answered that it was a whim, and nobody could persuade her to lay it aside; at this the young man laughed, but kept his thoughts to himself.

One hot day, however, he happened to be going toward home when he caught sight of his mother's waiting-maid kneeling by a little stream that flowed through the garden, splashing some water over her face. The helmet was pushed on one side, and as the youth stood watching from behind a tree, he had a glimpse of the girl's great beauty; and he determined that no one else should be his wife. When he told his family of his resolve to marry her, they were very angry and made up all sorts of wicked stories about her. However, they might have spared themselves the trouble, as he knew it was only idle talk. I have merely to remain firm, he thought, and they will have to give in.

It was such a good match for the girl that it never occurred to anyone that she would refuse the young man, but so it was. It would not be right, she felt, to make a quarrel in the house, and though in secret she wept bitterly for a long while, nothing would make her change her mind. At length one night her mother appeared to her in a dream, and bade her marry the young man. So the next time he asked her — as he did nearly every day — to his surprise and joy she consented. The parents then saw they had better make the best of a bad business, and set about making the grand preparations suitable to the occasion. Of course the neighbors said a great many ill-natured things about the wooden helmet, but the bridegroom was too happy to care, and only laughed at them.

When everything was ready for the feast, and the bride was dressed in the most beautiful embroidered dress to be found in Japan, the maids took hold of the helmet to lift it off her head, so that they might do her hair in the latest fashion. But the helmet would not come, and the harder they pulled, the faster it seemed to be, till the poor girl yelled with pain. Hearing her cries, the bridegroom ran in and soothed her, and declared that she should be married in the helmet, as she could not be married without. Then the ceremonies began, and the bridal pair sat together, and the cup of wine was brought them, out of which they had to drink. And when they had drunk it all, and the cup was empty, a wonderful thing happened. The helmet suddenly burst with a loud noise, and fell in pieces on the ground; and as they all turned to look, they found the floor covered with precious stones that had fallen out of it. But the guests were less astonished at the brilliancy of the diamonds than at the beauty of the bride, which was beyond anything they had ever seen or heard of. The night was passed in singing and dancing, and then the bride and bridegroom went to their own house, where they lived till they died, and had many children, who were famous throughout Japan for their goodness and beauty.

THE GIRL WITH THE WOODEN HELMET

The Enchanted Wreath

SWEDEN

Once upon a time there lived near a forest a man and his wife and two girls; one girl was the daughter of the man, and the other the daughter of his wife; and the man's daughter was good and beautiful, but the woman's daughter was cross and ugly. However, her mother did not know that, but thought her the most bewitching maiden that ever was seen.

One day the man called to his daughter and told her to come with him into the forest to cut wood. They worked hard all day, but in spite of the chopping they were very cold, for it rained heavily, and when they returned home, they were wet through. Then, to his vexation, the man found that he had left his axe behind him, and he knew that if it lay all night in the mud, it would become rusty and useless. So he said to his wife:

"I have dropped my axe in the forest. Tell your daughter to go and fetch it, for mine has worked hard all day and is both wet and weary."

But the wife answered:

"If your daughter is wet already, it is all the more reason that *she* should go and get the axe. Besides, she is a great strong girl, and a little rain will not hurt her, while *my* daughter would be sure to catch a bad cold."

By long experience the man knew there was no good saying any more, and with a sigh he told the poor girl she must return to the forest for the axe.

The walk took some time, for it was very dark, and her shoes often stuck in the mud; but she was brave as well as beautiful and never thought of turning back merely because the path was both difficult and unpleasant. At last, with her dress torn by brambles that she could not see, and her face scratched by the twigs on the trees, she reached the spot where she and her father had been cutting in the morning, and found the axe in the place he had left it. To her surprise three little doves were sitting on the handle, all of them looking very sad.

"You poor little things," said the girl, stroking them, "why do you sit there and get wet? Go and fly home to your nest, it will be much warmer than this; but first eat this bread, which I saved from my dinner, and perhaps you will feel happier. It is my father's axe you are sitting on, and I must take it back as fast as I can, or I shall get a terrible scolding from my stepmother." She then crumbled the bread on the ground, and was pleased to see the doves flutter quite cheerfully toward it.

"Good-bye," she said, picking up the axe, and went her way homeward.

By the time they had finished all the crumbs, the doves felt much better, and were able to fly back to their nest in the top of a tree.

"That is a good girl," said one; "I really was too weak to stretch out a wing before she came. I should like to do something to show how grateful I am."

"Well, let us give her a wreath of flowers that will never fade as long as she wears it," cried another.

"And let the tiniest singing birds in the world sit among the flowers," rejoined the third.

"Yes, that will do beautifully," said the first. And when the girl stepped into her cottage, a wreath of rosebuds was on her head and a crowd of little birds were singing unseen.

The father, who was sitting by the fire, thought that in spite of her muddy clothes, he had never seen his daughter looking so lovely; but the stepmother and the other girl grew wild with envy.

"How absurd to walk about on such a pouring night, dressed up like that," the stepmother remarked crossly, and roughly pulled off the wreath as she spoke, to place it on her own daughter. As she did so, the roses became withered and brown, and the birds flew out of the window.

"See what a useless thing it is!" cried the stepmother; "and now take your supper and go to bed, for it is near upon midnight."

But though she pretended to despise the wreath, she longed none-theless for her daughter to have one like it.

Now it happened that the next evening the father, who had been alone in the forest, came back a second time without his axe. The stepmother's heart was glad when she saw this, and she said quite mildly:

"Why, you have forgotten your axe again, you careless man! But now *your* daughter shall stay at home, and *mine* shall go and bring it back." Throwing a cloak over the girl's shoulders, she told her to hasten to the forest.

With a very ill grace the girl set forth, grumbling to herself as she went; for though she wished for the wreath, she did not at all want the trouble of getting it.

By the time she reached the spot where her stepfather had been cutting the wood, the girl was in a very bad temper indeed, and when she caught sight of the axe, there were the three little doves, with drooping heads and soiled, bedraggled feathers, sitting on the handle.

"You dirty creatures," she cried, "get away at once, or I will throw stones at you." And the doves spread their wings in a fright and flew up to the very top of a tree, their bodies shaking with anger.

"What shall we do to revenge ourselves on her?" asked the smallest of the doves. "We were never treated like that before."

"Never," said the biggest dove. "We must find some way of paying her back in her own coin!"

"*I* know," answered the middle dove. "She shall never be able to say anything but 'dirty creatures' until the end of her life."

"Oh, how clever of you! That will do beautifully," exclaimed the other two. And they flapped their wings and clucked so loud with delight, and made such a noise, that they woke up all the birds in the trees close by.

"What in the world is the matter?" asked the birds sleepily.

"That is *our* secret," said the doves.

Meanwhile the girl had reached home crosser than ever; but as soon as her mother heard her lift the latch of the door, she ran out to hear her adventures. "Well, did you get the wreath?" she cried.

"Dirty creatures!" answered her daughter.

"Don't speak to me like that! What do you mean?" asked the mother again.

"Dirty creatures!" repeated the daughter, and she could say nothing else.

Then the woman saw that something evil had befallen her, and turned in her rage to her stepdaughter.

"*You* are at the bottom of this, I know," she cried; and since the father was out of the way, she took a stick and beat the girl till she screamed with pain and went to bed sobbing.

If the poor girl's life had been miserable before, it was ten times worse now, for the moment her father's back was turned the others teased and tormented her from morning till night; and their fury was increased by the sight of the wreath, which the doves had placed again on her head.

Things went on like this for some weeks, when one day as the king's son was riding through the forest, he heard some strange birds singing more sweetly than birds had ever sung before. He tied his horse to a tree, and followed where the sound led him, and to his surprise he saw before him a beautiful girl chopping wood, with a wreath of pink rosebuds, out of which the singing came. Standing in the shelter of a tree, he watched her a long while, and then, hat in hand, he went up and spoke to her.

"Fair maiden, who are you, and who gave you that wreath of singing roses?" he asked, for the birds were so tiny that until you looked closely you never saw them.

"I live in a hut on the edge of the forest," she answered, blushing, for she had never spoken to a prince before. "And as to the wreath, I know not how it came there, unless it may be the gift of some doves whom I fed when they were starving." The prince was delighted with this answer, which showed the goodness of the girl's heart, and besides he had fallen in love with her beauty, and would not be content until she promised to return with him to the palace, and become his bride. The old king was naturally disappointed at his son's choice of a wife, as he wished him to marry a neighboring princess; but as from his birth the prince had always done exactly as he liked, nothing was said and a splendid wedding feast was prepared.

The day after her marriage the bride sent a messenger, bearing handsome presents to her father, and telling him of the good fortune that had befallen her. As may be imagined, the stepmother and her daughter were so filled with envy that they grew quite ill, and had to take to their beds, and nobody would have been sorry if they had never got up again; but that did not happen. At length, however, they began to feel better, for the mother invented a plan by which she could be revenged on the girl who had never done her any harm.

Her plan was this: In the town where she had lived before she was married, there was an old witch who had more skill in magic than any other witch she knew. To this witch she would go and beg her to make her a mask with the face of her stepdaughter. When she had the mask, the rest would be easy. She told her daughter what she meant to do, and although the daughter could only say "dirty creatures" in answer, she nodded and smiled and looked well pleased.

Everything worked out exactly as the woman had hoped. By the aid of her magic mirror the witch beheld the new princess walking in her gardens in a dress of green silk, and in a few minutes had produced a mask so like her that very few people could have told the difference. However, she counseled the woman that when her daughter first wore it — for that, of course, was what she intended her to do — she had better pretend that she had a toothache, and cover her head with a lace veil. The woman thanked her and paid her well, and returned to her hut, carrying the mask with her under her cloak.

In a few days she heard that a great hunt was planned, and the prince would leave the palace very early in the morning, so his wife would be alone all day. This was a chance not to be missed, and taking her daughter with her she went up to the palace, where she had never been before. The princess was too happy in her new home to remember all that she had suffered in the old one, and she welcomed them both gladly, and gave them quantities of beautiful things to take back with them. At last she took them down to the shore to see a pleasure boat that her husband had had made for her; and here, the woman, seizing her opportunity, stole softly behind the girl and pushed her off the rock on which she was standing, into the deep water where she instantly sank to the bottom. Then she fastened the mask on her daughter, flung over her shoulders the velvet cloak that the princess had let fall, and finally arranged a lace veil over her head.

"Rest your cheek on your hand, as if you were in pain, when the prince returns," said the mother; "and be careful not to speak, whatever you do. I will go back to the witch and see if she cannot take off the spell laid on you by those horrible birds. Ah! why did I not think of that before!"

No sooner had the prince entered the palace than he hastened to the princess's apartments, where he found her lying on the sofa apparently in great pain.

The Stepmother tries to drown the Princess

"My dearest wife, what is the matter with you?" he cried, kneeling down beside her, and trying to take her hand; but she snatched it away, and pointing to her cheek murmured something he could not catch.

"What is it? Tell me! Is the pain bad? When did it begin? Shall I send for your ladies to bathe the place?" asked the prince, pouring out these and a dozen other questions, to which the girl only shook her head.

"But I can't leave you like this," he continued, starting up. "I must summon all the court physicians to apply soothing balsams to the sore place." And as he spoke, he sprang to his feet to go in search of them. This so frightened the pretended wife, who knew that if the physicians came near her the trick would at once be discovered, that she forgot her mother's counsel not to speak, and forgot even the spell that had been laid upon her, and catching hold of the prince's tunic, she cried in tones of entreaty, "Dirty creatures!"

The young man stopped, not able to believe his ears, but supposed that pain had made the princess cross, as it sometimes does. However, he guessed somehow that she wished to be left alone, so he only said:

"Well, I dare say a little sleep will do you good, if you can manage to get it, and that you will wake up better tomorrow."

Now, that night happened to be very hot and airless, and the prince, after vainly trying to rest, at length got up and went to the window. Suddenly he beheld in the moonlight a form with a wreath of

THE PRINCESS RETURNS FROM THE SEA

roses on her head rise out of the sea below him and step onto the sands, holding out her arms as she did so toward the palace.

That maiden is strangely like my wife, he thought; I must see her closer. And he hastened down to the water. But when he got there, the princess — for indeed it was she — had disappeared completely, and he began to wonder if his eyes had deceived him.

The next morning he went to the false bride's room, but her ladies told him she would neither speak nor get up, though she ate everything they set before her. The prince was sorely perplexed as to what could be the matter with her, for naturally he could not guess that she was expecting her mother to return every moment, and to remove the spell the doves had laid upon her, and meanwhile was afraid to speak lest she should betray herself. At length he made up his mind to summon all the court physicians; he did not tell her what he was going to do, lest it should make her worse, but he went himself and begged the four learned leeches attached to the king's person to follow him to the princess's apartments. Unfortunately, as they entered, the princess was so enraged at the sight of them that she forgot all about the doves, and shrieked out, "Dirty creatures! Dirty creatures!" which so offended the physicians that they left the room at once, and nothing that the prince could say would prevail on them to remain. He then tried to persuade his wife to send them a message that she was sorry for her rudeness, but not a word would she say.

Late that evening when he had performed all the tiresome duties that fall to the lot of every prince, the young man was leaning out of his window, refreshing himself with the cool breezes that blew off the sea. His thoughts went back to the scene of the morning, and he wondered if, after all, he had not made a great mistake in marrying a lowborn wife, however beautiful she might be. How could he have imagined that the quiet, gentle girl who had been so charming a companion to him during the first days of their marriage could have become in a day the rude, sulky woman who could not control her temper even to benefit herself. One thing was clear, if she did not change her conduct very shortly, he would have to send her away from court.

He was thinking these thoughts, when his eyes fell on the sea beneath him, and there, as before, was the figure that so closely resembled his wife, standing with her feet in the water, holding out her arms to him.

"Wait for me! Wait for me! Wait for me!" he cried; not even knowing he was speaking. But when he reached the shore, there was nothing to be seen but the shadows cast by the moonlight.

A state ceremonial in a city some distance off caused the prince to ride away at daybreak, and he left without seeing his wife again.

"Perhaps she may have come to her senses by tomorrow," he said to himself; "and, anyhow, if I am going to send her back to her father, it might be better if we did not meet in the meantime." Then he put the matter from his mind, and kept his thoughts on the duty that lay before him.

It was nearly midnight before he returned to the palace, but instead of entering, he went down to the shore and hid behind a rock. He had scarcely done so, when the girl came out of the sea and stretched out her arms toward his window. In an instant the prince had seized her hand and though she made a frightened struggle to reach the water — for she in her turn had had a spell laid upon her — he held her fast.

"You are my own wife, and I shall never let you go," he said. But the words were hardly out of his mouth when he found that it was a hare that he was holding by the paw. Then the hare changed into a fish, and the fish into a bird, and the bird into a slimy wriggling snake. This time the prince's hand nearly opened of itself, but with a strong effort he kept his fingers shut, and drawing his sword cut off its head, which broke the spell and the girl stood before him as he had seen her first, the wreath upon her head and the birds singing for joy.

The very next morning the stepmother arrived at the palace with an ointment that the old witch had given her to place upon her daughter's tongue, which would break the dove's spell if the rightful bride had really been drowned in the sea; if not, then it would be useless. The mother assured her that she had seen her stepdaughter sink, and that there was no fear that she would ever come up again; but to make all quite safe, the old woman might bewitch the girl; and so she did.

After that the wicked stepmother traveled all through the night to get to the palace as soon as possible, and made her way straight into her daughter's room.

"I have got it! I have got it!" she cried triumphantly, and laid the ointment on her daughter's tongue.

"*Now* what do you say?" she asked proudly.

"Dirty creatures! Dirty creatures!" answered the daughter; and the mother wrung her hands and wept, as she knew that all her plans had failed.

At this moment the prince entered with his real wife. "You both deserve death," he said, "and if it were left to me, you should have it. But the princess has begged me to spare your lives, so you will be put into a ship and carried off to a desert island, where you will stay till you die."

Then the ship was made ready and the wicked woman and her daughter were placed in it, and it sailed away, and no more was heard of them. But the prince and his wife lived together long and happily, and ruled their people well.

The Boy Who Found Fear at Last

TURKEY

Once upon a time there lived a woman who had one son whom she loved dearly. The little cottage in which they dwelt was built on the outskirts of a forest, and because they had no neighbors, the place was very lonely, and the boy stayed at home with his mother to keep her company.

They were sitting together on a winter's evening when a storm suddenly sprang up, and the wind blew the door open. The woman started and shivered, and glanced over her shoulder as if she half expected to see some horrible thing behind her. "Go and shut the door," she said hastily to her son. "I feel frightened."

"Frightened?" repeated the boy. "What does it feel like to be frightened?"

"Well — just frightened," answered the mother. "A fear of something, you hardly know what, takes hold of you."

"It must be very odd to feel like that," replied the boy. "I will go through the world and seek fear until I find it." And the next morning before his mother was out of bed, he had left the forest behind him.

After walking for some hours he reached a mountain, which he began to climb. Near the top, in a wild and rocky spot, he came upon a band of fierce robbers sitting around a fire. The boy, who was cold and tired, was delighted to see the bright flames, so he went up to them and said, "Good greeting to you, sirs," and wriggled himself in between the men, until his feet almost touched the burning logs.

The robbers stopped drinking and eyed him curiously, and at last the captain spoke:

"No caravan of armed men would dare to come here, even the very birds shun our camp, and who are you to venture in so boldly?"

"Oh, I have left my mother's house in search of fear. Perhaps you can show it to me?"

"Fear is wherever *we* are," answered the captain.

"But *where*?" asked the boy, looking around. "I see nothing."

"Take this pot and some flour and butter and sugar over to the churchyard that lies down there, and bake us a cake for supper," replied the robber. And the boy, who was by this time quite warm, jumped up cheerfully, and slinging the pot over his arm, ran down the hill.

When he got to the churchyard, he collected some sticks and made a fire; then he filled the pot with water from a little stream close by, and mixing the flour and butter and sugar together, he set the cake on to cook. It was not long before it grew crisp and brown, and then the boy lifted it from the pot and placed it on a stone while he put out the fire. At that moment a hand stretched out from a grave, and a voice said:

"Is that cake for me?"

"Do you think I am going to give to the dead the food of the living?" replied the boy with a laugh. And giving the hand a tap with his spoon, and picking up the cake, he went up the mountainside, whistling merrily.

"Well, have you found fear?" asked the robbers when he held out the cake to the captain.

"No; was it there?" answered the boy. "I saw nothing but a hand that came from a grave, and belonged to someone who wanted my cake, but I just rapped the fingers with my spoon, and said it was not for him, and then the hand vanished. Oh, how nice the fire is!" And he flung himself on his knees before it, and so did not notice the glances of surprise cast by the robbers at each other.

"There is another chance for you," said one at length. "On the other side of the mountain lies a deep pool; go to that, and perhaps you may meet fear on the way."

"I hope so, indeed," answered the boy. And he set out at once.

He soon beheld the waters of the pool gleaming in the moonlight, and as he drew near, he saw a tall swing standing just over it, and in the swing a child was seated, weeping bitterly.

That is a strange place for a swing, thought the boy; but I wonder what he is crying about. And he was hurrying on toward the child, when a maiden ran up and spoke to him.

"I want to lift my little brother from the swing," she cried, "but it is so high above me that I cannot reach. If you will get closer to the edge of the pool, and let me mount on your shoulder, I think I can reach him."

"Willingly," replied the boy, and in an instant the girl had climbed to his shoulders. But instead of lifting the child from the swing as she could easily have done, she pressed her feet so firmly on each side of the youth's neck that he felt that in another minute he would be choked, or else fall into the water beneath him. So, gathering up all his strength, he gave a mighty heave, and threw the girl backward. As she touched the ground, a bracelet fell from her arm, and this the youth picked up.

"I may as well keep it as a remembrance of all the strange things that have happened to me since I left home," he said to himself, and turning to look for the child, he saw that both it and the swing had vanished, and that the first streaks of dawn were in the sky.

With the bracelet on his arm the youth started for a little town that was situated in the plain on the far side of the mountain, and as he entered its principal street, hungry and thirsty, a merchant stopped him. "Where did you get that bracelet?" asked the merchant. "It belongs to me."

"No, it is mine," replied the boy.

"It is not. Give it to me at once, or it will be the worse for you!" cried the merchant.

"Let us go before a judge, and tell him our stories," said the boy. "If he decides in your favor, you shall have it; if in mine, I will keep it!"

To this the merchant agreed, and the two went together to the great hall, in which the *kadi* was administering justice. He listened very

THE SEA-MAIDEN WITH A WICKED FACE !!

THE BOY SECURES THE BRACELET

carefully to what each had to say, and then pronounced his verdict. Neither of the two claimants had proved his right to the bracelet, therefore it must remain in the possession of the judge until its match was brought before him.

When they heard this, the merchant and the boy looked at each other, and their eyes said, "Where are we to go to find the other one?" But as they knew there was no use in disputing the decision, they bowed low and left the hall of audience.

Wandering he knew not where, the youth found himself on the seashore. At a little distance was a ship that had struck on a hidden rock, and was rapidly sinking, while on deck the crew were gathered with faces white as death, shrieking and wringing their hands.

"Have you met with fear?" shouted the boy. And the answer came above the noise of the waves.

"Oh, help! Help! We are drowning!"

Then the boy flung off his clothes, and swam to the ship, where many hands were held out to draw him on board.

"The ship is tossed here and there, and will soon be sucked down," cried the crew again. "Death is very near, and we are frightened!"

"Give me a rope," said the boy in reply, and he took it, and made it safe around his body at one end, and to the mast at the other, and sprang into the sea. Down he went, down, down, down until at last his feet touched the bottom, and he stood up and looked around him. There, sure enough, a sea-maiden with a wicked face was tugging hard at a chain that she had fastened to the ship with a grappling iron, and was dragging it little by little beneath the waves. Seizing her arms in both his hands, he forced her to drop the chain, and with the ship above remaining steady now, the sailors were able gently to float her off the rock. Then taking a rusty knife from a heap of seaweed at his feet, he cut the rope around his waist and fastened the sea-maiden firmly to a stone, so that she could do no more mischief, and bidding her farewell, he swam back to the beach where his clothes were still lying.

The youth dressed himself quickly and walked on, until he came to a beautiful shady garden filled with flowers and a clear little stream running through. The day was hot, and he was tired, so he entered the gate, and seated himself under a clump of bushes covered with sweet-smelling red blossoms, and it was not long before he fell asleep. Suddenly a rush of wings and a cool breeze awakened him, and raising his head cautiously, he saw three doves plunging into the stream. They splashed around joyfully, and shook themselves, and then dived to the bottom of a deep pool. When they appeared again, they were no longer three doves, but three beautiful damsels, bearing between them a table made of mother-of-pearl. On this they placed drinking cups fashioned from pink and green shells, and one of the maidens filled a cup from a crystal goblet, and was raising it to her mouth, when her sister stopped her.

"To whose health do you drink?" she asked.

"To the youth who prepared the cake, and rapped my hand with the spoon when I stretched it out of the earth," answered the maiden, "and was never afraid as other men were! But to whose health do you drink?"

"To the youth on whose shoulders I climbed at the edge of the pool, and who threw me off with such a jerk that I lay unconscious on the ground for hours," replied the second. "But you, my sister," she added, turning to the third girl, "to whom do you drink?"

"Down in the sea I took hold of a ship and shook it and pulled it until it would soon have been lost," she said. And as she spoke, she looked quite different from what she had done with the chain in her hands, seeking to work mischief. "But a youth came, and freed the ship and bound me to a rock. To his health I drink," and they all three lifted their cups and drank silently.

As they put their cups down, the youth appeared before them.

"Here am I, the youth whose health you have drunk; and now give me the bracelet that matches a jeweled band that surely fell from the arm of one of you. A merchant tried to take it from me, but I would not let him have it, and he dragged me before the kadi, who kept my bracelet until I could show him its match. And I have been wandering here and there in search of it, and that is how I have found myself in such strange places."

"Come with us, then," said the maidens, and they led him down a passage into a hall, out of which opened many chambers, each one of greater splendor than the last. From a shelf heaped up with gold and jewels the eldest sister took a bracelet, which in every way was exactly like the one that was in the judge's keeping, and fastened it to the youth's arm.

"Go at once and show this to the kadi," she said, "and he will give you the match to it."

"I shall never forget you," answered the youth, "but it may be long before we meet again, for I shall never rest until I have found fear." Then he went his way, and won the bracelet from the kadi. After this he again set forth in his quest of fear.

On and on the youth walked, but fear never crossed his path, and one day he entered a large town where all the streets and squares were so full of people, he could hardly pass between them.

"Why are all these crowds gathered together?" he asked of a man who stood next to him.

"The ruler of this country is dead," was the reply, "and as he had no children, it is needful to choose a successor. Therefore each morning one of the sacred pigeons is let loose from the tower yonder, and on whomsoever the bird shall perch, that man is our king. In a few minutes the pigeon will fly. Wait and see what happens."

Every eye was fixed on the tall tower that stood in the center of the chief square, and the moment that the sun was seen to stand straight over it, a door was opened and a beautiful pigeon, gleaming with pink and gray, blue and green, came rushing through the air. Onward it flew, onward, onward, until at length it rested on the head of the boy. Then a great shout arose:

"The king! The king!" But as he listened to the cries, a vision swifter than lightning flashed across his brain. He saw himself seated on a throne, spending his life trying, and never succeeding, to make poor people rich; miserable people happy; bad people good; never doing anything he wished to do, not able even to marry the girl that he loved.

"No! No!" he shrieked, hiding his face in his hands; but the crowds who heard him thought he was overcome by the grandeur that awaited him, and paid no heed.

"Well, to make quite sure, let fly more pigeons," they said, but each pigeon followed where the first had led, and the cries arose louder than ever:

"The king! The king!" And as the young man heard, a cold shiver that he knew not the meaning of, ran through him.

"This is fear, that you have searched for so long," whispered a voice, which seemed to reach his ears alone. And the youth bowed his head as the vision once more flashed before his eyes, and he accepted his doom, and made ready to pass his life with fear beside him.

The Magic Book

DENMARK

There was once an old couple named Peder and Kirsten who had an only son called Hans. From the time he was a little boy he had been told that on his sixteenth birthday he must go out into the world and serve his apprenticeship. So one fine summer morning he started off to seek his fortune with nothing but the clothes he wore on his back.

For many hours he traipsed on merrily, now and then stopping to drink from some clear spring or to pick some ripe fruit from a tree. The little wild creatures peeped at him from beneath the bushes, and he nodded and smiled, and wished them "Good morning." After he had been walking for some time, he met an old white-bearded man who was coming along the footpath. The boy would not step aside, and the man was determined not to do so either, so they ran up against one another with a bump.

"It seems to me," said the old fellow, "that a boy should give way to an old man."

"The path is for me as well as for you," answered young Hans saucily, for he had never been taught politeness.

"Well, that's true enough," answered the other mildly. "And where are you going?"

"I am going into service," said Hans.

"Then you can come and serve me," replied the man.

Well, Hans could do that; but what would his wages be?

"Four coins a year, and nothing to do but keep some rooms clean," said the newcomer.

This seemed to Hans to be easy enough; so he agreed to enter the old man's service, and they set out together. On their way they crossed a deep valley and came to a mountain, where the man opened a trap-door, and bidding Hans follow him, he crept in and began to go down a long flight of steps. When they got to the bottom, Hans saw a large number of rooms lit by many lamps and full of beautiful things. While he was looking around, the old man said to him:

"Now you know what you have to do. You must keep these rooms clean, and strew sand on the floor every day. Here is a table where you will always find food and drink, and there is your bed. You see there are a great many suits of clothes hanging on the wall, and you may wear any you please; but remember that you are never to open this locked door. If you do, ill will befall you. Farewell, for I am going away again and cannot tell when I may return."

No sooner had the old man disappeared than Hans sat down to a good meal, and after that went to bed and slept until the morning. At first he could not remember what had happened to him, but by and by he jumped up and went into all the rooms, which he examined carefully.

How foolish to bid me to put sand on the floors, he thought, when there is nobody here but myself! I shall do nothing of the sort. And so he shut the doors quickly, and only cleaned and set in order his own room. And after the first few days he felt that that was unnecessary too, because no one came there to see if the rooms were clean or not. At last he did no work at all, but just sat and wondered what was behind the locked door, till he decided to go and look for himself.

The key turned easily in the lock. Hans entered, half frightened at what he was doing, and the first thing he beheld was a heap of bones. That was not very pleasing; and he was just going out again, when his eye fell on a shelf of books. Here was a good way of passing the time, he thought, for he was fond of reading, and he took one of the books from the shelf. It was all about magic, and told how you could change yourself into anything in the world you liked. Could anything be more exciting or more useful? So he put it in his pocket, and ran quickly away out of the mountain by a little door that had been left open.

When he got home, his parents asked him what he had been doing and where he had gotten the fine clothes he wore.

"Oh, I earned them myself," he answered.

"You never earned them in this short time," said his father. "Be off with you; I won't keep you here. I will have no thieves in my house!"

"Well, I only came to help you," replied the boy sulkily. "Now I'll be off, as you wish; but tomorrow morning when you rise, you will see a great dog at the door. Do not drive it away, but take it to the castle and sell it to the duke, and he will give you ten coins for it; only you must bring the strap you lead it with back to the house."

Sure enough the next day the dog was standing at the door waiting to be let in. The old man was rather afraid of getting into trouble, but his wife urged him to sell the dog as the boy had bidden him, so he took it up to the castle and sold it to the duke for ten coins. He did not forget to take off the strap with which he had led the animal, and to carry it home. When he got there, old Kirsten met him at the door.

"Well, Peder, have you sold the dog?" she asked.

"Yes, Kirsten; and I have brought back ten coins, just as the boy told us," answered Peder.

"Aye! That's wonderful!" said his wife. "Now you see what one gets by doing as one is told; if it had not been for me you would have driven the dog away again, and we should have lost the money. After all, I always know what is best."

"Nonsense!" said her husband. "Women always think they know best. I should have sold the dog just the same whatever you had told me. Put the money away in a safe place, and don't talk so much."

The next day Hans came again; but though everything had turned out as he had foretold, he found that his father was still not quite satisfied.

"Be off with you!" he said. "You'll get us into trouble."

"I haven't helped you enough yet," replied the boy. "Tomorrow there will come a great fat cow, as big as the house. Take it to the king's palace and you'll get as much as a thousand coins for it. Only you must unfasten the halter you lead the cow with and bring it back, and don't return by the high road, but through the forest."

The next day when the couple rose, they saw an enormous head looking in at their bedroom window, and behind it was a cow that was nearly as big as their hut. Kirsten was wild with joy to think of the money the cow would bring them.

"But how are you going to put the rope over her head?" she asked.

"Wait and you'll see, Mother," answered her husband. Then Peder took the ladder that led up to the hayloft and set it against the cow's neck, and he climbed up and slipped the rope over her head. When he had made sure that the noose was held fast, they started for the palace, and met the king himself walking his grounds.

"I heard that the princess was going to be married," said Peder, "so I've brought your majesty a cow that is bigger than any cow that was ever seen. Will your majesty buy it?"

The king had, in truth, never seen so large a beast, and he willingly paid the thousand coins, which was the price demanded; and Peder remembered to take off the halter before he left. After he was gone, the king sent for the butcher and told him to kill the animal for the wedding feast. The butcher got ready his poleax; but just as he was going to strike, the cow changed itself into a dove and flew away, and

the butcher stood staring after it as if he were turned to stone. However, since the dove could not be found, he was obliged to tell the king what had happened, and the king in his turn despatched messengers to capture the old man and bring him back. But Peder was safe in the woods, and could not be found. When at last he felt the danger was over, and he might go home, Kirsten nearly fainted with joy at the sight of all the money he brought with him.

"Now that we are rich people we must build a bigger house," she cried; and was vexed to find that Peder only shook his head and said, "No; if we did that, people would talk and say we had gotten our wealth by ill-doing."

A few mornings later Hans came again.

"Be off before you get us into trouble," said his father. "So far the money has come right enough, but I don't trust it."

"Don't worry about that, Father," said Hans. "Tomorrow you will find a horse outside by the gate. Ride it to market and you will get a thousand coins for it. Only don't forget to loosen the bridle when you sell it."

Well, in the morning there was the horse; Kirsten had never seen so fine an animal. "Take care it doesn't hurt you, Peder," she said.

"Nonsense, Wife," he answered crossly. "When I was a lad, I lived with horses, and could ride anything for twenty miles around." But that was not quite the truth, for he had never mounted a horse in his life.

Still, the animal was quiet enough, so Peder got safely to market on its back. There he met a man who offered nine hundred and ninety-nine coins for it, but Peder would take nothing less than a thousand. At last there came an old, gray-bearded man who looked at the horse and agreed to buy it; but the moment he touched it the horse began to kick and plunge. "I must take the bridle off," said Peder. "It is not to be sold with the animal as is usually the case."

"I'll give you a hundred coins for the bridle," said the old man, taking out his purse.

"No, I can't sell it," replied Hans's father.

"Five hundred coins!"

"No."

"A thousand!"

At this splendid offer Peder's prudence gave way; it was a shame to let so much money go. So he agreed to accept it. But he could hardly hold the horse, it became so unmanageable. So he gave the animal in charge to the old man, and went home with his two thousand coins.

Kirsten, of course, was delighted at this new piece of good fortune, and insisted that the new house should be built and land bought. This time Peder consented, and soon they had quite a fine farm.

Meanwhile the old man rode off on his new purchase, and when he came to a blacksmith shop he asked the smith to forge shoes for the horse. The smith proposed that they should first have a drink together, and the horse was tied up by the spring while they went indoors. The day was hot, and both men were thirsty, and besides they had much to say; and so the hours slipped by and found them still talking. Then the servant girl came out to get a pail of water, and being a kindhearted lass, she gave some to the horse to drink. What was her surprise when the animal said to her, "Take off my bridle and you will save my life."

"I don't dare," she said. "Your master will be so angry."

"He cannot hurt you," answered the horse, "and you will save my life."

At that she took off the bridle; but nearly fainted with astonishment when the horse turned into a dove and flew away just as the old man came out of the house. As soon as he saw what had happened, he changed himself into a hawk and flew after the dove. Over the woods and fields they went, and at length they reached a king's palace surrounded by beautiful gardens. The princess was walking with her attendants in the rose garden when the dove turned itself into a gold ring and fell at her feet.

"Why, here is a ring!" she cried. "Where could it have come from?" And picking it up, she put it on her finger. As she did so, the hill-man lost his power over Hans — for of course you understand that it was Hans who had been the dog, the cow, the horse, and the dove.

"Well, that is really strange," said the princess. "It fits me as though it had been made for me!"

Just at that moment, up came the king.

"Look what I have found!" cried his daughter.

"Well, that is not worth much, my dear," he said. "Besides, you have enough rings, I should think."

"Never mind, I like it," replied the princess.

But to her amazement, as soon as she was alone, the ring suddenly left her finger and became a man. You can imagine how frightened she was, as indeed anybody would have been; but in an instant the man became a ring again, and then turned back into a man, and so it went on for some time until she began to get used to these sudden changes.

"I am sorry I frightened you," said Hans when he thought he could safely speak to the princess without making her scream. "I took refuge with you because the old hill-man, whom I have offended, was trying to kill me, and here I am safe."

"You had better stay here then," said the princess. So Hans stayed, and they became good friends; though, of course, he only became a man when no one else was present.

This was all very well; but one day as they were talking together, the king happened to enter the room, and although Hans quickly changed himself into a ring again, it was too late.

The king was terribly angry.

"So this is why you have refused to marry all the kings and princes who have sought your hand?" he cried.

And without waiting for her to speak, he commanded that his daughter should be walled up in the summerhouse and starved to death with her lover.

That evening the poor princess, still wearing her ring, was put into the summerhouse with enough food to last for three days, and the door was bricked up. But at the end of a week or two the king thought it was time to give her a grand funeral, in spite of her bad behavior, and he had the summerhouse opened. He could hardly believe his eyes when he found that the princess was not there, nor Hans either. Instead, there lay at his feet a large hole, big enough for two people to pass through.

THE PRINCESS IMPRISONED IN THE SUMMERHOUSE

Now what had happened was this:

When the princess and Hans had given up hope, and cast themselves down on the ground to die, they fell down into this hole, and right through the earth as well, and at last they tumbled into a castle built of pure gold at the other side of the world, and there they lived happily. But of this, of course, the king knew nothing.

"Will anyone go down and see where the passage leads to?" he asked, turning to his guards and courtiers. "I will reward splendidly the man who is brave enough to explore it."

For a long time nobody answered. The hole was dark and deep, and if it had a bottom, no one could see it. At length a soldier, who was a careless sort of fellow, offered himself for the service, and cautiously lowered himself into the darkness. But in a moment he too fell down, down, down. Was he going to fall forever, he wondered! Oh, how thankful he was in the end to reach the castle, and to meet the princess and Hans, looking quite well and not at all as if they had been starved. They began to talk, and the soldier told them that the king was very sorry for the way he had treated his daughter, and wished day and night that he could have her back again.

Then they all took a ship and sailed home, and when they came to the princess's country, Hans disguised himself as the sovereign of a neighboring kingdom, and went up to the palace alone. He was given a hearty welcome by the king, who prided himself on his hospitality, and a banquet was commanded in his honor. That evening while they sat drinking their wine, Hans said to the king:

"I have heard the fame of your majesty's wisdom, and I have traveled from far to ask your counsel. A man in my country has buried his daughter alive because she loved a youth who was born a peasant. How shall I punish this unnatural father, for it is left to me to give judgment?"

The king, who was still truly grieved for the loss of his daughter answered quickly:

"Burn him alive, and strew his ashes all over the kingdom."

Hans looked at him steadily for a moment, and then threw off his disguise.

"You are the man," he said; "and I am the one who loved your daughter, and became a gold ring on her finger. She is safe, and waiting not far from here; but you have pronounced judgment on yourself."

Then the king fell on his knees and begged for mercy; and as he had in other respects been a good father, they forgave him. The wedding of Hans and the princess was celebrated with great festivities that lasted a month. As for the hill-man, he intended to be present; but while he was walking along a street that led to the palace, a loose stone fell on his head and killed him. So Hans and the princess lived in peace and happiness all their days, and when the old king died, they reigned instead of him.

How Ian Direach Got the Blue Falcon

SCOTLAND

Long ago a king and queen ruled over the islands of the West, and they had one son, whom they loved dearly. The boy grew up to be tall and strong and handsome, and he could run and shoot, and swim and dive better than any lad of his own age in the country. Besides, he knew how to sail, and sing songs to the harp, and during the winter evenings when everyone was gathered around the huge hall fire shaping bows or weaving cloth, Ian Direach would tell them tales of the deeds of his forefathers.

So the time slipped by until Ian was almost a man, as they reckoned men in those days, and then his mother the queen died. There was great mourning throughout all the isles, and the boy and his father mourned her bitterly also. But before the new year came, the king had married another wife and seemed to have forgotten his old one. Only Ian remembered.

On a morning when the leaves were yellow in the trees of the glen, Ian slung his bow over his shoulder, and filling his quiver with arrows, went on the hill in search of game. But not a bird was to be seen anywhere, until at length a blue falcon flew past him, and raising his bow, Ian took aim at her. His eye was straight and his hand steady, but the falcon's flight was swift, and he only shot a feather from her wing. As the sun was now low over the sea, he put the feather in his game bag, and set out homeward.

"Have you brought me much game today?" asked his stepmother as he entered the hall.

"Nothing except this," he answered, handing her the feather of the blue falcon, which she held by the tip and gazed at silently. Then she turned to Ian and said:

"I am setting it on you as crosses and as spells, and as the fall of the year! That you may always be cold and wet and dirty, and that your shoes may always have pools in them, until you bring me the blue falcon on which that feather grew."

"If it is spells you are laying, I can lay them too," answered Ian Direach; "and you shall stand with one foot on the great house and another on the castle, until I come back again, and your face shall be to the wind, from wherever it blows." Then he went away to seek the bird, as his stepmother bade him; and looking homeward from the hill, he saw the queen standing with one foot on the great house and the other on the castle, and her face turned toward whatever tempest should blow.

On he journeyed, over hills, and through rivers until he reached a wide plain, and never a glimpse did he catch of the falcon. Darker and darker it grew, and the small birds were seeking their nests, and at length Ian Direach could see no more, and he lay down under some bushes and sleep came to him. And in his dream a soft nose touched him, and a warm body curled up beside him, and a low voice whispered to him:

"Fortune is against you, Ian Direach; I have but the cheek and the hoof of a sheep to give you, and with these you must be content." With that Ian Direach awoke, and beheld Gille Mairtean the fox.

Between them they kindled a fire, and ate their supper. Then Gille Mairtean the fox told Ian Direach to lie down as before, and sleep until morning. And in the morning when he awoke, Gille Mairtean said:

"The falcon that you seek is in the keeping of the Giant of the Five Heads, and the Five Necks, and the Five Humps. I will show you the way to his house, and I counsel you to do his bidding, nimbly and cheerfully, and above all, to treat his birds kindly, for in this manner he may give you his falcon to feed and care for. And when this happens, wait until the giant is out of his house; then throw a cloth over the falcon, and bear her away with you. Only see that not one of her feathers touches anything within the house, or evil will befall you."

"I thank you for your counsel," said Ian Direach, "and will be careful to follow it." Then he took the path to the giant's house.

"Who is there?" cried the giant as someone knocked loudly on the door of his house.

"One who seeks work as a servant," answered Ian Direach.

"And what can you do?" asked the giant again.

"I can feed birds and tend pigs; I can feed and milk a cow, and also goats and sheep if you have any of these," replied Ian Direach.

"Then enter, for I have great need of such a one," said the giant.

So Ian Direach entered, and tended so well and carefully all the birds and beasts that the giant was better satisfied than he had ever been, and at length he thought that he might even be trusted to feed the falcon. And the heart of Ian was glad, and he tended the blue falcon until his feathers shone like the sky, and the giant was well pleased; and one day he said to him:

"For a long time my brothers on the other side of the mountain have begged me to visit them, but I have never gone for fear of my falcon. Now I think I can leave her with you for one day, and before nightfall I shall be back again."

Scarcely was the giant out of sight the next morning, when Ian Direach seized the falcon, and throwing a cloth over her head, hastened with her to the door. But the rays of the sun pierced through the thickness of the cloth, and as they passed the doorpost, she gave a spring, and the tip of one of her feathers touched the post, which gave a scream, and brought the giant back in three strides. Ian Direach trembled as he saw him; but the giant only said:

"If you wish for my falcon, you must first bring me the White Sword of Light that is in the house of the Big Women of Dhiurradh."

"And where do they live?" asked Ian. But the giant answered:

"Ah, that is for you to discover." And Ian dared say no more, and hastened down to the plain. There, as he hoped, he met his friend Gille Mairtean the fox, who bade him eat his supper and lie down to sleep. And when he had awoken the next morning, the fox said to him:

"Let us go down to the shore of the sea." And to the shore of the sea they went. And after they had reached the shore, and beheld the sea stretching before them, and the isle of Dhiurradh in the midst of it, the soul of Ian sank, and he turned to Gille Mairtean and asked why he had brought him there, for the giant, when he had sent him, had known full well that without a boat he could never find the Big Women.

"Do not be downcast," answered the fox. "It is quite easy! I will change myself into a boat, and you shall go on board me, and I will carry you over the sea to the Seven Big Women of Dhiurradh. Tell them that you are skilled in brightening silver and gold, and in the end they will take you as servant; and if you are careful to please them, they will give you the White Sword of Light to make bright and shining. But when you seek to steal it, take heed that its sheath touches nothing inside the house, or ill will befall you."

So Ian Direach did all things as the fox had told him, and the Seven Big Women of Dhiurradh took him for their servant, and for six weeks he worked so hard that his seven mistresses said to each other:

"Never has a servant had the skill to make all bright and shining like this one. Let us give him the White Sword of Light to polish like the rest."

Then they brought forth the White Sword of Light from the iron closet where it hung, and bade him rub it until he could see his face in the shining blade; and he did so. But one day when the Seven Big Women were out of the way, he thought to himself that the moment had come for him to carry off the sword, and replacing it in its sheath, he hoisted it on his shoulder. But just as he was passing through the door, the tip of the sheath touched it, and the door gave a loud shriek. And the Big Women heard it, and came running back and took the sword from him, and said:

"If it is our sword you want, you must first bring us the bay colt of the King of Erin."

Humbled and ashamed, Ian Direach left the house, and sat by the side of the sea, and soon Gille Mairtean the fox came to him.

"Plainly I see that you have taken no heed to my words, Ian Direach," spoke the fox. "But eat first, and I will help you once more."

At these words the heart returned again to Ian Direach, and he gathered sticks and made a fire and ate with Gille Mairtean the fox, and slept on the sand. At dawn the next morning Gille Mairtean said to Ian Direach:

"I will change myself into a ship, and will bear you across the seas to Erin, to the land where the king dwells. And you shall offer yourself to serve in his stable, and to tend his horses, at length until he is so well content that he gives you the bay colt to wash and brush. But when you run away with her, see that nothing except the soles of her hoofs touch anything within the palace gates, or it will go ill with you."

After he had thus counseled Ian Direach, the fox changed himself into a ship, and set sail for Erin. And the king of that country gave into Ian Direach's hands the care of his horses, and never before did their skins shine so brightly or was their pace so swift. And the king was well pleased, and at the end of a month he sent for Ian and said to him:

"You have given me faithful service, and now I will entrust you with the most precious thing that my kingdom holds." And when he had spoken, he led Ian Direach to the stable where stood the bay colt. And Ian rubbed her and fed her, and galloped with her all around the country, until he could leave one wind behind him and catch the other that was in front.

"I am going away to hunt," said the king one morning while he was watching Ian tend the bay colt in her stable. "The deer have come down from the hill, and it is time for me to give them chase." Then he went away; and when he was no longer in sight, Ian Direach led the bay colt out of the stable, and sprang on her back. But as they rode through the gate that stood between the palace and the outer world, the colt swished her tail against the post, which shrieked loudly. In a moment the king came running up, and he seized the colt's bridle.

"If you want my bay colt, you must first bring me the daughter of the king of the Franks."

With slow steps Ian Direach went down to the shore where Gille Mairtean the fox awaited him.

"Plainly I see that you have not done as I bid you, nor will you ever do it," spoke Gille Mairtean the fox; "but I will help you yet again. For a third time I will change myself into a ship, and we will sail to France."

And to France they sailed, and as he was the ship, Gille Mairtean sailed where he would, and ran himself into the cleft of a rock, high on to the land. Then he commanded Ian Direach to go up to the king's palace, saying that he had been wrecked, that his ship was stuck fast in a rock, and that none had been saved but himself.

Ian Direach listened to the words of the fox, and he told a tale so pitiful that the king and queen and the princess their daughter all came out to hear it. And when they had heard, nothing would please them except to go down to the shore and visit the ship, which by now was floating, for the tide was up. Torn and battered she was, as if she had passed through many dangers, yet music of a wondrous sweetness poured forth from within.

"Bring a boat here," cried the princess, "that I may go and see for myself the harp that gives forth such music." And a boat was brought, and Ian Direach stepped in to row it to the side of the ship.

To the far side he rowed so that none could see, and when he helped the princess on board the ship, he gave a push to the boat so that she could not get back to it again. And the music sounded always sweeter, though they could never see where it came from, and searched for it from one part of the vessel to another. When at last they reached the deck and looked around them, no land could they see, or anything except the rushing waters.

The princess stood silent, and her face grew grim. At last she said:

"An ill trick you have played on me! What is this that you have done, and where are we going?"

"It is a queen you will be," answered Ian Direach, "for the king of Erin has sent me for you, and in return he will give me his bay colt, that I may take him to the Seven Big Women of Dhiurradh, in exchange for the White Sword of Light. This I must carry to the giant of

THE PRINCESS FINDS HERSELF A PRISONER ON THE SHIP.

the Five Heads and Five Necks and Five Humps, and in place of it he will bestow on me the blue falcon, which I have promised my stepmother so that she will free me from the spell that she has laid on me."

"I would rather be wife to you," answered the princess.

By and by the ship sailed into a harbor on the coast of Erin, and cast anchor there. And Gille Mairtean the fox bade Ian Direach to tell the princess that she must bide yet a while in a cave among the rocks, for they had business on land, and after a while they would return to her. Then they took a boat and rowed up to some rocks, and as they touched the land, Gille Mairtean changed himself into a fair woman, who laughed and said to Ian Direach, "I will give the king a fine wife."

Now the king of Erin had been hunting on the hill, and when he saw a strange ship sailing toward the harbor, he guessed that it might be Ian Direach, and left his hunting, and ran down the hill to the stable. Hastily he led the bay colt from the stall, and put the golden saddle on her back, and the silver bridle over her head, and with the colt's reins in his hand he hurried to meet the princess.

"I have brought you the king of France's daughter," said Ian Direach. And the king of Erin looked at the maiden, and was well pleased, not knowing that it was Gille Mairtean the fox. And he bowed low, and asked her to do him the honor to enter the palace; and, as he went in, Gille Mairtean turned to look back at Ian Direach, and laughed.

In the great hall the king paused and pointed to an iron chest that stood in a corner.

"In that chest is the crown that has waited for you for many years," he said, "and at last you have come for it." And he stooped down to unlock the box.

In an instant Gille Mairtean the fox had sprung on his back, and gave him such a bite that he fell down unconscious. Quickly the fox took his own shape again, and galloped away to the seashore where Ian Direach and the princess and the bay colt awaited him.

"I will become a ship," cried Gille Mairtean, "and you shall go on board me." And so he did, and Ian Direach led the bay colt into the ship, and the princess went after them, and they set sail for Dhiurradh. The wind was behind them, and very soon they saw the rocks of Dhiurradh in front. Then spoke Gille Mairtean the fox:

"Let the bay colt and the king's daughter hide in these rocks, and I will change myself into the colt, and go with you to the house of the Seven Big Women."

Joy filled the hearts of the Big Women when they beheld the bay colt led up to their door by Ian Direach. And the youngest of them fetched the White Sword of Light, and gave it into the hands of Ian Direach, who took off the golden saddle and the silver bridle, and went down the hill with the sword to the place where the princess and the real colt awaited him.

THE SEVEN BIG WOMEN FALL OVER THE CRAG

"At last we shall have the ride that we have longed for!" cried the Seven Big Women; and they saddled and bridled the colt, and the eldest one got upon the saddle. Then the second sister sat on the back of the first, and the third on the back of the second, and so on for the whole seven. And when they were all seated, the eldest struck her side with a whip and the colt bounded forward. Over the moors she flew, and around and around the mountains, and still the Big Women clung to her and snorted with pleasure. At last she leaped high in the air, and came down on top of Monadh, the high hill where the crag was. And she rested her forefeet on the crag, and threw up her hind legs, and the Seven Big Women fell over the crag, and were dead when they reached the bottom. And the colt laughed, and became a fox again and galloped away to the seashore where Ian Direach and the princess and the real colt and the White Sword of Light were awaiting him.

"I will make myself into a ship," said Gille Mairtean the fox, "and will carry you and the princess and the bay colt and the White Sword of Light back to the land." And when the shore was reached, Gille Mairtean the fox took back his own shape, and spoke to Ian Direach in this way:

"Let the princess and the White Sword of Light and the bay colt remain among the rocks, and I will change myself into the likeness of the White Sword of Light, and you shall bring me to the giant, and he will give you the blue falcon." And Ian Direach did as the fox bade him, and set out for the giant's castle. From afar the giant beheld the blaze of the White Sword of Light, and his heart rejoiced; and he took the blue falcon and put it in a basket, and gave it to Ian Direach, who bore it swiftly away to the place where the princess and the bay colt and the real Sword of Light were awaiting him.

So well content was the giant to possess the sword he had coveted for so many a year that he began at once to whirl it through the air, and to cut and slash with it. For a little while Gille Mairtean let the giant play with him in this manner; then he turned in the giant's hand, and cut through the Five Necks, so that the Five Heads rolled on the ground. Afterward he went back to Ian Direach, and said to him:

"Saddle the colt with the golden saddle, and bridle her with the silver bridle, and sling the basket with the falcon over your shoulders, and hold the White Sword of Light with its back against your nose. Then mount the colt, and let the princess mount behind you, and ride thus to your father's palace. But see that the back of the sword is ever against your nose, else when your stepmother beholds you, she will change you into a dry bundle of sticks. If, however, you do as I bid you, she herself will become a bundle of sticks."

Ian Direach hearkened to the words of Gille Mairtean, and his stepmother fell as a bundle of sticks before him; and he set fire to her, and was free from her spells forever. After that he married the princess, who was the best wife in all the islands of the West. Henceforth he was safe from harm, for he had the bay colt who could leave one wind behind her and catch the other wind, and the blue

How Ian Direach returned home and how his stepmother fell as a bundle of sticks.

falcon to bring him game to eat, and the White Sword of Light to pierce through his foes.

And Ian Direach knew that all this he owed to Gille Mairtean the fox, and he promised him that he might choose any beast out of his herds whenever hunger seized him, and that henceforth no arrow should be let fly at him or at any of his race. But Gille Mairtean the fox would take no reward for the help he had given to Ian Direach, only his friendship. Thus all things prospered with Ian Direach until he died.

Urashima Taro and the Turtle

JAPAN

There was once a worthy old couple who lived on the coast, and supported themselves by fishing. They had only one child, a son, who was their pride and joy, and for his sake they were ready to work hard all day long, and never felt tired or discontented with their lot. This son's name was Urashima Taro, which means in Japanese, "Son of the island," and he was a fine well-grown youth and a good fisherman, minding neither wind nor weather. Not the bravest sailor in the whole village dared venture so far out to sea as Urashima Taro, and many a time the neighbors used to shake their heads and say to his parents, "If your son goes on being so rash, one day he will try his luck once too often, and the waves will end by swallowing him up." But Urashima Taro paid no heed to these remarks, and as he was really very clever in managing a boat, the old people were very seldom anxious about him.

One beautiful bright morning as he was hauling his well-filled nets into the boat, he saw lying among the fishes a tiny little turtle. He was delighted with his prize, and threw it into a wooden vessel to keep until he got home, when suddenly the turtle found its voice, and tremblingly begged for its life. "After all," it said, "what good can I do you? I am so young and small, and I would so gladly live a little longer. Be merciful and set me free, and I shall know how to prove my gratitude."

Now Urashima Taro was very good-natured, so he picked up the turtle, and put it back into the sea.

Years flew by, and every morning Urashima Taro sailed his boat into the deep sea. But one day as he was making for a little bay between some rocks, there arose a fierce whirlwind that shattered his boat to pieces, and she was sucked under by the waves. Urashima Taro himself very nearly shared the same fate. But he was a powerful swimmer, and struggled hard to reach the shore. Then he saw a large turtle coming toward him, and above the howling of the storm he heard what it said:

"I am the turtle whose life you once saved. I will now pay my debt and show my gratitude. The land is still far away, and without my help you would never get there. Climb on my back, and I will take you where you will."

Urashima Taro did not wait to be asked twice, and thankfully accepted his friend's help. But scarcely was he seated firmly on the shell,

when the turtle proposed that they should not return to the shore at once, but go under the sea, and look at some of the wonders that lay hidden there.

Urashima Taro agreed willingly, and in another moment they were deep, deep down, with fathoms of blue water above their heads. Oh, how quickly they darted through the still, warm sea! The young man held tight and marveled where they were going and how long they were to travel, but for three days they rushed on, until at last the turtle stopped before a splendid palace, shining with gold and silver, crystal and precious stones, and decked here and there with branches of pale pink coral and glittering pearls. But if Urashima Taro was astonished at the beauty of the outside, he was struck dumb at the sight of the hall within, which was lighted by the blaze of fish scales.

"Where have you brought me?" he asked his guide in a low voice.

"To the palace of Ryukyu, the house of the sea god whose subjects we all are," answered the turtle. "I am the first waiting-maid of his daughter, the lovely princess Otohimé, whom you will see shortly."

Urashima Taro was still so puzzled with the adventures that had befallen him, that he waited in a dazed condition for what would happen next. But the turtle, who had talked so much of him to the princess that she had expressed a wish to see him, went at once to make known his arrival. And as soon as the princess beheld him her heart was set on him, and she begged him to stay with her, and in return promised that he should never grow old, neither should his beauty fade. "Is that not reward enough?" she asked, smiling, looking all the while as fair as the sun itself. And Urashima Taro said, "Yes," and so he stayed there. For how long? That he only knew later.

His life passed by, and each hour seemed happier than the last, when one day there rushed over him a terrible longing to see his parents. He fought against it hard, knowing how it would grieve the princess, but it grew on him stronger and stronger, until at length he became so sad that the princess inquired what was wrong. Then he told her of the longing he had to visit his old home, and that he must see his parents once more. The princess was almost frozen with horror, and implored him to stay with her, or something dreadful would be

sure to happen. "You will never come back, and we shall meet again no more," she moaned bitterly. But Urashima Taro stood firm and repeated, "Only this once will I leave you, and then will I return to your side forever." Sadly the princess shook her head, but she answered slowly, "There is one way to bring you safely back, but I fear you will never agree to the conditions of the bargain."

"I will do anything that will bring me back to you," exclaimed Urashima Taro, looking at her tenderly, but the princess was silent. She knew too well that when he left her, she would see his face no more. Then she took from a shelf a tiny golden box, and gave it to Urashima Taro, telling him to keep it carefully, and above all things never to open it. "If you can do this," she said as she bade him farewell, "your friend the turtle will meet you at the shore, and will carry you back to me."

Urashima Taro thanked her from his heart, and swore solemnly to do her bidding. He hid the box safely in his garments, seated himself on the back of the turtle, and vanished in the ocean path, waving his hand to the princess. Three days and three nights they swam through the sea, and at length Urashima Taro arrived at the beach that lay before his old home. The turtle bade him farewell, and was gone in a moment.

Urashima Taro drew near to the village with quick and joyful steps. He saw the smoke curling through the roof, and the thatch where green plants had thickly sprouted. He heard the children shouting and calling, and from a window that he passed came the twang of the koto, and everything seemed to cry a welcome for his return. Yet suddenly he felt a pang at his heart as he wandered down the street. After all, everything was changed. Neither men nor houses were those he once knew. Quickly he saw his old home; yes, it was still there, but it had a strange look. Anxiously he knocked at the door, and asked the woman who opened it about his parents. But she did not know their names, and could give him no news of them.

Still more disturbed, he rushed to the burying ground, the only place that could tell him what he wished to know. Here at any rate he would find out what it all meant. And he was right. In a moment he stood before the grave of his parents, and the date written on the stone was almost exactly the date when they had lost their son, and he had forsaken them for the Daughter of the Sea. And so he found that since he had left his home, three hundred years had passed by.

Shuddering with horror at his discovery, he turned back into the village street hoping to meet someone who could tell him of the days of old. But when the man spoke, he knew he was not dreaming, though he felt as if he had lost his senses.

In despair he remembered the box that was the gift of the princess. Perhaps this dreadful thing was not true after all. He might be the victim of some enchanter's spell, and in his hand lay the counter-charm. Almost unconsciously he opened it, and a purple vapor came pouring out. He held the empty box in his hand, and as he looked, he saw that the fresh hand of youth had grown suddenly shriveled, like the hand of an old, old man. He ran to the brook that flowed in a clear stream down from the mountain, and saw himself reflected as in a mirror. It was the face of a mummy that looked back at him. Wounded to death, he crept back through the village, and no one knew the old,

old man to be the strong handsome youth who had run down the street an hour before. So he toiled wearily back, until he reached the shore, and here he sat sadly on a rock, and called loudly on the turtle. But she never came back anymore. Instead death came soon, and set him free. But before that happened, the people who saw him sitting lonely on the shore had heard his story, and when their children were restless, they used to tell them of the good son who for love of his parents had given up the splendor and wonders of the palace in the sea, and the most beautiful woman in the world besides.

The Prince Who Sought Immortality

HUNGARY

Once upon a time in the very middle of the middle of a large kingdom, there was a town, and in the town a palace, and in the palace a king. This king had one son whom his father thought was wiser and cleverer than any son ever was before, and indeed his father had spared no pains to make him so. He had been very careful in choosing his tutors and governors when he was a boy, and when he became a youth, he sent him to travel so that he might see the ways of other people, and find that they were often as good as his own.

It was now a year since the prince had returned home, for his father felt that it was time that his son should learn how to rule the kingdom that would one day be his. But during his long absence the prince seemed to have changed his character altogether. From being a merry and lighthearted boy, he had grown into a gloomy and thoughtful man. The king knew of nothing that could have produced such an alteration. He vexed himself about it from morning till night, until at length an explanation occurred to him — the young man was in love!

Now the prince never talked about his feelings — for that matter he scarcely talked at all; and the father knew that if he was to get to the bottom of the prince's dismal face, he would have to begin. So one day after dinner he took his son by the arm, and led him into another room hung entirely with the pictures of beautiful maidens, each one more lovely than the other.

"My dear boy," he said, "you are very sad; perhaps after all your wanderings it is dull for you here all alone with me. It would be much better if you would marry, and I have collected here the portraits of the most beautiful women in the world of a rank equal to your own. Choose which among them you would like for a wife, and I will send an embassy to her father to ask for her hand."

"Alas! Your Majesty," answered the prince, "it is not love or marriage that makes me so gloomy; but the thought, which haunts me day and night, that all men, even kings, must die. Never shall I be happy again until I have found a kingdom where death is unknown. And I have determined to give myself no rest until I have discovered the Land of Immortality."

The old king heard him with dismay; things were worse than he thought. He tried to reason with his son, and told him that during all these years he had been looking forward to his return in order to resign his throne and its cares, which pressed so heavily upon him. But it was in vain that he talked; the prince would listen to nothing, and the following morning buckled on his sword and set forth on his journey.

He had been traveling for many days, and had left his fatherland behind him, when close to the road he came upon a huge tree, and on its topmost bough an eagle was sitting, shaking the branches with all his might. This seemed so strange and so unlike an eagle that the prince stood still with surprise, and the bird saw him and flew to the ground. The moment its feet touched the ground, he changed into a king.

"Why do you look so astonished?" he asked.

"I was wondering why you shook the boughs so fiercely," answered the prince.

"I am condemned to do this, for neither I nor any of my kindred can die until I have uprooted this great tree," replied the king of the eagles. "But it is now evening, and I need work no more today. Come to my house with me, and be my guest for the night."

The prince accepted gratefully the eagle's invitation, for he was tired and hungry. They were received at the palace by the king's beautiful daughter, who gave orders that dinner should be laid for them at once. While they were eating, the eagle questioned his guest about his travels, and if he was wandering for pleasure's sake, or with any special aim. Then the prince told him everything, and how he could never turn back until he had discovered the Land of Immortality.

"Dear brother," said the eagle, "you have discovered it already, and it rejoices my heart to think that you will stay with us. Have you not just heard me say that death has no power either over myself or any of my kindred until that great tree is uprooted? It will take me six hundred years' hard work to do that; so marry my daughter and let us all live happily together here. After all, six hundred years is an eternity!"

"Ah, dear king," replied the young man, "your offer is very tempting! But at the end of six hundred years we should have to die, so we should be no better off! No, I must go on until I find the country where there is no death at all."

Then the princess spoke, and tried to persuade the guest to change his mind, but he sorrowfully shook his head. At length, seeing that his resolution was firmly fixed, she took from a cabinet a little box that contained her picture, and gave it to him saying:

"As you will not stay with us, prince, accept this box, which will sometimes recall us to your memory. If you are tired of traveling before you come to the Land of Immortality, open this box and look at my picture, and you will be borne along either on earth or in the air, quick as thought, or swift as the whirlwind."

The prince thanked her for her gift, which he placed in his tunic, and sorrowfully bade the eagle and his daughter farewell.

Never was any present in the world as useful as that little box, and many times did he bless the kind thought of the princess. One evening it had carried him to the top of a high mountain, where he saw a man with a bald head, busily engaged in digging up spadefuls of earth and throwing them in a basket. When the basket was full, he took it away and returned with an empty one, which he likewise filled. The prince stood and watched him for a little until the bald-headed man looked up and said to him:

"Dear brother, what surprises you so much?"

"I was wondering why you were filling the basket," replied the prince.

The Baldheaded Man on The Mountain

"Oh!" replied the man. "I am condemned to do this, for neither I nor any of my family can die until I have dug away the whole of this mountain and made it level with the plain. But come, it is almost dark, and I shall work no longer." And he plucked a leaf from a tree close by, and from a rough digger he was changed into a stately bald-headed king. "Come home with me," he added; "you must be tired and hungry, and my daughter will have supper ready for us." The prince accepted gladly, and they went back to the palace, where the bald-headed king's daughter, who was still more beautiful than the other princess, welcomed them at the door and led the way into a large hall and to a table covered with silver dishes. While they ate, the bald-headed king asked the prince how he had happened to wander so far, and the young man told him all about it, and how he was seeking the Land of Immortality. "You have found it already," answered the king, "for as I said, neither I nor my family can die until I have leveled this great mountain; and that will take a full eight hundred years longer. Stay here with us and marry my daughter. Eight hundred years is surely long enough to live."

"Oh, certainly," answered the prince; "but all the same, I would rather go and seek the land where there is no death at all."

So the next morning he bade them farewell, though the princess begged him to stay with all her might; and when she found that she could not persuade him, she gave him as a remembrance a gold ring. This ring was still more useful than the box, because when one wished oneself at any place, one was there directly, without even the trouble of flying to it through the air. The prince put it on his finger, and thanking her heartily, went his way.

He walked on for some distance, and then he recollected the ring and thought he would see if the princess had spoken truly as to its powers. "I wish I was at the end of the world," he said, shutting his eyes; and when he opened them, he was standing in a street full of marble palaces. The men who passed him were tall and strong, and their clothes were magnificent. He stopped some of them and asked in all the twenty-seven languages he knew what was the name of the city, but no one answered him. Then his heart sank within him; what should he do in this strange place if nobody could understand anything he said? Suddenly his eyes fell upon a man dressed after the fashion of his native country, and he ran up to him and spoke to him in his own tongue. "What city is this, my friend?" he inquired.

"It is the capital city of the Blue Kingdom," replied the man. "But the king himself is dead, and his daughter is now the ruler."

With this news the prince was satisfied, and begged his countryman to show him the way to the young queen's palace. The man led him through several streets into a large square, one side of which was occupied by a splendid building that seemed held up on slender pillars of soft green marble. In front was a flight of steps, and on these the queen was sitting wrapped in a veil of shining silver mist, listening to the complaints of her people and dealing out justice. When the prince came up, she saw directly that he was no ordinary man, and telling her chamberlain to dismiss the rest of her petitioners for that day, she signed to the prince to follow her into the palace. Luckily she had been taught his language as a child, so they had no difficulty in talking together.

The prince told all his story and how he was journeying in search of the Land of Immortality. When he had finished, the princess, who had listened attentively, rose, and taking his arm, led him to the door of another room, the floor of which was made entirely of needles, stuck so close together that there was not room for a single needle more.

"Prince," she said, turning to him, "you see these needles? Well, know that neither I nor any of my family can die until I have worn out these needles in sewing. It will take at least a thousand years for that. Stay here, and share my throne; a thousand years is long enough to live!"

"Certainly," he answered. "Still, at the end of the thousand years I should have to die! No, I must find the land where there is no death."

The queen did all she could to persuade him to stay, but as her words proved useless, at length she gave it up. Then she said to him, "As you will not stay, take this little golden rod as a remembrance of me. It has the power to become anything you wish it to be, when you are in need."

So the prince thanked her, and putting the rod in his pocket, went his way.

Scarcely had he left the town behind him, when he came to a broad river that no man might pass, for he was standing at the end of the world, and this was the river that flowed around it. Not knowing what to do next, he walked a little distance up the bank, and there, over his head, a beautiful city was floating in the air. He longed to get to it, but how? Neither road nor bridge was anywhere to be seen, yet the city drew him upward, and he felt that here at last was the country that he sought. Suddenly he remembered the golden rod that the mist-veiled queen had given him. With a beating heart he flung it to the ground, wishing with all his might that it should turn into a bridge, and fearing that, after all, this might prove beyond its power. But no, instead of the rod, there stood a golden ladder, leading straight up to the city of the air. He was about to enter the golden gates, when there sprang at him a wondrous beast, whose like he had never seen. "Out sword from the sheath," cried the prince, springing back with a cry. And the sword leaped from the scabbard and cut off some of the monster's

HOW THE PRINCE ARRIVED AT THE CITY OF IMMORTALITY

heads, but others grew again immediately, so that the prince, pale with terror, stood where he was, calling for help, and put his sword back in the sheath again.

The queen of the city heard the noise and looked from her window to see what was happening. Summoning one of her servants, she bade him go and rescue the stranger, and bring him to her. The servant obeyed her orders, and the prince thankfully entered her presence.

The moment she looked at him, the queen also felt that he was no ordinary man, and she welcomed him graciously, and asked him what had brought him to the city. In answer the prince told all his story, and how he had traveled long and far in search of the Land of Immortality.

"You have found it," she said, "for I am queen over life and over death. Here you can dwell among the immortals."

A thousand years had passed since the prince first entered the city, but they had flown so fast that the time seemed no more than six months. There had not been one instant of the thousand years that the prince was not happy, until one night when he dreamed of his father and mother. Then the longing for his home came upon him with a rush, and in the morning he told the Queen of the Immortals that he must go and see his father and mother once more. The queen stared at him with amazement, and cried, "Why, prince, are you out of your senses? It is more than eight hundred years since your father and mother died! There will not even be their dust remaining."

"I must go all the same," he said.

"Well, do not be in a hurry," continued the queen, understanding that he would not be prevented. "Wait until I make some preparations for your journey." So she unlocked her great treasure chest and took out two beautiful flasks, one of gold and one of silver, which she hung around his neck. Then she showed him a little trapdoor in one corner of the room, and said:

"Fill the silver flask with this water, which is below the trapdoor. It is enchanted, and whoever you sprinkle with the water will become a dead man at once, even if he has lived a thousand years. The golden flask you must fill with the water here," she added, pointing to a well in another corner. "It springs from the rock of eternity; you have only to sprinkle a few drops on a body and it will come to life again, even if it has been dead a thousand years."

The prince thanked the queen for her gifts, and bidding her farewell, went on his journey.

He soon arrived in the town where the mist-veiled queen reigned in her palace, but the whole city had changed, and he could scarcely find his way through the streets. In the palace itself all was still, and he wandered through the rooms without meeting anyone to stop him. At last he entered the queen's own chamber, and there she lay, with her embroidery still in her hands, fast asleep. He pulled at her dress, but she did not waken. Then a dreadful idea came over him, and he ran to the chamber where the needles had been kept, but it was quite empty. The queen had broken the last over the work she held in her hand, and with it the spell was broken too, and she lay dead.

Quick as thought the prince pulled out the golden flask, and sprinkled some drops of the water over the queen. In a moment she moved gently, and raising her head, opened her eyes.

"Oh, my dear friend, I am so glad you wakened me; I must have slept a long while!"

"You would have slept until eternity," answered the prince, "if I had not been here to waken you."

At these words the queen remembered about the needles. She knew now that she had been dead, and that the prince had restored her to life. She gave him thanks from her heart for what he had done, and vowed she would repay him if she ever got a chance.

The prince took his leave, and set out for the country of the bald-headed king. As he drew near the place, he saw that the whole mountain had been dug away, and that the king was lying dead on the ground, his spade and bucket beside him. But as soon as the water from the golden flask touched him, he yawned and stretched himself, and slowly rose to his feet. "Oh, my dear friend, I am so glad to see you," he cried. "I must have slept a long while!"

"You would have slept until eternity if I had not been here to waken you," answered the prince. And the king remembered the mountain and the spell, and vowed to repay the service if he ever had a chance.

Farther along the road that led to his old home the prince found the great tree torn up by its roots, and the king of the eagles sitting dead on the ground, with his wings outspread as if for flight. A flutter ran through the feathers as the drops of water fell on them, and the eagle lifted his beak from the ground and said, "Oh, how long I must have slept! How can I thank you for having awakened me, my dear, good friend!"

"You would have slept until eternity if I had not been here to waken you," answered the prince. Then the king remembered about the tree, and knew that he had been dead, and promised if ever he had the chance, to repay what the prince had done for him.

At last he reached the capital of his father's kingdom, but on reaching the place where the royal palace had stood, instead of the marble galleries where he used to play, there lay a great sulphur lake, its blue flames darting into the air. How was he to find his father and mother, and bring them back to life if they were lying at the bottom of that horrible water? He turned away sadly and wandered back into the streets, hardly knowing where he was going, when a voice behind him cried, "Stop, prince, I have caught you at last! It is a thousand years since I first began to seek you." And there beside him stood the old, white-bearded, figure of Death. Swiftly he drew the ring from his finger, and the king of the eagles, the bald-headed king, and the mist-veiled queen, hastened to his rescue. In an instant they had seized upon Death and held him tight, until the prince should have time to reach the Land of Immortality. But they did not know how quickly Death could fly, and the prince had only one foot across the border, when he felt the other grasped from behind, and the voice of Death calling, "Halt! Now you are mine."

The Queen of the Immortals was watching from her window, and cried to Death that he had no power in her kingdom, and that he must seek his prey elsewhere.

"Quite true," answered Death; "but his foot is in *my* kingdom, and that belongs to me!"

"At any rate half of him is mine," replied the Queen, "and what

The Prince who would seek Immortality.

good can the other half do you? Half a man is no use, either to you or to me! But this once I will allow you to cross into my kingdom, and we will decide by a wager whose he is."

And so it was settled. Death stepped across the narrow line that surrounds the Land of Immortality, and the queen proposed the wager that was to decide the prince's fate. "I will throw him up into the sky," she said, "right to the back of the morning star, and if he falls down into this city, then he is mine. But if he should fall outside the walls, he shall belong to you."

In the middle of the city was a great open square, and here the queen wished the wager to take place. When all was ready, she put her foot under the foot of the prince and flung him into the air. Up, up, he went, high among the stars, and no man's eyes could follow him. Had she thrown him up straight? the queen wondered anxiously, for if not, he would fall outside the walls, and she would lose him forever. The moments seemed long while she and Death stood gazing up into the air, waiting to know whose prize the prince would be. Suddenly they both caught sight of a tiny speck no bigger than a wasp, right up in the blue. Was he coming straight? No! Yes! But as he was nearing the city, a light wind sprang up, and swayed him in the direction of the wall. Another second and he would have fallen half over it, when the queen sprang forward, seized him in her arms, and flung him into the castle. Then she commanded her servants to cast Death out of the city, which they did with such hard blows that he never dared to show his face again in the Land of Immortality.

In the Land of Souls

NORTH AMERICA

Far to the north in the Land of Snows there lived a beautiful maiden who was lovelier than any other girl in her whole tribe. Many of the young braves sought her in marriage, but she would listen to one only — a handsome chief who had taken her fancy some years before. So they were to be married, and great rejoicings were made, and the two looked forward to a long life of happiness together, when the very night before the wedding feast a sudden illness seized the girl, and without a word to her friends who were weeping around her, she passed silently away.

The heart of her lover had been set upon her, and the thought of her remained with him night and day. He put aside his bow, and went neither to fight nor to hunt, but from sunrise to sunset he sat by the place where she was laid, thinking of his happiness that was buried there. At last after many days a light seemed to come to him out of the darkness. He remembered having heard from the old, old people of the tribe that there was a path that led to the Land of Souls — that if you sought carefully, you could find.

So the next morning he got up early, and put some food in his pouch and slung an extra skin over his shoulders, for he knew not how long his journey would take, nor what sort of country he would have to go through. Only one thing he knew, that if the path was there, he would find it. At first he was puzzled, as there seemed no reason he should go in one direction more than another. Then all at once he thought he had heard one of the old men say that the Land of Souls lay to the south, and so, filled with new hope and courage, he set his face southward. For many, many miles the country looked the same as it did around his own home. The forests, the hills, and the rivers all seemed exactly like the ones he had left. The only thing that was different was the snow, which had lain thick upon the hills and trees when he started, but grew less and less the farther south he went, until it disappeared altogether. Soon the trees put forth their buds, and flowers sprang up under his feet, and instead of thick clouds there was blue sky over his head, and everywhere the birds were singing. Then he knew that he was on the right road.

The thought that he should soon behold his lost bride made his heart beat for joy, and he sped along lightly and swiftly. Now his way led through a dark wood, and then over some steep cliffs, and on the top of these he found a hut or wigwam. An old man clothed in skins, and holding a staff in his hand, stood in the doorway; and he said to the young chief who was beginning to tell his story, "I was waiting for you, wherefore you have come I know. It is but a short while since she whom you seek was here. Rest in my hut, as she also rested, and I will tell you what you ask, and where you should go."

On hearing these words the young man entered the hut, but his heart was too eager within him to let him rest, and when he arose, the old man rose too, and stood with him at the door. "Look," the old man said, "at the water that lies far out there, and the plains that stretch beyond. That is the Land of Souls, but no man enters it without leaving his body behind him. So, lay down your body here; your bow and arrows, your skin and your dog. They shall be kept for you safely."

Then he turned away, and the young chief, light as air, seemed hardly to touch the ground; and as he flew along, the scents grew sweeter and the flowers more beautiful, while the animals rubbed their noses against him, instead of hiding as he approached, and birds circled around him, and fishes lifted up their heads and looked as he went by. Very soon he noticed with wonder that neither rocks nor trees barred his path. He passed through them without knowing it, for indeed, they were not rocks and trees at all, but only the souls of them; for this was the Land of Shadows.

So he went on with winged feet until he came to the shores of a great lake, with a lovely island in the middle of it; while on the bank of the lake was a canoe of glittering stone, and in the canoe were two shining paddles.

The chief jumped straight into the canoe, and seizing the paddles, pushed off from the shore, when to his joy and wonder he saw following him in another canoe exactly like his own the maiden for whose sake he had made this long journey. But they could not touch each other, for between them rolled great waves, which looked as if they would sink the boats, yet never did. And the young man and the maiden shrank with fear, for down in the depths of the water they saw the bones of those who had died before, and in the waves themselves men and women were struggling, and but few passed over. Only the children had no fear, and reached the other side in safety. Still, though the chief and the young girl quailed in terror at these horrible sights and sounds, no harm came to them, for their lives had been free from evil, and the Master of Life had said that no evil should happen unto them. So they reached unhurt the shore of the Happy Island, and wandered through the flowery fields and by the banks of rushing streams; and they knew not hunger nor thirst, neither cold nor heat. The air fed them and the sun warmed them, and they forgot the dead, for they saw no graves, and the young man's thoughts turned not to wars, neither to the hunting of animals. And gladly would these two have walked thus forever, but in the murmur of the wind he heard the Master of Life saying to him:

"Return to where you came, for I have work for you to do, and your people need you, and for many years you shall rule over them. At the gate my messenger awaits you, and you shall take again your body that you left behind, and he will show you what you are to do. Listen to him, and have patience, and in time to come you shall rejoin her whom you must now leave, for she is accepted, and will remain ever young and beautiful, as when I called her here from the Land of Snows."

He Wins Who Waits

ARMENIA

Once upon a time there reigned a king who had an only daughter. The girl had been spoiled by everybody from her birth, and besides being beautiful, was clever and willful, and when she grew old enough to be married, she refused to have anything to say to the prince whom her father favored, but declared she would choose a husband for herself. By long experience the king knew that once she had made up her mind, there was no use expecting her to change it, so he inquired meekly what she wished him to do.

"Summon all the young men in the kingdom to appear before me a month from today," answered the princess. "The one to whom I shall give this golden apple shall be my husband."

"But, my dear —" began the king in tones of dismay.

"The one to whom I shall give this golden apple shall be my husband," repeated the princess in a louder voice than before. And the king understood the signal, and with a sign proceeded to do her bidding.

The young men arrived — tall and short, dark and fair, rich and poor. They stood in rows in the great courtyard in front of the palace, and the princess, clad in robes of green, with a golden veil flowing behind her, passed before them all, holding the apple. Once or twice she stopped and hesitated, but in the end she always passed on, till she came to a youth near the end of the last row. There was nothing especially remarkable about him, the bystanders thought; nothing

THE · PRINCESS · CHOOSES

that was likely to take a girl's fancy. A hundred others were handsomer, and all wore finer clothes; but he met the princess's eyes frankly and with a smile, and she smiled too, and held out the apple.

"There is some mistake," cried the king, who had anxiously watched her progress, and hoped that none of the candidates would please her. "It is impossible that she can wish to marry the son of a poor widow, who has not a farthing in the world! Tell her that I will not hear of it, and that she must go through the rows again and fix upon someone else." So the princess went through the rows a second and a third time, and on each occasion she gave the apple to the widow's son. "Well, marry him if you will," exclaimed the angry king, "but at least you shall not stay here." And the princess answered nothing, but threw up her head, and taking the widow's son by the hand, they left the castle.

That evening they were married, and after the ceremony they went back to the house of the bridegroom's mother, which in the eyes of the princess did not look much bigger than a henhouse.

The old woman was not at all pleased when her son entered bringing his bride with him.

"As if we were not poor enough before," she grumbled. "I dare say this is some fine lady who can do nothing to earn her living." But the princess stroked her arm, and said softly:

"Do not be vexed, dear mother; I am a famous spinner, and can sit at my wheel all day without breaking a thread."

And she kept her word; but in spite of the efforts of all three, they became poorer and poorer; and at the end of six months it was agreed that the husband should go to the neighboring town to get work. Here he met a merchant who was about to start on a long journey with a train of camels laden with goods of all sorts, and needed a man to help him. The widow's son begged that he take him as a servant, and to this the merchant assented, giving him his whole year's salary beforehand. The young man returned home with the news, and the next day bade farewell to his mother and his wife, who were very sad at parting from him.

"Do not forget me while you are absent," whispered the princess as she flung her arms around his neck, "and as you pass by the well which lies near the city gate, stop and greet the old man you will find sitting there. Kiss his hand, and then ask him what counsel he can give you for your journey."

Then the youth set out, and when he reached the well where the old man was sitting, he asked the question as his wife had bidden him.

"My son," replied the old man, "you have done well to come to me, and in return remember three things: She whom the heart loves, is ever the most beautiful. Patience is the first step on the road to happiness. He wins who waits."

The young man thanked him and went on his way. Early the next morning the caravan set out, and before sunset it had arrived at the first halting place, around some wells, where another company of merchants had already encamped. But no rain had fallen for a long while in that rocky country, and both men and beasts were parched with thirst. To be sure, there *was* another well, about half a mile away, where there was always water; but to get it you had to be lowered deep down, and no one who had ever descended that well had been known to come back.

However, till they could store some water in their bags of goatskin, the caravans dared not go farther into the desert, and on the night of the arrival of the widow's son and his master, the merchants had decided to offer a large reward to anyone who was brave enough to go down into the enchanted well and bring some up. Thus it happened that at sunrise the young man was aroused from his sleep by a herald making his round of the camp, proclaiming that every merchant present would give a thousand gold coins to the man who would risk his life to bring water for themselves and their camels.

The youth hesitated for a little while when he heard the proclamation. The story of the well had spread far and wide, and long ago had reached his ears. The danger was great, he knew; but then, if he came back alive, he would be the possessor of eighty thousand gold coins. He turned to the herald who was passing the tent:

"*I* will go," he said.

"What madness!" cried his master, who happened to be standing near. "You are too young to throw away your life like that. Run after the herald and tell him you take back your offer." But the young man shook his head, and the merchant saw that it was useless to try and persuade him.

"Well, it is your own affair," he observed at last. "If you must go, you must. Only, if you ever return, I will give you a camel's load of goods and my best mule besides." And touching his turban in a token of farewell, he entered the tent.

Hardly had he done so than a crowd of men were seen pouring out of the camp.

"How can we thank you!" they exclaimed, pressing around the youth. "Our camels as well as ourselves are almost dead of thirst. See! Here is the rope we have brought to let you down."

"Come then," answered the youth. And they all set out.

On reaching the well, the rope was knotted securely under his arms, a big goatskin bottle was given to him, and he was gently lowered to the bottom of the pit. Here a clear stream was bubbling over the rocks, and stooping down, he was about to drink, when a huge Arab appeared before him saying in a loud voice:

"Come with me!"

The young man rose, never doubting that his last hour had come; but as he could do nothing, he followed the Arab into a brilliantly lighted hall, on the far side of the little river. There his guide sat down, and drawing toward him two boys, he said to the stranger:

"I have a question to ask you. If you answer it right, your life shall be spared. If not, your head will be forfeit, as the head of many another has been before you. Tell me: Which of my two children do I think the handsomer?"

The question did not seem a hard one, for while one boy was as beautiful a child as ever was seen, his brother was exceedingly ugly. But just as the youth was going to speak, the old man's counsel flashed into the youth's mind, and he replied hastily:

"The one whom we love best is always the handsomest."

"You have saved me!" cried the Arab, rising quickly from his seat, and pressing the young man in his arms. "Ah! if you could only guess what I have suffered from the stupidity of all the people to whom I have put that question, and I was condemned by a wicked genius to remain here until it was answered! But what brought you to this place, and how can I reward you for what you have done for me?"

"By helping me to draw enough water for my caravan of eighty merchants and their camels who are dying for want of it," replied the youth.

"That is easily done," said the Arab. "Take these three apples, and when you have filled your skin, and are ready to be drawn up, lay one of them on the ground. Halfway to the earth, let fall another, and at the top, drop the third. If you follow my directions, no harm will happen to you. And take, besides, these three pomegranates, green, red, and white. One day you will find a use for them!"

The young man did as he was told, and stepped out on the rocky waste, where the merchants were anxiously awaiting him. Oh, how thirsty they all were! But even after the camels had drunk, the skin seemed as full as ever.

Full of gratitude for their deliverance, the merchants pressed the money into his hands, while his own master bade him choose what goods he liked, and a mule to carry them.

So the widow's son was rich at last, and when the merchant had sold his merchandise, and returned home to his native city, his servant hired a man by whom he sent the money and the mule back to his wife.

I will send the pomegranates also, he thought, for if I leave them in my turban, they may some day fall out; and he drew them out of his turban. But the fruit had vanished, and in their places were three precious stones, green, red, and white.

For a long time he remained with the merchant, who gradually trusted him with all his business, and gave him a large share of the money he made. When his master died, the young man wished to return home, but the widow begged him to stay and help her; and one day he awoke with a start to remember that twenty years had passed since he had gone away.

"I want to see my wife," he said the next morning to his mistress. "If at any time I can be of use to you, send a messenger to me; meanwhile I have told Hassan what to do." And mounting a camel he set out.

Now, soon after he had taken service with the merchant, a little boy had been born to him, and both the princess and the old woman toiled hard all day to get the baby food and clothing. When the money and the pomegranates arrived, there was no need for them to work any more, and the princess saw at once that they were not fruit at all, but precious stones of great value. The old woman, however, not being accustomed like her daughter-in-law to the sight of jewels, took them only for common fruit, and wished to give them to the child to eat. She was very angry when the princess hastily took them from her and hid them in her dress. Then the princess went to the market and bought the three finest pomegranates she could find, which she handed the old woman for the little boy.

The princess also bought beautiful new clothes for all of them, and when they were dressed, they looked as fine as could be. Next, she took out one of the precious stones which her husband had sent her, and placed it in a small silver box. This she wrapped up in a handkerchief embroidered in gold, and handed it to the old woman.

"Go, dear mother," she said, "to the palace, and present the jewel to the king, and if he asks you what he can give you in return, tell him that you want a paper, with his seal attached, proclaiming that no one is to meddle with anything you may choose to do." Then, as she now knew what it was to be poor, the princess filled the old woman's pockets with gold and silver pieces, and gave one last instruction: "Before you leave the palace, distribute the money amongst the servants."

The old woman took the box and started for the palace. No one there had ever seen a ruby of such beauty, and the most famous jeweler in the town was summoned to declare its value. But all he could say was:

"If a boy threw a stone into the air with all his might, and you could pile up gold as high as the flight of the stone, it would not be sufficient to pay for this ruby."

At these words the king's face fell. Having once seen the ruby, he could not bear to part with it, yet all the money in his treasury would not be enough to buy it. So for a little while he remained silent, wondering what offer he could make the old woman, and at last he said:

"If I cannot give you its worth in money, is there anything you will take in exchange?"

"A paper signed by your hand, and sealed with your seal, proclaiming that I may do what I will, without hindrance," she answered promptly. And the king, delighted to have obtained what he coveted at so small a cost, gave her the paper without delay. Then, to the king's amazement, the old woman took handfuls of gold and silver pieces from her pockets and distributed them to his servants. Amidst a chorus of grateful murmurs, the old woman took her leave and returned home.

The fame of the wonderful ruby soon spread far and wide, and envoys arrived at the little house to know if there were more stones to sell. Each king was so anxious to gain possession of the treasure that he bade his messenger outbid all the rest, and so the princess sold the two remaining stones for a sum of money so large that if the gold pieces had been spread out, they would have reached from here to the moon. The first thing she did was to build a palace by the side of the cottage, and it was raised on pillars of gold, in which were set great diamonds, which blazed night and day. Of course the news of this palace was the first thing that reached her father the king on his return from the wars, and he hurried to see it. In the doorway stood a young man of twenty, who was his grandson, though neither of them knew it, and so pleased was the king with the appearance of the youth, that he carried him back to his own palace, and made him commander of the whole army.

Not long after this the widow's son returned to his native land. There, sure enough, was the tiny cottage where he had lived with his mother, but the gorgeous building beside it was quite new to him. What had become of his wife and his mother, and who could be dwelling in that other wonderful place? These were the first thoughts that flashed through his mind; but not wishing to betray himself by asking questions of passing strangers, he climbed up into a tree that stood opposite the palace, and watched.

By and by a lady came out, and began to gather some of the roses and jasmine that hung about the porch. The twenty years that had passed since he had last beheld her vanished in an instant, and he knew her to be his own wife, looking almost as young and beautiful as on the day of their parting. He was about to jump down from the tree and hasten to her side, when she was joined by a young man who placed his arm affectionately around her neck. At this sight the angry husband drew his bow, but before he could let fly the arrow, the counsel of the wise man came back to him: "Patience is the first step on the road to happiness." And he laid it down again.

At this moment the princess turned, and drawing her companion's

BLIND·RAGE·FILLED·THE·HEART·OF·THE·WATCHER

head down to hers, kissed him on each cheek. A second time blind rage filled the heart of the watcher, and he snatched up his bow from the branch where it hung, when words, heard long since, seemed to sound in his ears:

"He wins who waits." And the bow dropped to his side. Then, through the silent air came the sound of the youth's voice:

"Mother, can you tell me nothing about my father? Does he still live, and will he never return to us?"

"Alas! my son, how can I answer you?" replied the lady. "Twenty years have passed since he left us to make his fortune, and in that time only once have I heard any news of him. But what has brought him to your mind just now?"

"Because last night I dreamed that he was here," said the youth, "and then I remembered what I have so long forgotten, that I *had* a father, though even his very history was strange to me. And now, tell me, I pray you, all you can concerning him."

And standing under the jasmine, the son learned his father's history, and the man in the tree listened also.

"Oh," exclaimed the youth when it was ended, while he twisted his hands in pain, "I am general of the army, you are the king's daughter, and we have the most splendid palace in the whole world, yet my father lives we know not where, and for all we can guess, may be poor and miserable. Tomorrow I will ask the king to give me soldiers, and I will seek him over the whole earth till I find him."

Then the man came down from the tree, and clasped his wife and son in his arms. All that night they talked, and when the sun rose, it still found them talking. But as soon as it was proper, he went up to the palace to pay his homage to the king, and to inform him of all that had happened and who they all really were. The king was overjoyed to think that his daughter, whom he had long since forgiven and sorely missed, was living at his gates, and was, besides, the mother of the youth who was so dear to him. "It was written beforehand," cried the monarch. "You are my son-in-law before the world, and shall be king after me."

And the man bowed his head.

He had waited; and he had won.

About the Stories

While the text of the stories is firmly based on that in Andrew Lang's Fairy Books, some modifications have been made both for the ease of today's reader and to correct obvious errors. For example, in the story "Urashima Taro and the Turtle," sharp-eyed readers will notice in Henry Justice Ford's drawings that the hero's name is spelled Uraschimataro, reflecting the origin of Lang's text in a German translation. The individual Fairy Book from which each story has been taken is noted after the titles that appear below.

The Boys With the Golden Stars *Violet*
This beautiful story was taken from *Rumänische Märchen* by Mite Kremnitz. It is a version of the tale type known to folklorists as "The Three Golden Sons."

The Princess Bella-Flor *Orange*
This story from Fernan Caballero's *Cuentos, Oraciones, y Adivinas* deftly combines the familiar tale of the young hero whose kindness to animals is rewarded by their help in impossible tasks with the motif of aid from the soul of a dead man for whose burial the hero has paid. "Grateful dead" type tales often require the hero to rescue the princess from slavery; in this version she is hiding from the king's unwelcome courtship when the hero finds her and carries her off.

The Two Caskets *Orange*
Taken from *Yule-tide Stories* by Benjamin Thorpe, this tale is a typical version of the internationally popular story known as "The Tale of the Kind and the Unkind Girls," familiar as the Grimms' "Mother Holle."

The Snake Prince *Olive*
This is one of the excellent stories sent to Lang from Feroshepore, India, by his correspondent Major Campbell. There are a number of fairy tales in which a prince is enchanted into serpent shape. Although the "rustling, writhing crowd of snakes" gives this particular story its poetic force, the essential motif is that of "Cupid and Psyche," in which the wife's discovery of her mysterious husband's secret causes him to vanish. In tales of this type the wife's steadfast love and bravery in the search for her lost husband eventually lead to a happy ending.

About the Stories

The Story of the Seven Simons *Crimson*
Folktales celebrating the talents of a "Master Thief" have always been popular. Sometimes, as in this Hungarian story, the thief is only one of several brothers whose skills resemble those of the helpers in the Grimms' story "Six Go Through the World."

Peter Bull *Pink*
This comic story was translated by W. A. Craigie from the Danish original in Svend Grundtvig's *Danske Folkeæventyr efter Utrykte Kilder*.

The King of the Waterfalls *Lilac*
This story was told to Hector MacLean by the blind fiddler James Wilson at Islay, Argyll, on the 9th of June, 1859, and published in J. F. Campbell's *Popular Tales of the West Highlands* the following year. The opening in which the hero puts himself in an ogre's power in settlement of a gambling debt can lead into a number of situations. Here the story develops along the lines of the Norse "The Giant Who Had No Heart in His Body."

The Knights of the Fish *Brown*
The story of "The Twins, or Blood-Brothers," incorporating a separate tale known as "The Dragon-Slayer," is one of the most popular of all European folktales. This version is from Caballero's *Cuentos, Oraciones, y Adivinas*.

The Prince and the Three Fates *Brown*
We know from a papyrus of around 1700 B.C. that the Emperor Cheops, builder of the great pyramid, was fond of folktales. Among the stories that survive from Ancient Egypt are a number of striking tales showing clear links with stories still told today. Andrew Lang found this one in G. Maspéro's *Les contes populaires de l'Egypte ancienne*.

The Story of the Hero Makóma *Orange*
This tale of a mighty hero was sent to Lang by his correspondent Mr. Fairbridge, from what was then Rhodesia.

Hábogi *Brown*
Die Neuisländischen Volksmärchen by Adeline Ritterhaus is the source of this brief tale of love, marriage, and sibling rivalry.

The Fairy of the Dawn *Violet*
Although rather literary in form, with its gods and goddesses somewhat ill at ease in a mere folktale, this story from Kremnitz's *Rumänische Märchen* is essentially a version of the well-known international tale type "The Sons on a Quest for a Wonderful Remedy for Their Father." The motif of the one laughing eye and the one weeping eye is typical of Eastern European versions of this tale.

The King Who Wanted to See Paradise *Orange*
This story was told to Major Campbell, Lang's correspondent in India, by a Pathan tribesman, in what is now Pakistan. The familiar motif of a man returning from the otherworld to find all he knew dead and forgotten is here given a distinct Islamic twist. A Christian equivalent can be found in "The Monk and the Bird," a story particularly popular in Ireland. In it, a monk who spends a few moments listening to the song of a bird discovers that years have passed.

Ian, the Soldier's Son *Orange*
This story was collected in July 1859 by Hector MacLean from Donald MacNiven at Bowmore, Islay, and printed in J. F. Campbell's *Popular Tales of the West Highlands.*

The Elf Maiden *Brown*
Not all marriages with fairy beings end as happily as this tale, which Lang took from *Lappländische Märchen* by J. C. Poestion.

The Girl With the Wooden Helmet *Violet*
This story of modesty rewarded comes from David Brauns's *Japanische Märchen und Sagen.*

The Enchanted Wreath *Orange*
This story type is known as "The Black and the White Bride," after the story of that name in Grimm. This version comes from Thorpe's *Yule-tide Stories.*

The Boy Who Found Fear at Last *Olive*
The story of the fearless youth is widespread, but this ending is unusual. The choice of a king or emperor by means of a bird is a common motif, but its use here is especially effective. The story comes from Ignaz Kúnos's *Türkische Volksmärchen.*

The Magic Book *Orange*
This story was collected by the great Danish folklorist Evald Tang Kristensen, and published in *Eventyr fra Jylland.* It was translated by Mrs. Skavgaard-Pedersen.

How Ian Direach Got the Blue Falcon *Orange*
This version of "The Search for the Golden Bird," a tale type in which the hero is often helped by a fox, was collected by John Dewar from Angus Campbell, a quarryman, at Rosneath in Scotland in April 1860; Lang found it in J. F. Campbell's *Popular Tales of the West Highlands.*

Urashima Taro and the Turtle *Pink*
This famous Japanese tale, taken by Lang from Brauns's *Japanische Märchen und Sagen,* may be compared with the Irish legend of Oisín, who returned from Tir na n'Og to make the same discovery as Urashima Taro. Washington Irving Americanized the motif in *Rip Van Winkle.*

The Prince Who Sought Immortality *Crimson*
In some versions of this tale type, "The Land Where No One Dies," the hero is allowed to revisit his home, but warned not to get off his horse; he does so, and dies. Stories in which Death is cheated of his due seem particularly popular in Hungary. This story comes from Elisabet Róna-Sklarek's *Ungarische Volksmärchen.*

In the Land of Souls *Yellow*
Lang credits this Native American tale simply to the Smithsonian Bureau of Ethnology. His exact source has not been confirmed.

He Wins Who Waits *Olive*
Stories about a lowly hero who wins the hand of a princess have always been a staple of the fairy tale tradition. In this moving and well-paced tale from *Contes Arméniens* by Frédéric Macler, winning his bride is just the beginning of the hero's journey into wisdom.